The road was dark, but there was sufficient moonlight to enable him to see where he was going. As a car came into view, he quickly stepped to the side of the road and half turned away. There was no cover and he was hoping not to be recognized.

There was a roar behind him as the car accelerated, and surprised, he began to turn his body to look at it. The lights blinded him and immediately afterwards he felt a blow as the car hit his thighs hard, knocking him upwards and backwards. Blood trickled from his wounded head down to the collar of his white shirt, the stain slowly spreading. The little plastic bag flew from his fingers and pirouetted into the thick undergrowth.

Margaret Moore

TUSCAN
TERMINATION

WORLDWIDE®

TORONTO • NEW YORK • LONDON
AMSTERDAM • PARIS • SYDNEY • HAMBURG
STOCKHOLM • ATHENS • TOKYO • MILAN
MADRID • WARSAW • BUDAPEST • AUCKLAND

TUSCAN TERMINATION

A Worldwide Mystery/October 2007

First published by Hilliard & Harris.

ISBN-13: 978-0-373-26614-2
ISBN-10:   0-373-26614-6

Printed in U.S.A.

TUSCAN
TERMINATION

PROLOGUE

HE STRUGGLED INTO consciousness and with it came terror. He was being dragged along by his legs, those useless weighty things that refused to rebel. He was helpless. He opened his eyes and saw the bent figure, a dark silhouette in the moonlight, intent on moving him.

"No, please," he whimpered.

His legs were dropped quite suddenly, and for a moment he hoped. He tried to raise his head, but the terrible throbbing there increased, and a wave of nausea made him drop back, dizzy and weak.

The dark figure knelt beside him and hissed, "You asked for it."

"No, no." He cursed as he felt the strong hands turn him and push his back hard. Then came the shocked realisation that he was in the water. It was cold, so cold. He tried desperately to struggle again as he felt the water close over his head. But it had entered his mouth, forcing out the air, and squashing his lungs, which burst painfully.

There was a loud roaring in his ears as his head exploded.

Then nothing.

ONE

WHEN HILARY WRIGHT woke up, she had no idea that within a very short time she would find herself in the middle of a murder investigation. Birds were singing and Hilary felt a surge of well-being. There had been a storm the evening before and this morning the air was crystal clear. Sunlight streamed through the curtains and had woken her early. Actually it had rained for most of June but now at last, after a sad start, July seemed to be reverting to what was normal summer weather for Tuscany. She had been offered the use of her neighbours' pool, and decided to take a day off, go swimming this morning, and perhaps have a sandwich lunch at the poolside. She felt guiltily glad that her neighbours, Nigel and Robin Proctor, were away.

Leaping out of bed, she went to stand naked in front of the mirror, running her hands through her short blonde hair. Thoughtful blue eyes stared back at her. Hilary Wright, at forty-seven, had a fine, lithe body and long slim legs. She pulled in her belly and patted it. "Not bad for an old lady," she murmured.

After a quick shower she dressed in shorts and a tee shirt. She opened the window and gazed down at the pool. As she lived at the top of a hill, her neighbour's land lay directly below her house. Actually she thought the pool was pretty hideous. A kidney-shaped, pink, Hollywood pool, it was a blot on the lush landscape, surrounded by pink tiles, pink chairs and dreadful pink raffia sun umbrellas. Cast iron tables with pink marble tops gave it a certain air of opulence and the huge terracotta urns of cascading pink geraniums were beautiful. But even so, she wrinkled her nose with distaste. How twee it was, how precious and ugly. Then she looked more carefully. There was something different about it today. Something large and dark floated idly in the pool. Without her glasses Hilary couldn't see clearly from that distance, but it seemed to her that someone was swimming, or floating there. She fetched her glasses from her bedside table, put them on, and returned to the window, bringing into focus a body, floating face downwards. She strained forward, leaning out of the window, to confirm what she thought she had seen. She concentrated hard, desperate to see movement, but there was none.

"Oh God, who can it be? What can have happened?" she muttered.

At that moment the sounds of a key turning and the front door opening made her jump.

"It's me Signora, Pia. Shall I feed the cat, only he's asking?" It was Pia, her comfortable, rather elderly cleaner.

"Yes. Please do. You're rather early aren't you?" she hoped her voice sounded normal, as she felt rather shaky.

"Yes," bellowed the voice, anxious to be heard upstairs, "I've come early, as I need to get away early. It's because of my poor old uncle what's in hospital. He needs spoon-feeding at lunchtime and I've got to go and do it. Maria can't go because her baby's ill, and Anna can't because it's her day for helping her mother-in-law, the one with funny legs, and Monica's starting her three month stint cleaning at the town hall this morning, so it's up to me. That's all right isn't it?"

Hilary cleared her throat and replied firmly, "Fine." She heard Pia open the kitchen door and start talking to the cat, promising him food, which meant she would be going into the larder. Swiftly she put on a pair of espadrilles, ran silently downstairs, and slipped out of the back door. She needed to be sure about what she had seen. She had to be wrong. It must be some kid taking advantage of the owners' absence to swim there. At top speed she crossed the garden and slipped under the wire that temporarily denoted the boundary between their land and entered the Proctors' garden. Then she slowed down as she became aware that her breathing was quite rapid and she could feel her heart thudding in her chest. She took a deep breath, squared her shoulders and went down the steps that led to the pool area.

"How grotesque," she said out loud.

It really was a body. Long black hair waved lazily in the water like some exotic plant, while the swifts and swallows swooped and dived around it, brushing the surface of the water as they caught insects and carried them away. Here was something quite tremendous, yet they were completely unconcerned, going about their daily business unafraid. Hilary felt absurdly shaken. She had no thought to go to the body, to turn it, or see it, or desperately try and reverse what nature had accomplished. It seemed so still and surely dead, that she recoiled physically, stepping back. As she breathed out slowly she became aware that she had been holding her breath. Ah, this horrible pink pool with this surreal obscenity in it. How revolting it all was, she thought. The body, unconcerned by her presence continued its almost imperceptible movements. The trousers billowed, swollen with air, and the hair lay gently along the surface of the water. She suddenly felt quite sick.

After that, the phone calls, the busily rushing police cars and the ambulance, made the whole thing easier to cope with. The *carabinieri* in their uniforms, booted and with guns in holsters, redolent of the fascist era, held no fears for her. She was well known here: a respectable English Signora, widow of a man from this town, Borgo San Cristoforo. While the police rushed about in response to barked orders, overwhelmed by the importance of this case (for a death of this sort was rare in this small town), Hilary felt herself becoming more and more removed from the whole thing, as though this farcical death in a pink pool had nothing to do with her at all. And it was true. After all, she was only a spectator. It was only chance that had involved her here. And she bitterly regretted that she had agreed to water the

Proctors' plants while they were away. This had made her the re-cipient of their favours and thus afforded her the use of the wretched pool. It seemed, too, that it put their relationship on a false plane. They were nothing to her, not even friends. She knew nothing about them other than what they had told her. As an English woman living in Italy, she was often thrown into intimate contact with people whom she would otherwise never have met and with whom she had little in common, people about whom she knew nothing other than what they had chosen to tell her of themselves. Nationality was the only bond and she knew it to be insufficient. The Proctors were a prime example of this. They were not her type at all. Nigel, in his early sixties, was a six-foot, blustering presence with an anachronistic way of interspersing his conversation with, "Jolly good" or "Righty ho." And Robin, his wife, who like many very tall women was ultra feminine, was always coated in make-up and jangling with bracelets. She was at least fifteen years his junior. She had a passion for gardening, which she would work at wearing all her jewellery much to Hilary's amusement. Hilary herself always wore rags while gar-dening as she got into such a mess. But Robin sailed forth dressed to the nines and returned after an afternoon's work looking ab-solutely pristine. Nigel, who was some kind of a computer con-sultant, would often be called away to distant parts for work, while Robin usually kept the home fires burning. She had chosen to accompany him this time, as she loved Hong Kong.

Actually, Hilary was quite angry with herself for not facing the Proctor problem in some final and resolute way. In a cowardly manner she went to their house under false pretences, in the guise of a friendly neighbour, when she was not inclined to be friendly and heartily wished not to be their neighbour. As it was she seemed doomed to a life of plant watering whilst in return she was to enjoy the dubious benefits of the pink swimming pool. The trouble was that while Nigel and Robin were so kind, thrust-ing their riches on her, she felt only an increasing irritation with herself for being so feeble as to not withstand these friendly advances. The alternative, of course, was something so unpleasant that she had been loath to have recourse to it. To refuse their advances would have been churlish and they would have been offended. Adjoining gardens would have made this even more unpleasant. So she was doing a balancing act, walking the tightrope of pleasant, uncommitted neighbourliness.

She shrugged away thoughts of the Proctors. It wasn't their fault that someone had died in their pool. She even felt a momentary pang for them. It would be awful for them to come home to this, to know that someone had died in the pool, which was intended to be the fulcrum of their life in Italy.

MARESCIALLO BIAGIONI, the local head of police, commented to his wife as he got into bed that night, at the end of what had been a very unusual and exciting day for him, "She's cool as a cucumber, that English woman. No, not cool, cold. I'm sure she would have behaved just like that if she'd killed the man herself."

"It's the English temperament. They hold it all in, even at funerals." She sounded slightly disapproving.

"Mmm," replied Maresciallo Biagioni who was tired and longing to sleep.

"Was he killed?"

"Well, there is a head wound, but it's hard to tell till after the autopsy. Anyway, I doubt it. I reckon he was drunk and hit his head on the side of the pool as he fell into it."

"What on earth was he doing there?"

"Your guess is as good as mine. Perhaps he wanted a quick swim in private."

"Don't be ridiculous. There was a storm early in the evening and it was cold. He'd never have gone swimming then and you know it."

"I know nothing of the sort. Now let me sleep, woman. I'm worn out and I've got to get up early as they're sending someone up from Lucca to take charge of the case. I've had my moment of glory." He sighed and turned on his side. Tomorrow, the case would be out of his hands. But today he had been in charge and he felt that he had acquitted himself well. With another sigh of contentment, he plunged into sleep.

DESPITE WHAT the Maresciallo thought, Hilary was very disturbed and had a dreadful night filled with unpleasant nightmares. The one that she remembered, the one that woke her at first light trembling and bathed in sweat, was of birds pecking mercilessly at a body in the pool while she helplessly watched the water turn as pink as the tiles that lined it.

Unable to rid herself of these images, she decided not to try and sleep again. At six she was sitting in her kitchen, gloomily drinking black coffee while Cassius, her belligerent Siamese tomcat, nibbled at her ankles. Thinking about the probably unpleasant day ahead, she unreasonably cursed the Proctors for having built the pool in the first place, as though that in itself had been sufficient to cause a man's death.

TWO

PIA PADDED ABOUT the kitchen, her soft heel-less slippers slapping the tiled floor. She was moaning to herself, "Who would have thought it? So young as well. Merely a boy. What a tragedy!"

Hilary, who now knew who it was that had drowned, found herself wondering if, instead of being a tragedy, this were not a rather heavy-handed case of divine justice. For he was the person in town that she was least likely to mourn. Apart from a general dislike of the man and what he stood for, she also had more personal reasons for disliking him intensely. So she took no part in the litany of regret that Pia felt necessary as a comment for any death.

The dead man was Ettore Fagiolo, a slim-hipped, flashily dressed young man with over-long black hair. He had favoured black silk shirts, heavy gold chains (worn round his wrist and neck, a medallion nestling in the black hair on his chest) and had driven a red Porsche at a somewhat reckless speed given the narrow winding roads in the area. Improbably he had been a real estate agent who dealt mainly with foreigners, usually British and German nationals who were either seeking to buy a summer-house, or sometimes looking for a permanent residence.

He had sold the Proctors their house, the now neat and trim, re-baptised, Villa Rosa, which had once been Casa Balduini, named after the 19th century owners. The origins of the house were much earlier than that, of course. But the Balduini family had been responsible for the complete renovation and enlargement of the house, which had given it its present day aspect. By the time the Proctors bought it, it was in urgent need of repair.

The roof had leaked for at least ten years, the period for which it had remained uninhabited. Successive storms and the heat and cold had taken their toll, wreaking havoc, especially to the north-facing wall, which had been severely damaged.

Despite the rather daunting amount of work needed, the Proctors had fallen in love with the house and had set about restoring it without counting the cost. Ettore Fagiolo had overseen all the work on the house as well as the construction of the pool, which he adored, giving total approval to Nigel's design.

What he had also done was to overcharge on everything. And gossip had been rife as to the comprehensive cost of the work. Fabulous sums had been bandied about by the town gossips as certain knowledge. Nigel, who appeared to have absolute trust in the man, had even given him power of attorney to buy the house for him as he was abroad when the time came for the final contract to be signed.

Ettore had also rented out the house for him the whole of the previous summer for agreeably high rents, even after he had taken a hefty whack for himself. "A perfect partnership," said Nigel, calling him a "jolly good chap," inviting him to dinner and generally proclaiming him as a friend, until later. Later being when he began to realise just how much he had been overcharged. And, at the same time, when he found out that planning permission had not been obtained for work that was now completed and for which, after numerous protests, he had been forced to pay a heavy fine. At one point there had even been the possibility of the council coming to bulldoze the changing hut at the swimming pool.

According to Ettore, there had never been the slightest risk of anything of the sort. He hadn't asked for permission, which he knew would be refused, and had just built the thing, knowing that the worst that could happen would be a fine, known as a *condono* (this fine meant that although what you had done was illegal, the payment of a suitable sum of money would condone illegal action, making it legal, a process which often took some years to achieve). Ettore explained that he had never bothered to tell Nigel about it as it was part and parcel of normal practice in protected areas. Build and be damned, or in this case, pay the *condono*.

He assured Nigel, over and over again, that everyone did it. But Nigel became very wary, and at the same time heard some of the horror stories about Ettore that were circulating among the ex-pats. There was the one about the German who had bought a house without an access road but had been promised that he could build one. He was now being sued by his neighbour for attempting to do so (the case was still laboriously going through the courts and the German still had access to his house, only on foot, via a steep mule track). Then there was the story of the family that had bought a barn for conversion in an area where such a conversion was impossible, as the area was strictly agricultural.

Even worse in some ways, although smaller sums of money were involved, was the house insurance scam whereby, without having signed anything, an insurance premium would be requested of a foreign house owner at triple normal rates. If the unfortunate house owner paid it he would then discover that although the insurance stipulated that it was yearly, the house was in actual fact only covered for a few months. While this could not, in all honesty, have been firmly laid at Ettore's door, it was a strange fact that the insurance company had its office not only in the same building as Ettore's office, but on the same floor, so that leaving Ettore's office brought one face to face with the door of the insurance office. No one had ever actually seen anyone enter this office and it appeared that all their work was done through the post.

So it was a gradual awakening that brought Nigel to a consciousness of the truth about Ettore. Once it happened though, that was it. He held forth frequently about Ettore and his dishonesty. The friendship was over, the perks were over, and Ettore was parading himself as the injured party, especially as Nigel was refusing to pay the last instalment for the work on the pool.

Nigel had been served with an injunction to pay. The next step would be to take Nigel to court. Others had already followed that route. Ettore often lost his cases but he carried on bringing them as a matter of course, fattening the lawyers' pockets, convinced that if he held out long enough people would pay up, no matter what the sum, rather than have the expense of going through the courts for years.

How strange that he should die there, in the pool he admired so much, at the house of a man who was once his friend, mused Hilary.

She could hear Pia continuing her lamentations, calling upon the Virgin to witness her horror and distress as she slopped a wet cloth over the kitchen floor. Hilary's thoughts continued in a diametrically opposed manner as she continued to feel that Ettore had in some way only got what he deserved. "The mills of God…" she muttered, surprising even herself at her satisfaction, although she knew that she would not be the only one to feel that way. More than one person had wished him dead, and had even, on occasion, threatened to kill him.

She puzzled over his presence at the Villa Rosa. Why had he gone there, and when? The Proctors had left at midnight for an early morning flight from Rome to Hong Kong. She, herself, had been their guest at dinner that evening. As usual the food had been simple but superb. Robin was an excellent cook and almost the only non-Italian of Hilary's acquaintance able to make good coffee. The dinner had been the occasion for the handing over of the key and Robin had given her detailed instructions about the watering of her cherished plants. Hilary thought back to that evening. She had slithered up their muddy drive in a very grumpy frame of mind. But when Robin opened the door to her and received her with such evident pleasure, and Nigel appeared shortly afterwards with a large gin and tonic, she had regretted her initial, rather acid, comments about the state of the drive. She had hated having to arrive in muddy Wellies and change her shoes in the hall. But it had all seemed a ridiculous thing to complain about once she was seated in their comfortable sitting room as they beamed on her and thanked her profusely yet again.

What a strange couple they were. Robin, who was nearly as tall as her six-foot husband, was obviously fit and even a little muscular, but seemed to feel the need to state her femininity through her choice of clothes, which were almost vulgar. Nigel, on the other hand, with his grey crew cut, tanned face, ruddy cheeks and very blue eyes, wore rather formal and old-fashioned clothes. His stilted, telegraphic manner of talking made him seem like a caricature. He seemed to drink rather a lot, too. However, she had to admit that so did most of the other ex-pats, who couldn't believe how cheap the booze was in Italy and were determined to drink as much of it as they could. Yesterday Hilary had given what information she could about them to the Maresciallo, though she didn't know their exact whereabouts.

She knew she would probably be called on to give a written statement about everything this morning. She was feeling nervy, irritable and restless, and attributed this to lack of sleep. Sighing she went out into the garden.

Looking at the view usually made her feel very peaceful. But this morning she was aware of furtive movements in the Proctors' garden. Men were combing the whole area, pouncing on things and popping them in plastic bags. She tried not to think what this might mean. One thing was certain, it would be impossible to forget the Fagiolo death for one minute. Everyone was talking about it, according to Pia. It seemed that while some thought it had been an accident, others had suggested it might be suicide, something which Hilary thought most unlikely given the man's monstrous ego. And there were even those who were saying that he had been killed. There had been a head wound, which had been mercifully hidden from Hilary's view by the wet hair. But one of the ambulance men had told his wife about it, under oath of secrecy, and she had rushed out to do her shopping and tell all her friends after requesting similar guarantees of secrecy, with the result that now everyone knew. The size and nature of this wound grew with each telling, and by the time that Pia heard about it, it was said that half his head was missing, a fact about which Hilary was able to reassure her. Still, it was strange that he should have a head wound, unless of course he had fallen, hit his head on the side of the pool, and thus drowned. Hilary hugged that version to herself. She didn't want to think it could be murder.

Murders didn't happen in Borgo San Cristoforo. It was a quiet hill town in Tuscany with a very low crime rate. Besides, who would murder Ettore Fagiolo? He was unpleasant, unscrupulous and out for all he could get, but so were many others. No, this was an accidental death, and no doubt a perfectly plausible reason would be found for his presence at the Proctors' pool. She couldn't think of one herself, but there had to be. The alternative was unthinkable.

THREE

THE GERMAN, 'FRITZY' as everyone called him, was actually called Herman Ganz. He was pacing up and down his living room wearing rather large shorts and leather sandals. He held a can of beer in one hand and drank from it. His large belly, reddened from incautious sunbathing and gilded with blonde hairs, rose from the waistband of his shorts upwards to flabby pectorals. The whole was surmounted by a round red face, very pale blue, large, round eyes, now rather blood-shot, and full pink lips. It was an adult baby-face crowned by a blonde crew cut. He looked like a strange and rather dissolute baby of gigantic proportions. He was the sole agent for a German product, which had huge sales in Italy, and this necessitated numerous trips to the country. So he had decided to buy himself a house, roughly in the centre of Italy, to use as his base. The area was beautiful and quiet and there were few other Germans in the area. He also used the house for frequent extra-marital escapades and was increasingly annoyed by the lack of an access road. Privacy was one thing; inconvenience another.

At the moment he was profoundly worried. The day had started with a hangover. In fact the day had merely been a prolongation of the dreadful night before. He had forced himself to the phone and started work. He was in front of the computer with a black coffee on his desk when he heard the door open and his domestic help arrive. She was a young girl who had recently finished agricultural college and was doing some house-help work for the summer before starting her apprenticeship in some sector of agriculture. She was hoping to go in with a landscape gardener and nurseryman. Ganz found her quiet and efficient, actually much better than his permanent cleaner, now on holiday with her children. She gave him a cheerful *"Buon giorno."*

He replied in his rather basic Italian, with a heavy German accent, "Have a coffee, Valeria. I just made some."

"Thanks, I will. I need it this morning."

"Don't tell me you have a hangover, too?" He looked at her. As usual she looked beautiful, her skin like a dusky peach. She was wearing cut off jeans and her legs were slim and tanned.

"No, nothing like that. I've just had a bit of a shock." She hesitated. "You know that estate agent Ettore Fagiolo?"

"Yes, I am sorry to say."

"Oh, of course you do. I forgot." She gave him a dubious look.

"Well, what is it he has done?"

"He's dead. It seems he drowned in the pool at Villa Rosa."

He froze at the computer, kept his face turned away from the girl and said, in what he hoped was a normal tone of voice, "Well, that is so terrible. Poor man. I was not a friend of his. This you know," he glanced over his shoulder at her, "but this is very sad."

"Yes, he was an only child you know. It is awful for his family. Also no one can understand why he was there in the dark. No wonder he fell in. He probably couldn't see where he was going." She took her cup into the kitchen and said, "Well, I'll get started."

His brain had worked feverishly all morning while he sat in front of the computer pretending to work. Now she had gone. He had turned off the computer, ripped off his sweaty tee shirt and lumbered over to the fridge for a cold beer.

He tried to put his thoughts in order. Last night he had been disgustingly drunk—again! He had finally had the opportunity to get that Italian bastard, Ettore, on his own and somehow he had messed it up. Sweat pearled his brow, ran down the sides of his face and dripped from his jawbone to fall onto his belly. He rubbed distractedly at the damp blonde hairs and his itching, burning skin. What a fool he'd been! His plump fingers tightened round the beer can. Also he had not only been foolish, but totally humiliated. And worst of all he had blacked out and didn't even know what he had or had not done.

He frowned, concentrating, trying to put some kind of order into the jumbled sequence of events the night before. His stupid bar crawl, of which he could only remember jolly faces and claps on the back and encouraging cries of "Bravo Fritzy" from anonymous voices, had given him the foolish idea of vengeance for all the wrongs he had suffered at the hands of that little shit Ettore. He remembered hearing a voice bellowing, "I'll kill the bastard" in heavily accented Italian and presumed it must have been his own. Then at some point he remembered following Ettore's car, running and stumbling. He'd actually fallen over and scratched his Rolex. The car hadn't gone that far and they hadn't even seen him. Ettore and that young faggot from the bar were just disappearing into the Villa Rosa when he finally reached the crest of the hill. It had seemed a good idea to creep round to the back of the house to spy on them. He could also remember sliding around in the muddy drive. And then, for some reason, he'd found himself at the pool. *Probably fell down the steps,* he thought. Then he'd crashed into a chair and knocked it over, and the noise had brought Ettore out, and they'd had a row. He had tried to strike the bastard, but his aim was off and he'd fallen over. He supposed he must have dozed off after that. No, that was later, after he had been kicked up the arse and laughed at and had crawled away to hide.

Oh God, the humiliation!

He took another swig of beer. At about five in the morning he had woken up behind the woodshed, cold and damp and miserable. He had dragged himself out of the garden of the Villa Rosa and started the trek home, pausing only to vomit copiously in a rubbish bin. Somehow he had got himself into the house after clambering up that dreadful track and once there he had fallen fully clothed on his bed for a very few hours. Too few hours. Now the thing was, what had he done in the meantime?

He recommenced pacing, thinking hard. Did he remember voices shouting, or was that himself earlier? Perhaps he heard a car start up. Why couldn't he remember?

Had he thrown Ettore into the pool? It was possible, but he had no memory of it. If he had done it, then who could know he had been there? Had anyone seen him enter the Villa Rosa grounds? Everyone knew he'd got it in for Ettore, so they were bound to suspect him. But had anyone actually seen him go to the Villa Rosa? Another swig of beer and he thought, *I can't have done it. I wouldn't have had the strength.* After all, he reasoned, he had been blind drunk. He sighed and looked out of the window at the wonderful view of the mountains and vowed he would sell the house and go as soon as the whole thing was over.

"I'll probably be in jail," he muttered gloomily. "Who's going to believe I didn't do it, if I don't believe myself?"

He took another swig at the beer can and emptied it. Suddenly he thought of all the awful things he had heard about Italian prisons, the police and justice in general. God, it was almost like a third world country. No, they wouldn't dare to ill-treat a German. Ah, but that was another thing, they all joked with him and let him buy them drinks and so on, but he knew damn well what his fellow countrymen had done in Italy, in this town even, during the last world war, and Italians have long memories.

He squeezed the beer can, crumpling it, and tossed it into the waste bin. It missed and clattered on the floor. He turned on his heels and went into the bedroom, pulled out the suitcase he'd wedged into the cupboard and started throwing all his clothes into it. He stopped when it was nearly full, taking out the stuff again until he managed to find a suit and clean shirt to wear for the journey. He was leaving, today, now. He'd drive to Pisa and get on the first plane for anywhere. It was too dangerous to stay, even if he had done nothing. The thought of prison and rubber truncheons was more than he could bear. He was moving towards the shower when the doorbell rang, and then he knew it was too late.

FOUR

THEY LET HIM shower and dress and were extremely civil, he thought. They had escorted him to the police station and almost apologetically taken his fingerprints. He vaguely remembered seeing a neighbour's shocked face as he left the house with his escort. Now he sat facing the senior police officer, a middle-aged man wearing a very expensive and well cut suit. He looked like a cultured and intelligent man. Nothing could have been further from the barbarians he had been imagining. He relaxed a little. He could hardly imagine a man like that wielding a truncheon. He glanced at the uniformed policeman, gun in holster and a hatchet face, and thought he looked more the type.

He was jerked out of his reverie by the magistrate's first question.

"Do you prefer to speak Italian or English Signor Ganz? I'm afraid I don't speak German," he said.

"Well, I think maybe I speak English better, what about you?" said Ganz in heavily accented Italian.

Ruggero Di Girolamo, who prided himself on his excellent English, had spent several study periods in England as a young man, replied, "I prefer English, too."

The German's Italian was obviously very basic. He paused and looked the German straight in the eyes.

"I understand that you wished to kill Ettore Fagiolo. Did you do so?"

"NO!" he gasped, a beached whale, helpless. "No, no, no."

"But you informed quite a lot of people last night of your wish to do so."

"I?"

"Yes, indeed. In fact, at Aristotle's bar you said 'I'll kill that bastard' or in your own words *"Amazzo quel bastardo."*

The Italian's English was better than his own. He knew he had a thick German accent though his vocabulary was quite good, as he used English for business.

"Ja, um—vell…it vas that I had some drinks. I did not really vant to kill him."

"But you also followed his car on foot, shouting in German. Is that not so?"

"Ach, I do this? Yes, vell it was just a stupid drunken thing that I do. Imagine a man to chase a car, on foot." He tried to laugh.

"The car was going very slowly and parked shortly afterwards. You could have followed him when he got out. I think you did."

"No!"

"Please do not shout." He paused. "I also think that you followed him to the Villa Rosa and killed him. Perhaps you had an argument or a fight with him. After all you had had too much to drink, as you yourself told me. And then somehow he hit his head and you threw him in the water. An accident?" he looked inquiringly at Fritzy.

"No, none of these things has happened. You must prove this. I haff done nothing. I vant a lawyer and I must contact the German Consul. You are to take me to prison?" he gabbled rather hysterically.

"Did you do it?"

"No."

"Then why should you go to prison?"

Ganz was silent.

"Perhaps you could explain what you did last night. Where did you go?"

"Novhere."

"Let me see. It says here," he consulted a folder, turned a couple of pages and went on "that you were seen running after

Ettore Fagiolo's car shouting in German. Unfortunately no one understood what you were saying, but I think we have a fair idea. You were angry with this man, who was a liar and a cheat. You had already said in Italian that you wanted to kill him. You tell me you did not do so, so I am asking you what did you do?"

"I vent to my home."

"It must have taken you a long time to get there, as I have you running after the car at twelve-thirty and starting along the track home at five in the morning. I have witnesses to these facts. So where did you spend the night?"

"Oh vell, I suppose I must to tell the truth. I fall asleep on the vay."

"Really, and whereabouts was that? I mean it was obviously before reaching the track."

"I'm afraid this I cannot remember."

Di Girolamo seemed to be consulting the folder again, though the German thought it was just a ploy. Ganz was sweating profusely again but didn't want to take off his jacket, as the man in front of him was still wearing his and looked cool and calm. It was not pleasant to be treated like a criminal. Earlier they had taken his fingerprints and left him to sit in a bare room, alone with his thoughts He felt as though he had been there for hours. He probably had. He realised he was hungry. His watch had actually stopped so he had no idea of the time. They had come to get him at his home before lunch, and he guessed it must be late afternoon. The window was completely obscured so he couldn't see how much light was left. That was part of it. They isolated him in space and time and then they would beat him up. He felt depressed. This was not going well.

The phone rang and Di Girolamo barked his name into the receiver, then said "Good, thank you." He put the receiver down again and closed the folder on his desk.

"I think we have nearly finished for today. It is late and I am sure you are tired and hungry." He glanced at the fat German and

continued, "I would like you to make a statement about your movements last night and sign it. By the way, I understand that you were
packing a case when my men arrived. Where were you going?"

"I am going home, I need to do, organise, some things out in
Germany, business things—ja? As you know, I come and I go all
the time." He felt more confident now. It was obvious they had
no proof. And, anyway, he hadn't done it. Also they wouldn't
want any trouble at a diplomatic level. They would have to have
sure and certain proof before arresting a German subject. "I am
free to go back to Germany, ja?"

"I think that we will contact your embassy. We cannot hold
you here. If you were an Italian subject I would take your
passport and limit your movements. I will arrange an escort to
the airport for you and request that the German police sequester
your passport on arrival in Germany. Then you will be required
to inform them of your whereabouts. If you wish to return here,
and I am sure that business matters will necessitate that, they will
escort you to a plane and you will be met on arrival here and your
passport will be in our hands during your stay here. I think you
will find that there is a great deal of collaboration between our
two countries. If you decide to remain in Italy, if your business
matters in Germany could possibly be deferred, I will ask you
for your passport and that you inform the police of your whereabouts. You are a suspect in a murder case, but I prefer not to
arrest you. You will be free to travel within Italy, but you must
let me know where you are. Is that quite clear?"

Ganz thought for a moment, then pulled his passport out of
his pocket. He suddenly felt quite sure that for some reason they
didn't really think he'd done it. He said "I giff you this, and traffel
to Florence now. Germany can vait. I tell the truth. I know you
vould suspect me, but I am innocent. I haff nothing to fear—nein?
I vill do my normal tour round in Italy. I vill need to go to Milan,
Venice, Rome and Naples. I shall be back here," he stabbed a
forefinger at the ground, "I think about the end of the month. But

I vill report to the police in every town. Also I giff the name of
the Hotel vhere I stay. Is vhat you vant—*nicht wahr?*"

"If you fail to do so, I will put out an alert and have you arrested
as a murder suspect. Now, the statement and your signature, and
then you are free to go, unless you change your mind."

"Change my mind?"

"Yes, and tell me that you did it. A confession."

"No, I do not. I cannot confess to vhat I do not do—*ja?*"

Some time later, Herman Ganz was accompanied to his house
to collect the ill-packed suitcase and then escorted to the station
in time for the train to Florence. As he closed the door on his
house and started down the track to the waiting police car, one
of the two *carabinieri* said to him, "It's pretty inconvenient not
being able to drive a car up to the house. You should ask for permission to build a road."

"I'm thinking about it," he replied. *"Ci sto pensando."*

FIVE

THE DAY AFTER Ettore's death, Hilary had made a statement at the police station and after that had been left in peace. She had watched a team of quiet men discretely examine every inch of the pool area, dusting for fingerprints and putting small objects into plastic bags. All the garden tools had been removed from the shed. Slowly the searchers had moved over the whole garden area and into the garage. They had been inside the house as well.

The newspaper headlines on the first day had screamed: *"Tragic Death of a Young Man"* and *"Autopsy to Be Performed on Young Real Estate Agent"* and *"Young Man Drowned in an Englishman's Pool."* It wasn't until the next day that the headlines changed to *"Foul Play Suspected for Real Estate Agent's Death."* Some more cautious ones said, *"Inquiry into Young Man's Death—Not an Accident?"* and *"Accidental Death or Suicide?"*

Now, four days after the event, it seemed evident that Ettore Fagiolo had been murdered. Gossip was rife in the small town as everyone tried to find a plausible explanation for his death.

The body had been returned to the family and the funeral was to be that afternoon. Ettore was to be buried in the town cemetery by the elderly priest who had married his parents and had baptised him.

The service would be held in the church used by his ancestors and his body laid to rest in the same graveyard as his grandparents and other relatives who had died before him. The whole town turned out to join his funeral procession, but Hilary stayed home. She had long ago decided not to attend funerals because to go to one meant to go to all or cause offence. This way it was just accepted as part of her foreignness. She could hear the bells tolling—able now to recognize the different calls, festive or funereal, and the joyful mid-day peal by which she used to time herself, the call for local council meetings, the toll for vigils and the quarter hourly tolling away of time.

Ettore was dead and now it seemed likely that he had been murdered. Speculation was pointless, for she had no idea who could have killed him or why. But others with more privileged information or insight, or inventive capacity, accepted no limits and the town heaved and bubbled with speculation. She had been honoured with many versions, mainly because she had found the body and was accepted by everyone as an important witness. "Witness to what?" she said. "I only had the misfortune to look out of the window, see a body and report it." Nevertheless, this morning she had been told that a wronged woman had killed him; a German resident had done it in a drunken rage; a jealous husband had found him in the Proctors' villa with his wife and had killed him; and countless variations involving thieves drug rings and even the Mafia.

She sat on her terrace. The town was silent now. No doubt the procession was shuffling down to the cemetery about half a mile from the town centre. The day was humid and she thought how marvellous it would be to bathe, but where? Maybe the river? It was three-thirty. She rushed around in the kitchen and took a bottle of water from the fridge, washed some fruit and made a cheese roll. She grabbed a book and her bag. Her towel was in the car.

What bliss to leave the cloying atmosphere of the town and drive, the car slicing the thick air into movement, creating the illusion of a breeze as she drove to the river. Then minutes later she walked across the scalding boulders and dropped her bag beside the torrent. The water was a clear blue-white colour and moved fast and transparent over boulders, smoothed by the water's passage over time. A yard from the bank it was about three metres deep and slower moving as it swirled into a natural pool overhung by a steep bank on the other side. The local boys used it as a diving platform, like miniature Tarzans. But today she was alone, the only person in the world. The water was bubbling, frogs were calling, and there were rustling noises in the trees on the other bank. Nothing else.

She swam in the icy water and felt refreshed. This affair had begun to dominate her life recently. She had been sleeping badly and having trouble relaxing and concentrating. Her work had fallen behind and the deadline for completion of the translation drew nearer without any appreciable reduction of the sheaf of paper still to be worked through. *This is ridiculous,* she thought, *I must get down to some work. It's not as though I even liked Ettore. I actively disliked him. He was an unscrupulous, and rather unpleasant young man, with his red Porsche, and dark glasses.*

As she recollected him, a memory of meeting him recently as she drove to the coast flashed into her mind. His Porsche had been parked on the roadside and Ettore was lounging against it talking to Marco, the son of a local bar owner. The two dark heads were bent towards each other as though earnestly exchanging important information. They had looked up at the same moment, straight at her, as her car drove slowly by them.

Since Ettore's death, Marco had been in obvious misery. She had seen him the day before in his father's bar, white faced with dark circles under his green eyes, his adolescent beauty somehow marred so that he looked prematurely aged. Could he be involved somehow in this business, or was he just grieving for the loss of an idol more than a friend? A friend almost twice his age and in many ways a bad influence on him. She knew that Marco had recently been caught smoking a joint, luckily before his eighteenth birthday. Had this been due to Ettore's influence? It was fortunate that no other drugs had been found on him, but Marco's father had reacted very badly. To him, smoking a joint was as unthinkable as shooting up.

She felt suddenly extremely cold. She climbed out of the water, her teeth chattering, to wrap herself in a wonderfully warm towel. Then she found a comfortable hollow in the boulders and began to eat her cheese roll and read her book. Another hour or so and the sun would dip behind the hill. Then she would go home and work.

SIX

Augusta Fagiolo settled her senile husband into bed for an afternoon rest. He would sleep for at least two hours and she had things to do. Her only child was dead and buried. In the room he used at home there was nothing, only some of his clothes and shoes. She had taken the keys to his office and knew she must go there now and sort out the debris of his life.

She wore black and tied the laces on her best shoes with gnarled hands. Arthritis after years of wear and tear was only to be expected. She was a simple woman; her parents had been peasants and she had left school at the end of the second year of elementary school. She had begged to be allowed to continue, but her father had been adamant. He needed her to look after the sheep, walk with them all day as they roved from pasture to pasture. So she had obeyed, spending lonely days in the country with only the dogs for company and the bells of the sheep clanging their whereabouts. But she was stubborn. Although she had had little schooling she had continued to read and to learn.

As a woman there was not much for her but marriage and work in the house or on the land. But she could help her son who was a slow learner. She wanted something better for him. She had done her best by this son, forced him to continue his studies to become a *geometra* and given him her savings to start up as a real estate agent. Now she must do her best to protect his memory.

The key turned easily in the lock and for only the second time in her life, she went in. The day before the official opening he had shown her round, but there had been no reason to return. She glanced at the office where he received his clients. There was a huge desk, carpets on the floor, a soft sofa, a low table with some copies of architectural magazines. She walked through to the back office. Here were the worktables and computers and the drawing boards. He employed two young men barely out of school to do the designs, which he signed as his own.

There was one other room in which Ettore used to keep a change of clothes and shoes and also all his bills, invoices and bank account statements. This was the room she needed to look in. She had brought a roll of black rubbish bags with her. She opened the wardrobe and began removing his clothes. There were quite a lot. She folded them and put them in a bag for charity, but she ran her hands into every pocket and emptied them out first. When she had finished she had two packets of condoms (one half empty); a very small, very sharp pen-knife; an empty biro pen; two little packets of powder; some book matches from night clubs; a half empty packet of black, gold tipped cigarettes and several keys with name tags on them. These last she took through to the work room and put into a drawer in a desk. After some thought she took the packets of powder and put them into her pocket. The rest went into another black bag.

She opened a cupboard door and checked the contents on each shelf. There were folders containing bank statements that went back several years. These she ignored after checking that their contents tallied with what was written on the outside. There were bills, invoices and other paper work concerned with the financial or the bureaucratic side of his work. There were the customers' files for work in progress. All these she methodically checked and replaced.

It was hot in the office, so she turned on the overhead fan and opened a window. She found a locked cupboard door and after trial and error with the keys on the bunch, opened it. She knew immediately that this was what she had come here for. There were videocassettes with disgusting illustrations on the covers. The titles gave no illusion as to their contents. *Well,* she thought, *I find it revolting, but these days things are different.*

Her hand sketched the sign of the cross on her breast as she began throwing the videos into a rubbish bag. She had put on a pair of cotton gloves and had brought a cloth with her. She would wipe his fingerprints off each one, even though they were going to be destroyed, just in case. As she removed them from the shelves she glanced at them and gave an involuntary cry. The one she was holding had two men on the cover locked in sexual congress. She muttered a prayer, threw it in the bag and stoically continued. There were others, some with young boys, so young as to be just out of childhood. She felt a terrible shame. Who was this son of hers?

She did not know him; she did not want to know him.

She threw the last one in and picked up a box containing photos of men, naked men alone or with other men, or with a woman, or more than one woman. They were graphically obscene. She felt ill. In a separate envelope was a dreadful photo of a creature that was neither man nor woman. It was wearing a red curly wig and laughing. The mouth was open wide, the head thrown back. Large golden hoops dangled from its ears, and it was wearing heavy make-up, but nothing else. She looked at it thoughtfully, averting her eyes from the lower half, concentrating on the face. It reminded her of someone but she couldn't think whom. She put it on one side. Then she found a small folder of photos of children, little boys. They were brown skinned and thin, their eyes resigned.

"Not the children, dear God," she wept. All the photos she set aside in a separate bag. She would tear them into a thousand shreds, and then burn them and bury the ash. She hoped God would forgive him. And she would try to herself, but the images seemed burned into her retina and she experienced such horror that she felt there could be no forgiveness. A locked drawer contained a bag of loose pills, which she put in with the photos. There were also a few non-professional photos. She took them out and Marco smiled up at her, naked and erect, his face impudent and inviting.

SEVEN

As SHE HAD expected, Hilary had been called to the police station the day after the discovery of the body to sign a formal statement. But she was rather surprised to receive a request to return there for further questioning the day after the funeral. When she arrived, the local Maresciallo greeted her quite kindly and escorted her to a room where a man wearing a well cut, linen suit was sitting behind a desk. He rose to his feet and courteously asked her to be seated, introducing himself as Dottor Ruggero Di Girolamo, the magistrate in charge of the case.

"Good morning, please be seated. You are Signora Hilary Odescalchi née Wright?"

"Good morning, and yes, I am."

They spoke in Italian. He was very attractive, fairly tall, slim and very well dressed. He smiled, his dark blue eyes engaging hers. They shook hands and he indicated a chair, and then sat down himself. Di Girolamo had a case file in front of him to which he referred.

"This is just a formality. I know you have already made a statement but I would like to go over one or two things with you." He looked at her, gave another brief smile and continued.

"You were born in Great Britain in 1957, on December 25th and were married in 1974 to Guido Odescalchi, born in Italy in the Province of Lucca in the town of Borgo del Castello, on 5th September 1935, by whom you had two children, a female in 1978 and a male in 1981. Guido Odescalchi subsequently died on January 8th 1987 as the result of injuries sustained in a car crash, is that correct?" He looked up at her again.

"Yes, quite correct." *The sum of my life in two sentences,* she thought.

"So you have two children, Alexander, aged 20, and Amanda, aged 23. Where are they now? Do they live here?"

"No, no, they don't. Alex is at university in Kent, though he's on holiday in Greece now, and Amanda is a social worker in London.

They do come here for holidays when they can, but not more than two or three times a year."

"Were they, either of them I mean, here on the 8th of July?"

"No." She felt it to be a strange question.

"I see. Now, your address is No.1, Via del Sole, and you work as a translator, correct?"

"Yes."

"Could I see your passport please, or identity card? I presume you have both."

"Yes, I do, have both, I mean. Do you want to see both?"

"Yes," he looked at her again. "This is merely a formality, as I said before."

She handed him her documents. Somehow she felt a little uneasy, not that she had any reason to, but being in a police station was always a little unnerving.

He looked at her British passport and Italian identity card, and handed them back without comment.

"Signora Wright," he said following the Italian custom of using a woman's maiden name when calling her Signora, "I am sorry to have to ask you this, but I will have to ask you to allow us to take your fingerprints. We need the fingerprints of anyone who frequented the house, the Villa Rosa, so that we can eliminate all the known ones. And who knows, maybe find some unknown ones! It was overlooked when you came here to make your statement and I am afraid I still have unidentified fingerprints." He smiled reassuringly as though guessing at her discomfort.

She tried to sound unconcerned as she replied, "Of course, I understand."

"Good. But before we do that I would like to ask you a few questions just so that I can get a general idea of things. As you know, I am not in service in this area. Perhaps you could tell me something about your friends, the Proctors?"

"Well, that's just it," she replied, "I can't much, as I know so little of them myself. And I must tell you that they are neighbours, not friends."

"Not friends," he paused "I must have misunderstood. I thought you were very friendly. I understood that you were given the run of the house and use of the pool during their absence." His tone sounded a little harsh. He paused again and then suddenly said, "Were you there on the night of the 8th of July?"

"What!" She took a deep breath thinking, *I don't believe this,* and said, "No I was not. If you wish me to sign a statement to that effect, I will."

"Yes, I will ask you to do that," he replied calmly. "Now, about these neighbours," he paused significantly, "not friends. I would like you to tell me everything you know about them, their lives, their friends and their activities."

"Everything won't take long, I assure you. About three years ago they came to Italy looking for a house to buy. They know Italy quite well, speak the language reasonably and decided they wanted to live here as residents. I think they looked in several areas before someone put them on to Ettore Fagiolo, the real estate agent. They fell in love with the house, Casa Balduini, which they later painted pink and then re-named Villa Rosa. It was falling to pieces when they bought it and had been empty for ten years, which was when the previous owner, Signorina Rossi, died. Um, they bought it, renovated it, built the swimming pool and want to live in it most of the year. He is some kind of computer expert and sometimes goes abroad for brief periods, and she loves the house and garden and looks after them. They are my neighbours, nothing more, and as a good neighbour, I said I would water the plants while they're away, and they said, "Use the pool" and that's about it. By the way, I'm worried about the plants. If you haven't finished with the house could one of your men water them?"

"I think I can allow you into the house by tomorrow. You have the keys of course?"

"Yes, Robin, Mrs. Proctor that is, gave them to me that evening. I had dinner there, then they left at about midnight I suppose, as they were catching an early morning flight to Hong Kong from Rome."

"At what time?"

"I think it was at about 6.30 a.m."

"It only takes a little over three hours to get to Rome. Why did they leave so early?"

"Well, they had to be there an hour and a half before takeoff and Nigel likes to drive slowly and have time in hand, in case of a puncture or an act of God or whatever."

"I see. Now, tell me about their relationship with Ettore Fagiolo. You say that they bought their house from him and that he did the work on it. But I understand that their relationship changed at some point. Why was that?"

"Well the reason was that Nigel thought that he had been overcharged, as he had, in my opinion, and he'd heard stories from other foreigners who had had unfortunate experiences with him. Ettore that is. And he, Nigel I mean, felt he'd been made a fool of, especially as he had totally trusted Ettore up till then." She felt flustered and knew that she sounded as though she was.

"I see. So what you are telling me is that it would be very unusual for Ettore to be in their house?"

"Was he? In the house I mean?"

Dottor Di Girolamo smiled at her and said, "I ask the questions." He waited.

"Ettore has not been in the house for some time to my knowledge. But I don't know if I would know, if you see what I mean. They argued some time ago, but as work on the pool had been started by then, Ettore carried it through. And that was finished by June. I do know that Nigel had decided not to pay the last instalment for the work, as he felt he'd been cheated so much."

"You see, you do know quite a lot about their affairs. Let's see what else you know. Had Nigel expressed animosity towards this man?"

"Animosity! Really! If you mean did he want to injure him physically, I would think not. He doesn't seem a very violent sort of person to me. He was angry, but within normal limits. I mean, he wasn't obsessed by it or anything."

"So if Ettore had been invited to the house, he would have felt it safe to go there to talk things over?"

"Well yes, I suppose so. But isn't this all very hypothetical? How could Nigel invite him to the house if he wasn't there? Oh, I see. You mean as a trap or something. That sounds a bit far-fetched."

"Perhaps you invited him there in Nigel's name and then killed him for some reason of your own. You had the keys to the house." He said this in a very mild and reasonable tone of voice.

"What! Ah, so this is the theory that whoever finds the body committed the crime. I find that laughable." But she was shaken and he smiled at her discomfort.

"Yes, perhaps I am joking." There was a silence. Then he got up quickly out of his chair, his hand pressing the bell to summon an officer. Hilary rose to her feet, and he, speaking English, said to her, "Come, we'll take the fingerprints of this dangerous criminal."

He turned to young police officer who had entered the room and said, "Take her down and print her, and then get her to sign the brief statement I'm sending down." To Hilary he said, "Thank you for your help. You will be accompanied to have your fingerprints taken, you will sign a statement, and then," he paused, "you are free to go and water your flowers. But not until tomorrow. *Buon giorno Signora.*"

EIGHT

TWO DAYS LATER nothing much had happened. Hilary had been in to water Robin's plants the day before but had stayed in the house only briefly. Nigel and Robin were due back in about ten days' time and Hilary thought they would have an unpleasant shock, unless perhaps they had already been informed. She thought that maybe Nigel would be pretty calm after a bit of bluster, but she was sure Robin would have qualms about swimming in the pool now. At least they hadn't actually seen the body floating there.

She sat outside Gino's bar, a newspaper in front of her, vaguely aware of twittering American ladies at the next table. The words "cute" and "quaint" spattered their conversation. A group of young girls passed by and gazed in horror at the fat American women who were wearing large shorts, and designer tee shirts. Their cameras and bags were slung on the chairs. They both wore large straw hats and incredibly large sunglasses that covered the sides of the eyes. Both wore ankle socks and walking shoes. The girls laughed quietly and whispered to each other. Their linen dresses and shorts were cool and elegant. They were tanned and their hair looked perfectly natural, which Hilary knew meant that great care had been taken to make it look so. They wore thong sandals and their toenails were delicately varnished. Hilary loved to see these beautiful girls and had always thought it incredible that they all seemed to take such care of themselves. Even when she was younger she had never managed to achieve this seemingly effortless grace. Now she admitted defeat, but neither would she ever look like these women at the next table.

Marco came out with her cappuccino and brioche. He was still looking ill. The girls glanced at him once and then away as they murmured quietly. Marco, aware of their disdain, looked down at his feet. Then, he raised his eyes and met Hilary's and he abruptly banged the cup and plate on the table and bolted back into bar, the bead curtain clattering as he passed. From inside the bar she heard his father's voice call, "Marco," but there was only the sound of a slamming door in answer. The girls languidly walked on. The American women were calling, "Hey Ronnie, Ed, would you two just come over here and siddown. It's shady here…come on outta that sun."

Two large red-faced men with cameras slung round their necks that banged on their bellies as they moved waddled to join their wives. They were sweating profusely, their shirts quite damp, and Hilary wondered if they were having a good time. They looked pretty cheerful. She finished her brioche and drank the rest of her coffee, then folded the newspaper and left it on the table. The Americans had removed their hats and glasses and were discussing what to drink as she walked by them and went into the bar. Inside it was dark and cool. A fan hummed quietly. Sitting motionless at a table gazing at nothing with a neglected newspaper in front of him was Gino, Marco's father. He slowly brought his gaze round to meet hers, heaved himself to his feet and went behind the counter to the till.

"One euro fifty, Signora," he said, giving her an empty smile. She felt great compassion for this man, had known him for years and would have liked to offer words of comfort, as though words could comfort a father who could feel his son slipping away from him, distancing himself in every way. This was a son, cherished as possibly only an Italian child can be, adored, cosseted and spoilt: an only child born late to these two kind people. Something was very wrong and every one of them appeared to be suffering. She said nothing, paid, took her change and said "Ciao Gino."

He sighed. "Arrivederci," he said, looking her full in the eyes, which she knew meant, "You know and I know, but let's leave it there."

Outside, the Americans, like gaudy butterflies on their seasonal run through a foreign country, were calling hopefully in uncertain voices as she went past, "Cam-eri-air-ray. Does that sound right, Ed?"

"Yeah, I think that's about it, try it a bit louder."

She hoped they would enjoy Italy. They were hot, sticky and tired and couldn't speak the language. They were probably doing Italy in a week before moving on to do the rest of Europe. No doubt the folks back home would receive an edited account of their travels. She never helped English-speaking tourists as she felt they should make their own discoveries. And finding ways to make oneself understood was part of it. As she walked away she could hear them talking to Gino and his kind voice replying.

Walking through the old town on her way to Miriam Greene's house, Hilary passed groups of music students carrying their instruments. The St. Christopher Music Festival was on again and for the next four weeks the whole town would be filled with music as musicians and singers practised and gave informal afternoon concerts. Then would come the evenings in the newly restored theatre with small operas, often the first performance of a piece that had been neglected for well over two hundred years, and sacred music in the Duomo, which dominated the town and was dedicated to St. Christopher. In one of the small piazzas, chairs were already set out for that afternoon's concert and she made a mental note to go, and to phone Sue Browne, a friend of hers, to remind her.

Miriam Greene was a writer who had lived nearly the whole of her adult life in Italy. She lived on the opposite side of town to Hilary, in a large 19th century house, which she jokingly referred to as "the Mausoleum." The house was set back from the main road into town behind massive gates and was almost hidden from the road by enormous trees. It had a huge front door that was gained by ten stone steps of diminishing width and was overlooked by a stone balcony. Hilary pressed the brass doorbell and was admitted by a young Italian woman who smiled at her and said in Italian with a strong southern accent, "She's longing to see you, wants all the sordid details and says you should have come ages ago."

"Oh does she! Well, I only came now to bring her those documents. I suppose I'll have to see her. Where is she, in the writing room?"

"Of course, go on up."

Hilary always felt that Assunta was a little over-familiar and disliked herself for feeling that way.

She moved towards the staircase, which was rather wide and had carpeted stone steps and a French window on the landing that stood open. The boughs of an enormously overgrown cherry tree almost entered the house. A dog's barking heralded her entrance. The writing room was really a large corridor on the first floor, which had French windows at the end and a decorative cast iron railing, so that with the windows open it looked like an enclosed terrace. The window looked onto the mountains and the famous view of the Apuan Alps. A rock formation known as "the Dead Man" that resembled a sleeping giant lying on his back with his knees drawn up, was clearly visible. Miriam had put her desk here and an enormous chair. The corridor was lined with bookcases on one side and there was a sofa for visitors. In an alcove facing the desk was a television hooked up to a stereo and C.D. player. On the massive desk was her computer. She had satellite T.V. and was linked to the Internet.

She had been writing romantic novels for years and had published an incredible amount, roughly a book a year, for the last fifty years. She sat now in her massive chair; she was a huge woman, vastly fat. Hilary had often wondered if the chair had been made to measure. As always, a cigarette burned in an ashtray. Miriam was not allowed to smoke, so she left a cigarette burning and just had an occasional illicit puff. Her puffy feet were on a footstool under the desk. Beside them were the little pink goblin slippers she wore. On the sofa, on a pink cushion, sat a white poodle, her inseparable companion. Her name was Cherry (a pun on Cherie). She stopped barking, decided it wasn't worth attacking Hilary and curled up on the cushion. The television was on and, as usual, Hilary saw that Miriam had been watching an American soap opera. Apparently she considered them a source of inspiration.

"Darling," she said, "I thought you would never come and I am simply longing to know all about it. That Fagiolo thing I mean."

"There's nothing to tell. You know more than I do. You read all the papers and have your spies out to get all the gossip," she paused. "I see you are still watching rubbish."

"My dear, how else would I manage to write this drivel? I find them stimulating. I run out of ideas you know and I am reduced to stealing other people's ideas. And if I live much longer I shall be reduced to stealing from real events. Perhaps I could put Fagiolo in a book. I could make him bi-sexual and have him killed by his jealous lover, male of course."

"I didn't know characters in your books knew about sex, especially what you might call…deviant sex. I thought a discrete veil was drawn across or something."

"My dear, I move with the times. But you are trying to distract me. I want to know all about it."

"But you do know all about it. You're bound to have heard more gossip than me because you go out of your way to hear it and I don't."

"Quite true, but that's not quite the same as from the horse's mouth. Tell all, or have they told you not to. The cops, I mean."

"Miriam, they don't call them 'the cops' anymore. And no, they haven't, because I really do know nothing. I looked out of my bedroom window, saw the body and reported it. That's all."

"Well that's a fat lot of bloody good. You sound like a Girl Guide doing her good deed for the day. I thought you must have seen something. Didn't you even hear anything, voices, a car, a splash.... I mean, why did they keep you down there so long if you didn't have something to tell them?"

"How did you know? No, don't tell me. Listen, I didn't see or hear anything. I was in bed asleep." But thinking back, she had heard a car; in fact she seemed to remember hearing car doors slam and a car starting up.

"Miriam, I'm sorry to disappoint you. Look, I've brought you your stuff, it's quite simple. So unless there's anything else, I've got to go. I'm behind with my work and I want to get some done and then go to the concert this afternoon."

"What! You're not even staying for a cup of coffee? I don't know why you bothered to come in the first place."

"I came because you said you wanted the translation. I promise I'll come back and stay longer next time."

She could have stayed longer, but she didn't want to talk about Ettore Fagiolo, or as Miriam called him "the Bean." She had been feeling a little uneasy since her visit to the police station and preferred to keep off the subject.

"All right, bugger off then, but make sure that you bring me some interesting gossip next time. I feel quite thwarted. Are you sure you didn't do it yourself? I can't think why you should, but you certainly had the opportunity! Oh wait a minute...didn't he do something rather nasty to your daughter once? There you are, there's your motive," she cackled and wheezed and coughed, tears coursing down her face. "Don't look like that! You'll only make me laugh more."

Hilary supposed that her face showed the shock she felt, that Miriam should so casually refer to something she had thought was a secret. She said calmly "You'll choke yourself to death if you carry on like that and then I'll be accused of a double murder."

Miriam wheezed and coughed even more at that, but finally

got herself under control and said, "Tell that bloody lazy girl to bring me a gin and tonic." And, after a stern look from Hilary, "Okay, just a tonic. But with lots of ice and lemon. And come back soon. Ciao." The fat hand was raised in salute, rings glinting, and bracelets clanking on her plump wrists.

Hilary went down the stairs reflecting. Oh yes, he'd done something nasty to her daughter all right; he'd more or less raped her. But he had been drunk, and so had her daughter, at a rather wild party. And it had been some years ago. "Forget it and forget all about it. It never happened," her daughter had insisted, and so it had been. Hilary wondered how Miriam knew about it. Because if *she* did, then how many others had the same knowledge? Maybe Ettore had bragged about it. Also, had Miriam just said what other people were maybe saying behind her back? Did everyone discuss her and judge her? Did people think she had killed Ettore? *No, this is paranoia,* she said to herself.

While she was letting herself out of the gates, a police car drove slowly past and she saw Di Girolamo in it. He turned his head a fraction and looked at her. Was he having her watched, she wondered? As she hurried on she heard the car accelerating away on the road to Lucca.

MIRIAM LOOKED UP as Assunta came in with her tonic water. She had found Assunta and her husband Salvatore, both Sicilians, through an agency three years previously when her elderly housekeeper had died and her gardener/chauffeur had decided to retire. They had good references from a family in Catania. Their previous employer, an ancient noblewoman, had died and the couple were interested in moving further north. She had grown used to the southern lilt in their speech but found them incomprehensible when they spoke together in dialect. Assunta was a good housekeeper, cooked well and saw to it that the house was well cleaned, harrying the cleaners mercilessly. Also, Miriam sent her to the shops every morning to glean gossip for her. Salvatore drove well, and was able to do a thousand small jobs, as well as look after the garden. There was an extensive vegetable garden at the back of the house and a chicken run for eggs, and now and then a capon. She employed a local boy, slow-witted but strong, to help him. Assunta and Salvatore seemed to have integrated well into the small town. There were not the racial prejudices here about southerners or *terroni,* a derogatory name some people used, that unfortunately were being fomented by the Northern League in some of the towns in the north of Italy. Yes, on the whole she thought she had made a lucky choice. They were young enough to get out and about, "ears to the ground," as Miriam put it, and they brought her a plentiful supply of local gossip. She chuckled inwardly, remembering Hilary's face when she had let her know that she had knowledge of the incident between Ettore and Amanda. It had been brought to her by Salvatore after an evening in a bar drinking and swapping stories.

Miriam came from a well-to-do family in Sussex. Her maternal grandparents had been Italian, her grandmother a member of the aristocracy, and the links with Italy had been maintained. Her family had spent many summers touring Italy during the years of her childhood and adolescence. Then, of course, she had fallen in love with Tommaso Bargellini when she was only eighteen and had married him. They had lived for years in Rome but came to Borgo San Cristoforo every summer to this house. Her husband's grandfather built it at the turn of the century with the wealth he had accumulated over the years by exploiting *mezzadri,* victims of a system that bound tenant farmers to the land, which they tilled in exchange for half their produce. He had owned fifty-two *poderi,* or small farms, as he had always reinvested his money by buying up any small farms that became available. Tommaso had become a lawyer, and on his retirement they had come to live here permanently. He had died eight years earlier.

Miriam had started writing early on in the marriage. They had wanted children but, by the age of twenty-five, she had realised there would be no children. So she had begun to fill her time with writing, at first as a hobby. She wrote romantic novels that sold well, a more modern version of the servant-girl novels of her youth. She was surprised to find that her books were read by people from many spheres of life, and she had sold well. This additional income had been welcome, as death duties and land reforms had diminished Tommaso's family fortune. As a lawyer he had not been exceptionally successful, but their life style had always been what Miriam jokingly called "gracious." The only exception to their life in Italy had been their self-imposed exile during the Second World War. She and Tommaso had lived in Sussex for that period and had worked hard raising money for Italy's reconstruction. It had been in that period of her life that she had started to write in earnest. Now as she sat surrounded by technological paraphernalia she continued to write, not for the money it brought her, but because she did not know what else to do.

"Assunta, *mia cara,*" she smiled winningly, "Please bring me just a tiny drop of gin to put in this."

"Tiny it will be," grumbled Assunta. "I don't want your death on my hands."

"Heaven forbid. I've no intention of dying just yet. Life is much too interesting. Now come here and tell me what they are saying in the shops this morning."

AT SIX THAT EVENING, Hilary sat in the piazza listening to Baroque music. Susan Browne, a new young friend, had come with her, and they were both invited to dinner that evening with mutual friends. There were about fifty people sitting on white plastic chairs. A computer printout programme had been placed on each chair, and some members of the audience were fanning themselves with them. It was still hot in the square. The concert had attracted the usual culture tourists as well as a cross section of the local inhabitants. There were several children in the audience and even a few babies in pushchairs. The concerts in the theatre in the evening attracted a different public. But these were informal concerts, and rather fun. Hilary had gotten through a fair amount of work that day and now, relaxing, she began to hope that life would soon be back to normal. A light breeze sprang up and ruffled peoples' hair and sent sheets of music flying.

"The standard seems a bit higher this year," said Sue as they enthusiastically applauded two young oboists. Seven trumpets took the stage next and played something more modern. When the concert had finished, chairs were stacked and carried off and everyone dispersed. The next informal concert in two days' time was to be held in the cloisters of the convent.

"It's the only chance I get to go into the convent and it's so charming there." Sue was pleased. She loved the Music Festival. They started walking through the old town, pausing only to read posters that announced art exhibitions and other summer activities, which were mostly focussed on food.

"Shall I call for you to go to John and Terry's house tonight?" asked Sue.

"Yes, at about eight-thirty, okay?"

They separated. Hilary only had an hour in which to water the garden and change, so she walked briskly and, turning a corner at a smart pace, bumped into someone. Excusing herself, she looked up and saw it was Di Girolamo.

"*Buona sera,*" they said simultaneously.

"How fortunate that I should meet you," he said. "I wanted to ask you something, informally."

"Oh, well, yes, please do." She was sure her face was pink. He seemed to have the ability to make her feel very unsure of herself.

"I just wondered whether you liked Ettore Fagiolo."

"If I say 'no,' does that mean I did it?" She tried to smile as she spoke. "Of course if I say 'yes,' I could be lying."

"I knew you wouldn't like the question, but it is informal. I just wanted your opinion about him. I'm not writing it down, as you can see."

"Yes, I see. Well at the risk of an imminent arrest, I'll answer truthfully. I didn't like him at all. I thought him very unpleasant." She looked him straight in the eyes as she said this, as though to say, "I'm not afraid of you, and I'll say what I think no matter what the consequences."

"Well, well. That's very interesting." He smiled at her, which she found rather disconcerting. "Did you have a personal motive for this dislike?"

She felt herself go cold. "No, not all. I just dislike his sort."

"Thank you for your honesty," he said, and for one awful moment she thought he was being sarcastic, that he must know that she had a very strong, personal motive for disliking Ettore Fagiolo. She bit her lip and made no reply.

He looked as though he was going to ask her something else, but as the seconds passed and he said nothing at all, she wondered how she could leave him without it looking as though she wanted to run away from him. There was no way she could be the one to take the initiative given his position. She would just have to stand there for as long as he chose to make her.

He was wearing cream slacks and a shirt to match with a darker linen jacket, and had slotted his dark glasses into his open shirt neck. Hilary thought he must be about her own age or a little older, and very attractive. But she banished thoughts of his attractions from her mind as she reminded herself who he was and what he represented. They still stood there in silence. Once more, he seemed to be about to say something. But finally all he did say was, "I'm sorry to have taken up your time. As I am sure you are in a hurry. I'll say goodbye, Signora."

He turned abruptly and walked away quickly. Hilary didn't know what to think of him. What did he want from her? He might be attractive, but she found him almost menacing. She began walking home slowly, turning things over in her mind. Di Girolamo had been very strange. *Perhaps he thinks I did it,* she thought, *and I must be mad to have answered him like that. I should have just said, "Oh, I thought him a charming young man. What a tragedy!" like everyone else does. I wish I had. All I want is to be left alone, but I suppose there's not much chance of that now. How could I be so stupid, and why do I find it so hard to lie?*

Worst of all was the terrible thought that he might somehow come to know about Ettore and Amanda and seriously begin to think that she had a motive to kill him. Perhaps he already knew and was playing a cat and mouse game with her. Why else ask if she had a personal motive for disliking Ettore? She thought of the way the cards were stacked against her. She had the keys to the house, she had known exactly when the Proctors would be away, and she had a reason for killing him. What could have been easier than to ask Ettore to the Villa Rosa under some pretext and then kill him? Also, she had been the one to find the body and she knew that that in itself was suspicious.

On the other hand, had she really wanted to kill Ettore, would she have waited years to do so? Also, how could she have got him into the pool? She wasn't that strong and Ettore was quite a big man. She wouldn't have stood a chance against a man. *No, she reassured herself, there is no way they could suspect me.*

She had reached her front door by now and saw it was already nearly five past eight. There wouldn't really be time to water the garden, so she rushed upstairs for a shower. Sue was bound to be punctual, or worse still, come early.

After a tepid shower, she padded into the bedroom. The wardrobe held little as she mainly wore jeans, which were folded in a drawer. She chose a linen dress and jacket, and sandals of the same cream colour. Looking in the mirror, when she was ready, she saw a slim, still youthful and attractive woman. She was tanned and had blue eyes. Her hair was a silvery blonde and very short. Her dress was simple, classic and unadorned. She wore no jewellery, not even a ring, ever.

NINE

DINNER WITH FRIENDS was on the terrace as the night was warm and the air in the house was stifling. Terry and John were old friends of hers. They had been frequent visitors from the States, spending almost every summer in Italy for the last ten years since Terry (Theresa) had inherited her grandmother's house and decided to come and see the birthplace of her parents. What she had found was a dilapidated farmhouse with a large adjoining barn set in a charming area. She had fallen in love with the whole thing and had set to work to restore it with an attention to detail that had turned the farmhouse and barn into quite a large house with a separate flat in the area that had once housed the cows. She had turned the large cantinas into a fabulous kitchen, which was cool and spacious, and had paved a large area outside, reached by French windows, which she called the *La Terrazza*. That was where they always ate, weather permitting. To her great surprise she had also found some relatives and so felt that she belonged here. Her own parents had died together in a car crash fifteen years earlier when she was already married and had two small children. They had been her only family as there were no brothers and sisters. Her husband, an only child like herself, had only his mother still alive. But here in Italy they had found an extended family, and quite a large one. In fact two of Terry's cousins and their wives were already seated on the terrace, a glass of wine in one hand and an antipasto in the other. They all embraced and kissed cheeks as always, a custom that even the British seemed to have adopted recently. On her last trip back, Hilary had been quite surprised to be clasped to bosoms by usually undemonstrative people. Here it felt normal. Francesco, Terry's cousin, and his wife Giulietta, had children of the same age as her own. In fact, they were friends, especially the girls, who had been in the same class at school. Monica, another cousin, and her husband Pietro were younger, and their children were teenagers, roughly the same age as Terry and John's. Anne Gwent, an American friend of Terry's, arrived a moment later with her new man, Tom Wilcox.

"There's only Ben still to come," said Terry, greeting them. "He said he'd be a bit late."

"I'm afraid we were discussing 'the Bean,'" said Francesco, translating Ettore Fagiolo's surname.

"What a slime he was," said Terry.

"Do not speak ill of the dead," replied John as he came out with more glasses.

"Okay, Okay. But don't expect me to say anything good about him. Somebody swiped him with a shovel or something, so I'd take a bet he deserved it."

"Nobody deserves to be murdered," said Hilary.

"Yeah. I know it, but I don't feel a bit sad about it. Do you?"

"No," she admitted. "But if it's murder, there has to be a murderer, and I can't imagine who that could be. Has anyone got any ideas, realistic ones, not the wild theories I hear every day in the grocers?"

"I have," cried Ben, who had just arrived. "*Buona sera*, everybody! I have a splendid theory. It was that crazy German in the next village, the one who was so furious about the farm he bought without an access road. He's always getting drunk and muttering curses. That court case is dragging on and he has to carry every single thing to the house on his back; all those damned great gas cylinders and his wood for the fire. It takes him hours with a small wheelbarrow. Well, I think he arranged a midnight tryst, pretending to be a woman, and when 'the Bean' arrived, he whammed him and threw him in the pool."

"Very ingenious. Apart from the fact I can't see Ettore being taken in like that, I happen to know that the German isn't even here at the moment," said Francesca.

"I know, but he was here. He left on the day the body was discovered. I know because I asked the old crone who looks after his house while he's away, in a very casual and round about manner, I assure you. Also, I didn't mean that he lured him there with a phone call, but with a note."

"Does he write in Italian?" asked Giulietta.

"All right, I give in. My theory lets in water. Has anyone else got any ideas?"

"Not me," said John "I'll get you a drink; you deserve one for trying. What about you, Hilary? You found the body, you must have thought up some explanation. Besides, you should be an expert with all those detective stories you translate."

"At first I thought he'd had an accident, and even now I can't really believe someone murdered him. I can't think of anyone who would. I still like to think it must have been accidental. Maybe he had a fight with someone and hit his head, and later fell into the pool. I suppose that's murder as well, but it's the only kind I could possibly imagine. It still doesn't explain why he, and the hypothetical other person, were there."

"No, no, no," said Pietro, "you are too kind hearted. You think too well of people. Lots of people here could be murderers. Even I. Any of us could, depending on the circumstances."

"I suppose you're right, but I agree with Hilary. Are we absolutely sure that it couldn't have been an accident? I mean, I know the police are still investigating, but they haven't said very much, and they don't seem to have any suspects," said Monica hopefully, as if to contemplate murder in her hometown made her uneasy.

"Hey Monica, set your mind at rest. It was suicide, the guy whacked himself with something and then threw himself in the water," said John. "Come on, girls, this is a murder, and that's what's so good about it. I want everyone to think of a plausible, or even an implausible solution, by the end of the evening. Except Ben, of course, he's already given us his solution. Now, let's eat."

Meals at John and Terry's were simple and wholesome. They had wild mushroom soup served with toasted bread rubbed with garlic followed by potato, chickpea and onion salad. There was a platter of Parma ham, and one of mozzarella and tomatoes with fresh basil and the local cold-pressed olive oil. A huge bowl of mixed green salad was set on the table and seemed to contain an enormous and colourful variety of lettuces as well as rocket, radishes and sliced cucumber. The bread was wholemeal and had been cooked in a wood oven. Her children were eating out with their friends, but Terry always felt that even so called fast food in Italy, which was usually a pizza, was pretty wholesome.

The long table was set with an orange tablecloth and in the centre was a simple terracotta bowl of orange, red and yellow nasturtiums. There were four fat red candles set along the table and the plates were yellow.

At the end of the meal, Terry and John brought to the table two beautiful fresh fruit tarts. The fruit was set on custard, which covered the rich pastry base, and was coated with a slightly sticky fruit gelatine. They were made by the local *pasticceria* and were absolutely delicious.

"I hope you're all thinking hard because after coffee you will all be called upon for your solutions. I'm sure we're all a darned sight brighter than the local Chief of Police, Maresciallo Biagioni, so we'll solve his case for him," said John. "I mean, that guy is the original of all those *carabinieri* jokes, he's so slow."

"Hey, he's better than the last one. That guy spent four nights a week harassing courting couples in country lanes, according to my builder Piero, who got pounced on. Piero also said the policeman would have been better off doing something of the same sort himself at home instead of wasting precious time and stopping other people from doing it," Francesco laughed.

"That jerk! He probably got more thrills that way. Did any of you ever see his wife," said Tom, and they all laughed. *Carabinieri* have always been the butt of jokes in Italy. Hilary had heard, and promptly forgotten, thousands over the years.

She said, "I think this one is a little better, but that's besides the point. The whole thing has been handed over to plainclothes men from Lucca and all those little men with plastic collecting bags certainly aren't from this area."

"Look, we only got here two days ago," said Tom "What is the official version? I haven't even seen a newspaper and I got a tearful version from Pia which was *'Che tragedia—così giovane'* etc., etc."

"Yes, we've all had that," said Hilary. "According to the papers, they think he may have disturbed intruders, I suppose burglars, and as a good citizen he went to investigate and got himself killed."

"I suppose that is barely possible, but Ettore was hardly a good citizen as far as I know. I'd say, if he was there, he was up to no good." Terry said firmly.

"Okay let's take that as our starting point," said John. "He was there and he was up to no good."

"Then our next question is, what sort of no good?" said Tom.

"Poisoning the pool, to take revenge on Nigel for blackening his name," said Sue.

"No, no, no," said Ben. "He was there to meet a woman, to bed her in Nigel's house and defile it, or that's what he thought he was going to do. But he met up with the German who had drunk too much in order to get up the courage to kill him."

"Okay, Ben, your theory sounds lovely. A German with Dutch courage: fitting for Fagiolo, but hard to swallow. I mean, if he'd planned it so meticulously he wouldn't have risked spoiling it by getting drunk. And he was drunk. Everyone in town saw him earlier that evening," said Francesco.

"True, I agree with you," said John. "But I like the idea of a tryst with a woman, a midnight dip in the pool and love-making on the sun-loungers."

"Bit cool for that, John," said Terry. "You forget the storm finished at about ten o'clock and it was a chilly night."

"Okay, maybe he did plan to bed a woman in Nigel's bed, as Ben says. But he hadn't actually got her into the house when," he paused, "when he was surprised by someone with whom he had a violent argument and got his head bashed in. Maybe even intruders, as the police put it."

"Or a peeping Tom," suggested Anne.

"Or," said Giulietta, "someone who thought *he* was an intruder and went to investigate. But I don't see why they would kill him."

"I've got it!" cried Terry. "He had the midnight tryst as you said, Ben, with a woman, but a jealous lover or husband followed them and called him down to the pool to talk and killed him."

"Perhaps it was a woman. 'Hell hath no fury.' He met up with her at the Villa Rosa for one last time to break off the relationship. When he told her, she threw something at him, which hit him on the head, and he fell into the pool. A crime of passion," Giulietta said triumphantly.

"Could an Ettore Fagiolo really inspire all this passion?" asked Ben. "I can't see it myself. He seemed a pathetic thing to me. I'll give you my second hypothesis now, a more sinister one. Fagiolo deals in drugs and decides to use the Villa Rosa garden as a hiding place for the stuff, as he knows the Proctors are away. He's there hiding it, when someone kills him for it."

"A bit far-fetched, Ben," said Sue. "Why would he risk dealing in drugs? He made a lot of legitimate money selling houses."

"That shows how little you understand. Drugs are big money, houses are peanuts," replied John. "That's a good one Ben, I like it better than the German."

"Really, you two, I think that's ridiculous. Who would he sell drugs to around here? Grass maybe, but heroin or coke, which are the money makers, I think not," said Terry "I don't think there are too many heroin addicts round here."

"How could you possibly know that, Terry? They don't wear placards round their necks," said Anne.

"Yeah, I know that. But surely he would need to have a big outlet for drugs. No, Ben, I vote your first theory impossible, and your second improbable."

"Well, I still like my German theory best," said Ben. "I am the only one here with a little imagination and a profound knowledge of human nature based on thirty-five years of medical practice. My credentials are good, my mind nimble, and while all of you are younger than I, I see no signs of the mental agility one would expect from such a mixed bunch. All I can say is that if the German didn't do it, he certainly wanted to. But perhaps someone else got there first!" They all laughed.

"Okay, Okay. Ben wins, but I shall be very interested to see what Nigel 'the computer' has to say when he gets back next week. I bet he puts it all in a computer and comes up with the answer."

"My dear John," said Ben. "A computer can only compute the facts with which it has been supplied. It is inferior to the human brain in cases where intuition or imagination is called for. What facts could Nigel feed it with? Very few, I'm sure." Ben began to list the facts, as they knew them...

"Ettore was murdered. His death was caused by a blow to the head, and the police haven't made public the manner in which that was achieved, and subsequently by drowning.

"His murder took place at the Villa Rosa, at some time between 12:30 a.m. and 3:00 a.m. according to the newspaper reports.

"He had many enemies. I suppose one could add a list of names here.

"One of his enemies was threatening to kill him that very evening.

"This enemy, the German, was seen to leave a bar very drunk

and in apparent pursuit of Ettore. Though how successful he was at following a car on foot in that condition we can only imagine. At all events, the car only went 300 metres or so, so it is possible that he could have managed it.

"The owners of Villa Rosa were away. Having left at midnight for Rome. Did the German know this?"

"You bet he did," said Terry

"I said facts, Terry," said Ben. "Not what you are willing to bet on. Well, if you give a computer these facts, it will no doubt come up with the same answer I did."

"Well, if it's so simple, how come they haven't arrested Fritzy? He's even been allowed to leave town," said John.

"Proof. There is no proof. And without proof, a fingerprint, a footprint, a hair, there can be no arrest," replied Ben.

"You mean it's possible that he did it and is free to kill again?" asked Monica, sounding worried.

"If there's no proof, then he probably didn't do it. I wouldn't worry too much about it, Monica," said Giulietta. "Anyway, even if he did do it, he'd never kill again. This was a once in a lifetime murder. One could almost forgive him for it."

"I know you think I worry too much, but the thought of a murderer at large in the community is awful," Monica said.

"At large! Just the right term for old Fritzy," laughed Terry.

"Well, I think that we probably don't have all the facts. There must be some things that the police know and don't tell the general public," said Hilary.

"Like the murder weapon. The papers haven't said what it was, but I bet they have it. Perhaps they're waiting for Nigel and Robin to return to get their fingerprints for elimination purposes," said Pietro.

"Yeah, and they were combing the grounds, and the house. Maybe they found something there. Until we know the facts, all of them, I'm afraid we'll have to give up trying. I mean, we're all talking about the German, but suppose they found a long blonde hair or a woman's shoe print, or a lipstick or something?" said Terry.

"Maybe the German is a cross-dresser," said Ben.

They all laughed. "You're determined to make it the German," said Hilary. "Forget him. And Terry, could I have some more coffee?"

Most of them were drinking coffee and some were 'correcting' it with the local dark rum. Others were drinking home-distilled grappa, as an aid to digestion. They moved on to talk of other topics. The Duomo bells tolled out every fifteen minutes, cicadas rhythmically crrr crrr-ed, and a crazed hornet did a death dance round the light set high over the kitchen door. Food, wine, good friends, voices raised excitably, or laughing companionably.

This was summer.

It was late when they all got up to go. They had caught up on news, told funny stories and discussed the St. Christopher Music Festival, mutual friends and, of course, their children. Now they all called their good-byes at the end of a relaxing evening. The night air was warm. Moths battered themselves against the light bulbs in the kitchen and bats were patrolling the area near the hay barn as always. The sky was filled with stars and the moon was nearly full and almost orange. Hilary, the last to leave, thanked John and Terry, saying, "When I've finished this wretched translation I'll invite you two. It really is my turn. Bruno should be back next week, so it will probably be for the week after that. Anyway, I'll call you." As she walked down the garden path she passed Franny and Jake, John and Terry's children, coming home.

She felt really relaxed, back to normal. She resolved that the next day she was going to get through a lot of work. She had let the Ettore Fagiolo case upset her whole rhythm.

The air was scented and filled with the sounds of cicadas. As the moon was almost full, she didn't even need to use her torch on the country lane that would bring her to the church and her house by the little used back road. Her house was the last on a road that led from the main gate of the town into the country. *How I love walking at night here,* she thought. The sky was velvet black, with too many stars, as she had once exclaimed, newly arrived from London, where the sky was a dull vermilion and stars were hard to see. That had been over twenty-five years ago and she still felt the same way about it.

She turned the corner briskly and walked along between the wall of her garden and the church, where there was the first street light. The bats seemed insanely driven to excesses by the light, and swooped very low and fast, grazing the garden wall. But she even felt benevolent towards them this evening.

She found herself thinking about Di Girolamo. She felt that he didn't really think she had anything to do with the murder, so she couldn't explain to herself what he wanted from her. Why had he stood there in silence looking at her? Was that police tactics, and if so, should she be worried? It had certainly been unnerving. Once again she berated herself for truthfully saying what she thought of Ettore. That had been a mistake, but surely he couldn't possibly think that she had killed a man because she disliked him? Then she remembered what Miriam had said, but shrugged it off. He'd never find out about that. Impossible. And even if he did, what did it matter? It was history.

Her house was the first on her road from this end, and next to it was Villa Rosa, with all the lights on. *It can't be the police again at this time of night,* she thought. *Could it be Nigel and Robin back early?*

She walked a little further down the road and saw that their garage was open, their car was parked in it with two doors open, and the door from the garage into the house was also open. *So,* she thought, *they are back. I'll leave them to it. I suppose they know about what happened. As the owners of the house they must have been told. Maybe that's why they're back early.* She hesitated, uncertain whether or not to call out to them. But then she heard Nigel's voice, raised belligerently. "For God's sake, Robin," followed by a lengthy mumble, and she moved decisively towards her own front door, inserted the key into the lock and went in.

AT THE OTHER END of town, Augusta Fagiolo stared at a photograph and asked herself for the hundredth time what she should do. She felt sure that this boy was involved, might even be the killer of her son, but to make her son's perversion public was impossible for her. She had ripped all the other photos, with one exception, into tiny pieces and burned them in the garden that night with the rubbish from the garden. The next morning she had dug the ashes into the earth. If it hadn't been for this photograph, the secret would be safe. Should she send it to the police anonymously, and write a note saying 'This boy killed Ettore Fagiolo?' If she did that, it might still put her son in a bad light. Perhaps this boy was a pervert who had pestered her son. Would they think that? Could she put them on the right track? She put the photo back in the bottom drawer of the credenza under the electricity bills. She was certain this boy was responsible for her son's death. Ettore must not die un-avenged. She would pray to God for guidance.

Deliver us from evil, she prayed to herself.

TEN

THE NEXT MORNING Hilary went shopping early. She passed Villa Rosa but there were no signs of life. She did not call on the Proctors, feeling it would be best to wait until they contacted her. Not that she was looking forward to seeing them anyway, as they would have to talk about the whole thing, and she knew it must be awful for them. In fact she hoped they would leave her alone for a bit, at least until they'd seen the police, as she felt sure they would. Besides, she had some strange uneasy feeling that she should not discuss anything with them at all and she felt almost decided to say something that would halt any discussion, like, "I know it's awful for you and it was for me, and I would prefer not to talk about it," or something of the sort.

She paused outside the greengrocer's to admire crates of fresh vegetables, but only bought two melons, as she had a good vegetable garden, and was hard put to eat all her produce. Ettore Fagiolo was still a topic of conversation there, but there was little speculation about his death now. Things were sliding towards a more mundane treatment of the subject, as though the wild speculation of the first few days had exhausted the collective imagination, and the intruder theory was taken as correct. The discussion over the vegetables was mainly about burglaries.

In the grocer's shop, however, the die-hard gossips were still at it.

"To think I only saw him that evening buying cigarettes," commented one woman, as though that would have been sufficient to ward off death. And there seemed to be some sort of resentiment in her voice. Perhaps she thought he should have given notice of his intended demise. Signora Pastore held forth from behind the high counter. She stood on a raised dais, which invested her with an air of authority. Like a public speaker, she praised and condemned, always with an eye to commerce. Obviously the Fagiolo family were not among her customers, as she felt quite safe in saying, "Well he was a wild one, that Ettore, and I always knew he'd come to a bad end."

Then as a sop to convention, "Of course, it's a terrible thing for his mother, all the same. He was an only son."

She finished parcelling up some *prosciutto crudo* and handed it with a flourish, bending down slightly, to a wizened old lady. She banged on her till and pronounced triumphantly, "Two euros and fifty cents," brandishing the fiscal receipt that it had immediately disgorged. And without which no one would dare to leave the shop for fear of being fined. She began energetically cutting into a huge piece of Parmesan for her next customer, her eyes raised at intervals to assess the worth of her clients.

"What do you say, Signora," she threw at Hilary. "Of course you found the body and spoke with the police."

Her knife smashed through the last inch of cheese with a tremendous thud and she began hacking it into smaller pieces. All the other customers now turned towards her, and Hilary felt coerced into saying something. "I think the police feel sure that he'd gone to investigate a noise in the garden, um—burglars or something," she mumbled, annoyed to have been forced to answer.

"Hmph," came the reply. Signora Pastore gave a triumphant glance around her clientele. "Well, I see it this way. If you mind your own business you don't get into any trouble and you don't get yourself killed." She brandished her knife and continued, "You wouldn't catch me going into someone else's garden and that's a fact, no matter what I heard or saw. Besides, whoever heard of the police getting it right? It would be a miracle if they did." She paused to allow her admiring customers to consent with a smile. "And if they did get it wrong, then I'd like to know what he was doing there."

The Parmesan was weighed and wrapped and joined by a packet of pasta and a jar of cherry jam. The till disgorged another piece of paper, and then it was Hilary's turn. The two women, who had been there when she came in, were only there to gossip. While her *prosciutto crudo* was being cut, the monologue continued, "It wouldn't be the first time he was in someone's house while they are away," she added cryptically. "These foreigners are too trusting. They leave him their keys and he does what he likes."

Luckily, a customer who had just come in went off on a tangent with a story about the gullibility of some foreigners, and how one particular couple had learned the hard way to be more cautious. Under the cover of that, Hilary paid and left the shop. She bumped into Sue Browne as she came out and exclaimed, "Really that woman is monstrous," and told her what had been said.

Sue laughed and said, "Come on, you know you usually enjoy her. She's just playing the Fagiolo story for all it's worth. Besides, she's right, actually. I know he was using that house up in Altamura because I saw him there. With someone, of course."

"Well he couldn't have been using Nigel's house surely; he didn't have the keys."

"He might have, you know. Don't forget that last year he rented the house out for them. And I bet he had duplicates made."

"I can't believe it. Nigel had only just left. He would have been mad to go there. Nigel would have killed him if he…oh no, I didn't mean that, but he would have been furious!"

"So would anyone."

"I wonder if he was there with someone, then, and perhaps heard a noise in the garden and so on. I mean, the burglar theory would still fit. What am I saying? Of course if he was there. Then there had to be somebody with him."

"Well, I would think so. I can't see him sitting in there on his own, listening to music or watching the telly. I mean what would be the point?"

"Yes, of course, but don't you see? If somebody was with him, then perhaps she saw the murderer or, as no one has said anything, perhaps that person was the murderer," said Hilary following through her train of thought.

"Should we tell the police, I mean, do you think they know that he used peoples' houses while they were away?"

"I don't know. Perhaps they do know. Otherwise why did they go through the house like that, dusting for fingerprints? I didn't tell you but they took mine, too, for purposes of elimination."

"Did they? How unpleasant. Anyway, I expect they do know then, don't you? I don't really want to go and tell them something they probably already know. Besides I don't think it's vital information. I mean, I didn't see who was with him that time, I just saw that there was another person. Also, I don't really feel like spending half the morning in the police station giving them information that they already have, which will be laboriously typed by a barely literate junior officer with one finger on an ancient typewriter.

"It's not like that anymore. They have computers now," said Hilary laughing. "And I think you're right. They must know already. I haven't much time to waste either, though I am going to have a cappuccino before I go back home to start work, are you coming?"

"No, I'm off to the dentist. In fact, I'm already late. Ciao." She rushed off, narrowly avoiding a motor scooter driven expertly by a beautiful youth with long golden curls and no crash helmet.

ELEVEN

SHE STEPPED THROUGH the bead curtain and into the cool, dark, silent bar. The only sound was the quiet hum of machinery.

"Gino," she called

"Coming."

"No hurry, I'll be outside, can you send me out a cappuccino and a brioche?" She looked around and then called again, "Where's the newspaper?"

"I've got it back here. I was just checking my lottery numbers. I'll bring it out in a minute."

She went back outside and sat at a table that was still in the shade. Tubs of freshly watered geraniums added to the sensation of coolness, though by now at ten o'clock, the sun was already hot. It was going to be a very hot day. Marco, Gino's son, came out with her order, "Is this paper okay? My mother's got the other one upstairs."

"Yes, that's fine, thank you." She glanced up at the boy. He was just eighteen, dark and very pretty, his long hair curled to his shoulders. He had full lips and incredibly green eyes. He often reminded her of a long dead rock-star, but she realised that the similarity was contrived, as she had heard from his parents that his bedroom walls were covered with posters of this singer, whose death had guaranteed him the status of a mythical figure. Had he lived he would have been as old as Marco's father, and like others who valiantly rocked on, would have become a little pathetic. As it was, he would never age, and could never disappoint. This beautiful boy, Marco, looked as troubled as his hero often had. He still had dark circles under his eyes and he looked even thinner than usual. His father stepped out of the bar and clapped his hand on the boy's shoulder. Hilary saw Marco wince and tense himself as though something horrendous was touching him, something that might threaten or damage him. His face remained blank.

"Marco's a bit down at the moment, he's been very upset by this dreadful business." Gino coughed and said, "You know— the murder. He was a great friend of Ettore, who, I must say, always took a great interest in him even though he's only a boy. Eh, Marco?" His big hand patted the boy's shoulder again. "He used to take him out in that car of his, and now and then even take him and his friends down to coast. He was a night-clubber, was *povero* Ettore, God rest his soul."

This belated and rather pathetic attempt at acceptance of a relationship of which his parents had disapproved was too much for Marco, who wriggled free and rushed back into the bar, rattling the bead curtain violently.

Gino turned to watch him go, and then, heaving a sigh, lowered his plump body onto the chair next to Hilary. Lowering the tone of his voice he said, "I'm not sorry he's dead. I suppose you know that. The boy is suffering now, but he'll get over it given time. He followed that man around like a little dog. He grew his hair long to be like him, he hero-worshipped him, wore clothes like him, even spoke like him. I know Ettore was a bright young man, making money and a name for himself, but I never liked him, and I never trusted him. It wasn't healthy. What did he want with a young boy like Marco? He was ruining him, and I hope that now I can start trying to get him back, if it's not too late."

"It will take time and patience," she said, feeling that the words were banal as she said them, but no others came to mind.

"The truth is, I'm glad he's dead. I often felt like getting rid of him myself. I wouldn't have needed a hammer or whatever to do it with either. I'd have done it with my bare hands. I'd have put my hands round his neck and squeezed."

"Come on," said Hilary. "I've never thought of you as a violent man. You're just not that sort of person. I can't believe you're saying things like this." She was really surprised. He never even spoke ill of anyone, though, of course, that could have been just a sort of bar-owner's form of diplomacy.

"A man can be driven to anything. I think even the calmest, most God-fearing person could murder to protect his child. Anyway, someone else has done it for me. *Non tutto il male viene a nuocere.*"

Hilary paid her bill and left. Yes, it would be a good thing for Marco to be set free from Ettore's hold. He was a weak boy. An unsuccessful scholar, he had left school early to work for his father. But he did little work and his father kept making excuses for his lazy, pampered son.

"He's young. He'll get into it as he gets older," he would say in a forgiving tone. But Marco often disappeared when he was needed most. And last spring he had been caught by the police smoking a joint. His friendship with Ettore had been the most worrying development, as this was an older person whose hold had been stronger than that of his peer group. He often took the boy out in his Porsche and even let him drive it on occasion.

When he took him down to the coast for the evening, they never came back until five the next morning, which meant the boy would spend the whole day in bed, only getting up in the late afternoon to make a pasty-faced, token appearance in the bar and then, by ten, he would be off again. He was certainly in a bad way now, and she wasn't sure his father would be capable of regaining his affection. He didn't know how. That heavy-handed attempt he'd made in the bar, though obviously well meant, seemed patronising and was most unlikely to be effective.

There was a police car parked outside Villa Rosa and as Hilary went by, Nigel and Robin came out of the house escorted by two policemen. They got into the car and it drove off. She had just time to see Robin's anxious face look out of the car window at her. She thought, *It's almost over for the rest of us, but for them it's just beginning.*

TWELVE

MARCO WENT OUT into the kitchen. He was sweating and his hands were shaking. He reached up to the medicine cupboard and shook out twenty drops of his mother's Valium into a glass. He added a tiny amount of water and swilled the mixture down. The Valium might make him a little sleepy, though he doubted it. He would almost welcome it. Anything would be better than the way he was feeling at the moment. He clenched his fists and muttered, "I have to get out of here—but how?" He couldn't take the car, his father's car. Since he'd been busted for smoking a joint, his father had forbidden him to use it. Maybe someone would be going to the coast and could give him a lift. He hadn't got much money left; they kept him short on purpose. God, what shits they were. His father was pathetic, pretending to be nice and normal about Ettore when he knew damn well he'd hated his guts. He'd have killed him himself if he'd had the chance.

Perhaps he had.

He thought about that for a bit and then laughed out loud, murmuring, "I can just see that flabby old man assaulting someone. Pathetic!"

Then there was his mother, stupid cow. She must be senile already. God, she'd had him when she was ancient. She was always pawing him and gazing at him tearfully. Why couldn't she leave him alone? He had a sudden memory of himself as a young child and his parents' pride in him. Well, they weren't proud of him now.

He had a little money stashed away from his birthday. They

gave him money now that he was a big boy. And his aunt had coughed up, too, which his parents hadn't realised. Then there was the odd ten or twenty euros pinched here and there, from the till or his mother's bag. He thought they hadn't noticed since he was careful not to do it too often, but maybe they had, as his father had started hovering around the till lately. Still, he'd said nothing. The Valium was starting to kick in. He felt calmer now.

He scratched his chest and moved towards the table where his mother's bag was lying. He opened it. Her wallet was bulging; she never went short for sure. You'd think she'd be a little more generous to her only son. All because of a stupid joint. These people, their generation, were so out of touch; they were from another planet. Another galaxy!

He quickly took two twenty-euro notes from the wallet and replaced it in the bag. He went to the sink and splashed cold water on his face. He suddenly shivered and dried himself on some paper towels. Then he moved towards the back door, and looked at himself in the mirror his mother had put there for last minute checks before leaving the house. He saw a thin pale face, dark mauve shadows under his green eyes and dark curls framing the whole. He looked like a desperate little boy who had suddenly grown old. He looked both vulnerable and at the same time capable of hurting others. But as he moved to leave, a shadow fell on his face and softened its harshness and he looked almost like a girl. He pouted at the mirror, yeah—almost like a girl.

THIRTEEN

THE PHONE RANG. Hilary pressed the save button on her computer and glared at the phone. She picked it up saying, *"Pronto."*

"Darling, it's me. I'm back."

"Bruno! You're back! How nice. I'd forgotten you were due back today. I've so much to tell you. I need to talk to you."

"If it's about Fagiolo, I know. The first person I saw when I was lugging my suitcase up the garden path stopped me and told me all, in detail. You know what small towns are like. Was it awful?"

"Yes. I wish you'd been here."

"Well I'm here now. Do you want me to come round?"

She looked at the clock. It was already ten-thirty "No, you must be tired. I'm on the last pages of this damned book, so you go to bed and I'll finish this tonight and see you tomorrow. Evening, that is, as I want the day to myself."

"If you're sure."

"I'm sure. We're both tired now, and from tomorrow I'll be free—till the next job. So we can celebrate."

"I'll think of something nice to do and phone you tomorrow. Good-night."

"Good-night."

She put the phone down; Bruno was back. Now her life really would return to normal. She hadn't realised just how much she had missed him. She was so used to being alone after Guido's death that she had been reluctant to allow a man back into her life. When she had, it had been on her terms. She was very wary. Losing her husband so early in a marriage with young children to support and provide a future for had made her strong and independent. She had clung to the children at first; they were all survivors after a natural disaster. Then slowly she had gained strength and given them strength, and then she had let them go.

So she had come to enjoy living alone. She had to consult no one. She did as she pleased, when she pleased. Although she knew she had been pitied by many women. Watching them, she saw that many were slaves to their families, often household drudges, most of them unable to make decisions alone, usually not allowed to make decisions alone, and she felt glad of her independence. Their whole lives revolved around their men. She had come to really appreciate her solitary life, and when she met Bruno, had been quite disconcerted. She felt that to allow him into her life would mean changing it so radically that it would become unbearable. Things that were precious to her would be lost. She was uncertain about what she would gain. Slowly she had accepted him and a part of her was his. But she would not live with him. She remained her own person, as he did, and only a part of their lives was communal. She was really glad he was back, but now she put him out of her mind and started working again. Tomorrow she would send off the completed work and give herself a break for a couple of weeks.

UP IN THE OLD TOWN at two o'clock in the morning when Bruno got up to close a window that was letting in too much of a draught, he could see her light still on—a small beacon across the little valley. He knew she would work through till dawn, if necessary, once she had decided to finish. He worried that although she was tough, she drove herself too hard. He would have liked her to let him take some of her burdens, but he knew it was hopeless. She lived as she pleased and he supposed he was lucky to be allowed whatever part of her life she felt able to give him. He had hoped that this holiday would make her miss him enough to want him more. But the cool voice at the other end of the phone dashed this hope. Nothing had changed.

MARCO WIPED his sweaty fingers down his tee shirt, picked up the phone and dialled a local number. When he heard an answer he said in a gruff voice, "I saw you do it."

"What!"

"I saw you kill him." He heard breathing but there was no answer. His hands felt sweaty again.

"I need money. If you agree, I will forget what I saw."

"How much," said the voice tersely.

"A thousand euro, for now."

"When and where?"

"Leave it behind the little Madonna on the corner of the street near Palazzo Guelfi at midnight tonight."

The line went dead. He wiped his hands again and let out a sigh. It was easy, so easy. A thousand euro was nothing for people like that. He should have asked for more. Well, he would of course, later. Ettore was dead and he had loved him, but Marco knew he would have approved of this. Let that fat bastard sweat and suffer. Sooner or later he would be made to pay the legal price for what he had done. But before that, he would squeeze him dry.

He was feeling very isolated. Ettore had been the most important person in his life for the last two years. His parents, whom he had always exploited shamelessly, had seemed to him to be the enemy. They were always on at him, first about school, then about going out at night, (especially with Ettore), then the joint. Why couldn't they leave him alone? They knew nothing about him, or who he really was. Not like Ettore. Ettore had been so smart. He took the foreign suckers for all he could, and he really knew how to live. Now that he was dead, Marco asked himself who really cared about him? Also he wasn't feeling too good, and he had to sort out one or two things. Bleeding those two suckers would take care of that. He went back into the bar and started stacking the dishwasher.

His father smiled benignly at him and thought that things were looking better already.

That evening Marco left the bar and made his way to the main piazza. It was eleven o'clock. This part of town was always full of people until midnight or even later. Families were returning home with sleepy children; televisions blared from open windows; older children were still bicycling or whizzing about on roller-skates. Outside the two main bars there were tables and chairs, many occupied by tourists, grateful for the cool night air. Groups of people were laughing and talking.

Around the edge of the piazza in dark corners or on benches around the grassy area were groups of young people. Motor scooters zoomed from group to group. Cigarettes glowed in the dark. Loud laughter would suddenly break out and seated figures would spring up and gesticulate and shout, arguing, or describing with a wealth of action.

Marco edged towards the darkest area where five or six youths were sprawling on the school steps; two others were seated on their scooters, ready to move on. They stopped talking as Marco approached. He sat down on the steps beside a boy whose head was shaved and whose ears were decorated with several studs and a ring. Another ring pierced the outer extremity of his left eyebrow. Marco pulled out his cigarettes, offering them around. Two of the boys took an additional cigarette and put it behind their ear. Another boy passed his beer can along and Marco took a swig and passed it back. They sat in silence for a bit, watching the movement in the square, occasionally commenting, "Look at that jerk" or "She's not bad." The beer can passed round again, was emptied out, and another one took its place. Marco had downed some more Valium before coming out and had already had two shots of his father's whisky. He began to feel sleepy.

"Is anyone going down to the coast?" he asked

"Yeah, me and Ricky," said the shaven headed youth. "You coming?"

"When, tomorrow night?"

"Yeah, about ten. Pick you up here."

Marco rose to his feet and said, "See you then," and slouched off.

They watched him leave, their faces white in the darkness.

FOURTEEN

NIGEL PUT DOWN the phone. He looked a little paler than usual.

Robin said, "What is it? Who was that?"

He turned and walked to the sideboard, poured himself a whisky, shot it down and replied, "I'm not sure but I think it was Marco."

"Well, what did he want?"

He looked at her "He wanted money, a thousand euro to keep his mouth shut."

"About what?"

"Three guesses," he said.

"Oh, he knows?"

"Yes, he saw me that night. His actual words were, 'I know you did it.'"

"Oh God, he must have been there. Nigel, if you give him money he'll only come back for more, again and again. You're not supposed to give in to blackmailers."

"What's the alternative? He saw us come back. Do you want me to tell the police we came back? That's the only alternative. Otherwise we jolly well pay up."

"We could get in first and say we saw him do it. Or at least that we saw him there, and hadn't wanted to compromise ourselves by telling them the truth."

"You think they'd believe me? Our position is awful enough as it is. He drowned in our pool after being hit with our spade, which probably has my fingerprints on it. They know I couldn't stand the sight of him. Now you want me to say I was there.

You're crazy. No, for now we pay up, and wait. Maybe they'll arrest someone and then we'll be free. If they find someone else it won't matter if they know we came back."

"That's not very likely is it?"

"No, but I need time to think. So for now we give him the money. I'll go and get the cash now and put it where he said. I'll watch him get it, though. I want to be sure I know who we're dealing with. Then we'll see."

THE LITTLE MADONNA was set in a niche in the sidewall of the palazzo. She was illuminated by a tiny light and had an expression of sorrow. A potted plant with trailing flowers was in front of her and two small posies had been set in tiny vases at her side. Nigel slid his hand behind the statue and left the small, brown packet there. He walked off slowly. The little road in the old town was deserted. Even if someone had been watching from a window, he had been so quick they would not have realised what he was doing.

He turned a corner and then ran swiftly up steep steps, and at the top of them turned back along a road that was parallel to the road he had just walked along. Shortly afterwards he found himself directly above Palazzo Guelfi, looking down more, and even steeper, steps. He remained immobile in a doorway. There were no street lights near him, so he was sure he could not be seen, but he had a good view of the Madonna. He waited. As the bells of the Duomo tolled out the quarter past the hour, he saw the boy approach the statue, apparently touch it and then cross himself and move on. *So I was right,* he thought. He also thought how wonderful it be would to rush down the steps and beat Marco to a pulp.

He sighed and retraced his steps. Robin was waiting for him at home. She was very wrought up at the moment. That damn policeman was needling them both. They'd been down there for hours. They had answered innumerable questions, and he had managed to remain true to his image of himself. But Robin was more fragile. That business with the passport, which was none of their business, had really finished her off. They really had no right to go into things like that. And he had threatened them, pleaded with them and reminded them of the laws governing privacy, but she was terrified of exposure. Now this interfering little dago druggie had made things even worse.

He wished he'd never met Ettore Fagiolo.

FIFTEEN

PIA WAS SLOPPING a very wet mop over the floor when Hilary came down in her dressing gown the next morning.

"You're late down this morning," she said.

"Yes, I was working till gone three. I wanted to finish."

"I've been meaning to tell you. There's one of them black wasp things, you know, those long ones with a double body. It's made a nest on top of the wardrobe in the spare bedroom, and another on the beams. You'll have to get someone in to get rid of it."

"I'll ask Aldo when he comes to clean the gutters."

"You make sure you do, or we'll have the house full in no time."

Hilary went into the kitchen. The door to the garden was open and the sun had nearly dried the floor. Pia had given a summary wipe over the surfaces. *She's getting past it,* thought Hilary. Her eyesight wasn't too good now, and her energy levels were low. Bending and stretching were limited. She was nearly seventy and had been a cleaner all her working life. She had worked for Hilary for over fifteen years and she was loath to get rid of her. So she put up with it. Every so often she had what she called a blitz on the house herself, so that things didn't get too bad. Pia had been great when the kids were younger and they were all fond of her. She grumbled at them all and shared her joys and sorrows with them. Now she said, "I hope you're eating a proper breakfast after working all night like that. You're too thin as it is."

"Yes I will. Porridge, bread and marmalade and milky coffee, that all right?"

The bread was fresh as a van delivered it to the house every morning, and the marmalade was homemade by a friend who had come to stay last year and wanted to make herself useful. Hilary said a mental 'Thank you' to her every morning. She cleared away the breakfast things and told Pia she was going up for a shower and to get dressed.

"You shouldn't shower after a meal, it's bad for you. You'll block your digestion. I've told you before."

"Well it has never happened before so I don't see why it should happen now. Don't worry."

"You're not getting any younger," she replied

"Well, that's true, but I'll take the risk."

Pia looked unconvinced. Her generation had a firm set of beliefs and stuck rigidly to them. She had been brought up on an isolated farm in the mountains above Borgo San Cristoforo, the eldest of three sisters. The other two were called Maria and Immacolata, their names, like Pia's, a testimony to their parents' simple faith. Pia's whole life had been regulated by taboos, and a strange mixture of Christian faith and pagan rites. The one superimposed on the other, but never entirely taking its place. The elements were all powerful, and strict adherence to rituals and the prescribed norms were necessary in order to avoid unpleasant, or even life-threatening consequences.

One of the most dangerous elements was water. Daily contact with it was strictly regulated and taboos on bathing were frequent: after eating, when menstruating and after giving birth (the proscribed period was 40 days). Blood was a mysterious substance and water had an effect on its flux.

The younger generation had only a vestigial interest or belief in these taboos, which had passed down over the centuries with little modification. The young were embracing modern and foreign ideas, but those of Pia's generation had little choice but to placate deities and the elements, as if their lives depended on it.

The moon also played a large part in governing life: the planting of seeds, the conception of children, the start of labour, even the re-growth of cut hair, were all affected by the phases of the moon. According to Pia her father had only fathered female children, as his wife was only fecund during the female phase of the moon. Another woman, one of seven girls, had told Hilary that her own parents had had the same problem.

The devil was omniscient and was always causing trouble. Pia had once made the sign of the cross over Hilary's blackberry jelly "so as the devil won't take a part." Babies' prams often had a red horn dangling over the baby, cheek to jowl with an image of the Virgin Mary.

Probably these rituals gave a sense of security. The ability to navigate a course through life manoeuvring through a wealth of hazards, knowing that strict adherence to the governing norms would ensure one's survival, must make one feel less vulnerable, more in control of one's destiny. Pia had long ago decided that Hilary must be exempt from these, as a foreigner, for she seemed to survive flagrantly breaking taboos. But, every now and then, she still felt obliged to warn her of the risks she was taking.

When Hilary came downstairs again, Pia was polishing the dining room table and humming to herself. Hilary asked, "Pia, did you go to the doctor about that rash?"

"Yes I did. He says it's St.Antony's Fire, and I've got tablets to take."

"I hope you're taking them. And don't stop when it feels better, take them all."

Pia had a habit of stopping any course of medicine as soon as she felt the benefit. Each of the two women was conversant with her own sphere and instructed the other who was less expert.

"Anyway, I went to Benito's wife to be on the safe side." Benito's wife, never called by her own name, which Hilary couldn't even remember, was a white witch who would 'sign' warts and other ailments, muttering strange words and making crosses in the air. Pia gave Hilary a look, which meant each to his own.

Hilary said, "Well you're well covered, then. I'm sure you'll get well soon. But take the medicine just to 'be on the safe side.'"

She laughed and Pia laughed, too and said, "Well, two's better than one."

The phone rang. She knew it was Bruno. He was so predictable.

"Good morning. You finished late, I saw your light was still on at two this morning."

"Yes, I finished just after three, so I only got up half an hour ago. I'm going out to post the wretched thing now. I can't wait to get rid of it."

"You always say that," he laughed "Look, about tonight, I thought we could go down to the coast to that concert, Uto Ughi is playing. I thought we could eat at La Morosa on the way down, if we leave early."

"That sounds lovely."

"All right, I'll book then for seven-fifteen-ish. See you at six-thirty. Ciao."

She put the phone down and stood lost in thought for a few moments, gazing out of the window. Now that she knew Bruno was back and available, she suddenly realised that she didn't really care whether she saw him or not. Good dependable Bruno, always the same, always there for her. Why didn't she feel more excited about his return? What did she really feel about him? Telling herself it was still too early in the morning to answer questions like that, she shrugged and went off to the kitchen to make some more coffee and wake up properly. She felt as though she was moving in slow motion and even her thought process seemed slowed down. A strange dissatisfaction weighed on her while a feeling of unease troubled her. The thought of Ettore's death crept between her and everything else.

SIXTEEN

PIA SEEMED TO be hovering about, like the embodiment of Hilary's worries. The thought of hearing of some family trouble seemed too enormous to bear. So, hoping to avoid whatever Pia was about to tell her, Hilary picked up her package and said brusquely, "I'm going out. See you tomorrow."

Pia took a deep breath and blurted out, "Something's been worrying me." She paused, "I don't know if I should say anything or not." She ground to a halt, looking flustered. Hilary turned from the door and came back into the kitchen. She sat down and put her bag on the table.

"What is it Pia? Sit down and tell me what's wrong."

Pia wrung her hands together and then sat down abruptly.

"It's probably nothing. But you remember that night that Ettore Fagiolo got himself killed? Well, I'd been to my cousin's house to take a present for her daughter who's getting married and I stayed a bit late. Anyway, I came home by your house. Your lights were out, but the Proctors' car was in the garage. And I think it was about one o'clock because I remember thinking how late it was and how I was coming to you earlier than usual the next morning. You remember?"

"Yes, I remember. Your uncle was in hospital. But are you sure it was that late?"

"Oh yes. I'm pretty sure it was. Or near enough. Because either before or after I passed the house, somewhere along the road, I know I heard the Duomo bells. That's when I remember thinking about having to get up earlier than usual."

"Well, why didn't you say something before?"

"I don't know. The murder sort of put it out of my mind. But when my cousin's daughter got married on Sunday, then it all came back to me."

"I see. But it can't be. You mean the Proctors were here? No, wait a minute. I saw them leave at midnight. Nigel always sticks to his plans and I did actually see them go." She paused, "They must have come back."

"I suppose so. That's what's worrying me. If they came back, then perhaps they were there when Ettore was killed."

"Not necessarily. I don't think the police know precisely at what time he died. Perhaps they came back for something and then whizzed off again."

"Yes, but should I say something, you know, to the *carabinieri*. I don't want to get them into trouble, but if they were there maybe they saw something."

"You mean if they were there, then maybe they did something. Look, if they did nothing they have probably already told the police that they had to come back. If they haven't told the police it doesn't look too good for them. Either way, you have to tell the police. You can't risk them not knowing."

"So I've got to go there." Pia looked utterly miserable.

"Yes. Look, don't worry. They'll be pleased that you came. I saw the magistrate from Lucca and he was a very nice person."

"But everyone will see me go there," she wailed, and that, Hilary knew, was the real problem.

"Listen, do you want me to phone and talk to them for you? Perhaps they could fix it so you don't have to go there."

"I'm not having them come to the house!" Pia cried, horrified.

"No, no. Let me think. Shall I see if someone could come here while you are here, at my house? Then people would think they were coming to see me?"

"Do you think they would?" She turned it over in her mind. "Well if they agree, I suppose that's all right. Hey! Don't tell them my name or they'll be waiting for me at home when I get there."

Hilary picked up the phone and dialed while Pia hovered anxiously beside her.

"*Pronto,* could I speak to Dottor Di Girolamo please? I am Hilary Wright, yes, yes, thank you." Silence. "Good morning, yes, it's Hilary Wright."

"Ah! You have called to confess?" Di Girolamo sounded quite jovial.

"No, of course not!"

"What a disappointment." He chuckled. "How can I help you?"

"I wanted to ask you something."

"Yes. Ask."

"If someone had some information that might be important, but they were unwilling to be seen coming to the police station, or to have you seen going to their house, would you consider meeting that person on neutral ground?"

"This is not hypothetical, I presume."

"Do I have to answer that one?"

"No. Let's say that I would be willing."

"Good." She smiled encouragingly at Pia.

"Good, and what? Are you going to tell me more?"

"Yes, of course. This person has some information concerning the Fagiolo murder that might be important."

"May I know the name of this person?"

"No, I'm afraid not."

"It's not you, I presume?"

"No. This person has asked me to fix a meeting with the police and I have suggested my house as neutral ground."

"I see. You should inform this person that, while we are grateful for information from the public, it is a criminal offence to withhold evidence."

"I don't see the necessity to threaten. This person has only just remembered something and is anxious to inform you, but is worried about others being aware of that fact. This is a small town."

"I understand. I hope you will understand that I would like this information as soon as possible."

"Would tomorrow morning do?"

"This morning if you please."

"Oh, I don't know if that is possible as I still have to contact the person in question. It might be possible this afternoon." She looked at Pia, who looked back at her and nodded with a resigned expression on her face.

"I'll get in touch and phone you back about the time."

"Please do that as soon as possible or I will be forced to pay you an unexpected visit. And I might just do it with an escort of cars and the sirens going." He laughed. "I would hazard a guess that the person is standing beside you right now."

"I'm glad you have a sense of humour," she risked saying. "I'll phone back within a quarter of an hour."

"I wasn't joking," he said, and the line went dead.

SEVENTEEN

PIA WENT OFF home for lunch, muttering and moaning. "I wish I'd never told you," she said to Hilary. "I know I'll live to regret it."

"No, you won't. You're doing the right thing. It might be very important. But even if it's not, then your conscience is clear. You can sleep at night. You don't have to worry anymore."

She had fixed up with Di Girolamo for him to come at four-thirty, as she knew Pia always had a rest in the afternoons before going shopping. It would look quite normal for her to be dressed to go shopping rather than cleaning, and popping in to see Hilary for a cup of tea was also normal. Not many people would notice Di Girolamo. He was coming alone. And if they did see him, well, he was going to Hilary's house, not Pia's. All these things were repeated over and over to Pia but she still didn't feel happy about it. The only certain thing was that she would be there.

Hilary heated up some leftovers in the oven. The day before she had stuffed a large number of marrow flowers from the garden with a mixture of her own vegetables, an egg and Parmesan cheese, garlic and basil and placed them in an oven dish, having added a trickle of olive oil. She had baked them for an hour. She liked to eat them piping hot with a plate of her home-grown tomatoes dressed simply with oil, aromatic vinegar and a little fresh basil. Fresh crusty bread and some local sheep's cheese completed the meal.

She ate out on the little terrace overlooking the garden. The terrace was shady and cool in the summer, as it was almost totally covered by an ancient but extremely vigorous wisteria.

Huge lilac blooms hung down from the supporting structure and long tendrils waved about in search of new areas to cover. It had to be ruthlessly pruned at frequent intervals. On the table, wedged against her plate and propped up by the fruit bowl, she had an open book. But she barely glanced at it today, as she was thinking about the implications of Pia's information. What she mainly did was to ask herself if she thought it possible that Nigel had killed Ettore. On the whole she thought it possible, but not very likely. She imagined that Nigel had come back to fetch some forgotten item, found Ettore there for whatever reason and had accidentally killed him, during an argument perhaps. And had then gone off as though nothing had happened.

She munched on her bread and cheese. Why had Ettore been there and why by the pool? It didn't seem likely that he would be down by the pool; it was much too cool for swimming that evening. There had been a storm, which had lasted until about nine o'clock and the temperature had dropped considerably after that. Perhaps the burglar theory was correct. And in that case, it had not been Nigel who had killed him. Why else should Ettore be down by the pool? Or perhaps Ettore had been in the house and Nigel had found him there and had given chase. Perhaps they had had an argument. It seemed much more probable to her that Nigel had come back before Ettore was there, had retrieved his stuff and driven off, not thinking it worthwhile enough to mention. Or maybe he had already told the police, in which case she was wasting their time. She turned back to her book, an improbable detective story set in Italy.

At four-fifteen p.m., Pia arrived dressed in her shopping dress, a flowery short-sleeved frock with a white collar. She was wearing black sandals that covered most of her misshapen feet, and stockings, which Hilary knew were rolled down to just below the knee even though Pia knew how bad that was for her varicose veins. She had brought her shopping bag with her and had even bought a few things on the way. As usual, her grey hair was made into a plait that was then wound around her head and fixed with pins. She also wore a very anxious expression and her plump face twitched a little, obviously under stress.

"Come in, Pia. We'll start making tea, shall we? You look as though you need something. Did you eat lunch?"

"Not really. I wasn't very hungry."

"Did you have a rest?"

"Sort of."

"I see." Hilary was busy with the kettle and cups. She pulled out a packet of biscuits and put them on the table. "Come on, start with a biscuit. The tea won't be a minute."

"What? It won't look very good, us sitting here eating, when he arrives."

"Never you mind about that, I'll offer him a cup, too."

Ruggero Di Girolamo was punctual, and if he was a little surprised to see a couple of ladies having tea, he gave no sign of it. He accepted a cup himself, which he took with neither milk nor sugar, nor even lemon. He sipped the tea and looked at the two women. The old lady was obviously the key witness. Ha ha, he thought, *I hope they haven't brought me here to hear senile chattering. She looks to be in a bit of a state.* He had been introduced to her as Pia Pieri and he guessed her to be at least seventy. He would be very cautious, as they often got muddled at that age. Hilary Wright seemed very protective of her, and he wondered what the connection was. He decided to leave the direction of the meeting entirely in the Englishwoman's hands.

He leant back in his chair and said, "This tea is very good."

"Thank you," she said. "Would you like a biscuit? They're very nice ones."

He took one and was surprised to find they were his favourites. He kept wanting to laugh. It was absolutely ridiculous, him sitting here having tea with them. The Englishwoman was very cool, and seemed completely at her ease. He'd needled her a bit in her interview at the station, but she had come through it well.

And now look at her, offering him tea and biscuits as though they were old friends. Of course, he realised it was all for the benefit of the old lady, who every now and then dared to glance quickly at him and then away again, as though he were dangerous.

He felt strangely attracted to Hilary. He gave her an apprais-ing look, which she intercepted before looking away from him and turning her attention to Pia.

She patted her hand and said in an encouraging tone, "Well Pia, do you feel ready to tell Dr. Di Girolamo what you saw?" She smiled at her and spoke to her, as one would to encourage a shy child.

He smiled himself in what he hoped was a benevolent manner and said, "When you're ready."

Hilary gave him a glance of approval. It was going to be all right, and it was. Pia got the whole story out with the minimum of fuss.

And she was much more straightforward than usual, as though his presence had given her the ability to become concise. He thanked her very much at the end and left without commenting on her statement.

Hilary accompanied him to the door and said, "Thank you for being so kind to her. I hope we haven't wasted your time."

"As I told you before, I ask the questions."

She looked down and then hesitantly added, "By the way, I have heard something that you probably already know."

He waited.

"Well, it's just that apparently Ettore had the keys to several people's houses, foreigners' houses I mean, and it seems he sometimes used them when they were away. The houses I mean, not the keys. Oh well, of course I mean, he had to use the keys to get into the houses. Sorry, I'm not being terribly clear am I?"

He remained silent, staring at her.

She was beginning to feel rather stupid. Feeling that she must be turning pink, she took a deep breath and finished rapidly.

"Well, I mean he wasn't alone when he did so, so I thought I should tell you in case you didn't know…if he was using Nigel's house, then he wouldn't have been alone, and so…" she trailed off.

As he still said nothing she added hesitantly, "I just thought that if someone had been with him, they might have seen the murderer, or even be the murderer."

"When did you hear this?"

"Yesterday, I think."

"I see. Where did you hear this?"

"Oh it was just gossip in the shop. But a friend confirmed that she had seen him in a house, and not alone. And she's not going to be happy if I tell you her name."

"Ah, you keep finding me reluctant witnesses." He smiled at her. "Well, I will not ask you for now. Perhaps you could tell this person that I might like a signed statement, as I do like everything in writing, just for the record."

"Yes, I'll do that."

She watched him walk to his car. He looked back at her and smiled before putting on his sunglasses and setting off. As the car passed her, he actually grinned, and she thought how absolutely silly she must seem to him. A middle-aged, flustered idiot. No wonder he grinned. What must he think of her? Well, what did it matter anyway? At least she had done what she wanted to do. Then she went back in to congratulate Pia and to reassure her once again.

EIGHTEEN

FRANNY AND JAKE were playing cards on the terrace. Terry, their mother, came out with some homemade lemonade and glasses.

"Are you kids going swimming today?" she asked.

"Maybe. We're waiting for Roberto to phone. It's nicer if we go in crowd. Giulia has already said she'd like to come, too."

"What about this evening, are you eating here or what?"

"Definitely 'or what,'" said Jake. "I'm playing in the five-a-side football tournament tonight and I'm eating with the other guys afterwards."

"Here," said Franny. "Is it okay if Giulia eats here, too, Mom?"

"Of course. I was just counting heads."

The phone rang and Jake jumped up shouting, "I'll get it!" He spoke fluent Italian, as did Franny, because they had spent long periods of their childhood in the local schools. They had a lot of friends in Borgo San Cristoforo and loved the time they spent in Italy.

Jake came back. "Okay everybody, we're on for the pool. Roberto's coming round to pick us up in a quarter of an hour."

"Do you kids ever see Marco these days?" asked Terry. He had been a frequent visitor at the house when the kids were younger and had been in the same class as Jake.

"Uh-uh!" said Jake.

"I suppose that means 'no' and you don't want to talk about it."

"Brilliant. I'm going up to get my swimming gear." He raced back into the house and up the stairs.

"Franny?"

"Yeah?"

"Well, why don't you two see him anymore?"

"Oh Mom, he's changed so much. He hangs around with these awful kids, and they're doin' stuff, and anyway everyone says he's a faggot. Sorry, I mean gay."

"You're kidding."

"No. No, I'm not. He's always stoned or worse. And he was Ettore's 'boy.'"

"Why, I had no idea. I never knew Ettore was gay."

"Well, we reckon he was what dad calls 'ambidextrous,' you know, swinging on both sides of the bed."

"Bi-sexual, dear, is the correct term."

"Really, mom, do we always have to be so damn 'correct'? Anyway, that's why we don't see Marco anymore." She looked uncomfortable, got up and slouched off to get her gear.

Jake came back downstairs, looked at his mother and said, "No, don't tell me Franny's been spilling the beans. Ah, I see you blush...so 'bean' is the operative word, eh? Just please keep your mouth shut on this one. Don't go telling all your friends."

"As if I would."

He gave her a long hard look. "I mean it, Mom."

A car drew up and hooted. Franny rushed downstairs to join her brother and then they all drove off, shouting their good-byes, leaving Terry to digest what she'd just heard.

A metallic clanging noise startled her and she ran to the back of the house. Their nearest neighbour, Poldo, was vigorously bashing a saucepan with a metal ladle. His bees had swarmed and this was the method guaranteed to halt their flight, ensuring that they stopped in a nearby tree and did not head off to the woods, where retrieval would be impossible. She could see the gigantic black swarming mass hanging in a tree near their common boundary, on her side of the fence.

Poldo came puffing over to her, red in the face, and said, "I'll come and get them later when it's cooler. Can I bring my ladder round, through to your side? I promise I'll drive carefully this time."

A week earlier he had driven his three-wheeled truck right through her flower border in order to reach the tree where his bees had swarmed.

"Of course you can."

The bees swarmed every summer, and as he had ten hives, this was a fairly frequent occurrence.

He gave her a smile and said, "I'll bring you over some honey. Do you need eggs? We've got a glut."

"That would be lovely, thanks. But you must let me pay for them this time."

"No. I shall be very offended if you pay for them. After all, the bees are on your land, and.I have to disturb you to come and get them. And then there was the flowerbed last week. So we're quits."

She gave in. She never seemed to manage to pay for anything and was worried that one day there would be some kind of monumental repayment in the form of a favour or a permission of some kind that she would be hard put to refuse after months of kindness received. John kept telling her not to worry, but her grandmother had taught her Italian proverbs that seemed to apply to the situation, and she knew that 'all chickens come home to roost' and *'non si prende niente per niente'* both of which meant that sooner or later, she would have to repay what she had been given.

Later, towards evening, she was presented with a jar of chestnut flower honey. Nearly black in colour with a very strong, distinctive taste, it was her favourite. She also received a basket containing twenty large brown eggs which she knew would have deep yellow yolks and be wonderful, and totally unlike anything she could buy in the shops. She desperately rummaged in the cupboard searching for something with which to repay these gifts, and finally hit on a jar of green tomato pickle that she had made the previous autumn. It was at least a partial re-payment, though she knew she risked something else arriving within the next few days; some unbidden, but none the less welcome gift of superb vegetables to supplement her own unhappy ones, a jar of homemade jam, or a plate of succulent figs, and she would be back where she started, in some kind of debt.

NINETEEN

NIGEL HAD CAUGHT a summer cold. His eyes watered, his nose ran, his head throbbed; he felt hot and feverish, and he coughed incessantly. Robin had given him aspirin and tucked him into bed. On his bedside table were packets of paper handkerchiefs, orange juice (freshly squeezed with a little lace doily over the glass), aspirin, cough syrup, a thermometer and a small ice bucket full of ice cubes.

"Well, that's me done for," groaned Nigel. "No going to the concert for me." He miserably blew his nose, and looked at Robin with watering eyes. "But I want you to go."

"No, I'll stay here with you."

"Look, I've got all I need, and I know how much you wanted to go. It'll do you good to get out of here. The only place you've been since we got back is the police station. Please go. It'll take your mind off things."

"You're probably right, but I'll stay all the same. I can't face going alone."

"Look, Robin, you're bound to meet someone down there. I know John and Sebastian are going and you haven't seen them for ages, so you won't be alone."

"Mmm, I'll think about it."

"Well don't think too long, you haven't that much time. And you know how long it takes you to get ready."

Robin fussed around tidying up. It was true she was longing to get away, but she wanted to go miles away and forever. She couldn't tell Nigel that she didn't want to live here any longer, wished they'd never come here, wished they'd never met Ettore, wished things could be as before, and never would be again.

Tears sprang to her eyes. Everything was ruined. The murder had changed their lives irrevocably, and now there was this police-man with his embarrassing questions. And, almost worse, there was the blackmail. If they had to, maybe they could bluff that one out, but she couldn't help feeling that Nigel should never have given in to him. It looked so bad. It made him look guilty. Oh God! If only it had never happened. But it had, and living with it was destroying her. She had to pull herself together. She had no desire to go out and talk to people but, on the other hand, to get into the car and go down the coast might pull her out of it. She turned to Nigel and said, "If you're really sure you'll be all right, then I'll go. I'll phone you when I arrive and again after the concert."

"I'll be fine, really. I'll probably read a bit and then doze off, so don't worry about phoning. Just go!"

She went off to shower and change. Riffling through the clothes in the huge wardrobe in her dressing room, she decided to wear a knee-length silk dress with buttons down the front in a wonder-ful golden beige colour that shimmered as she walked. Her long legs were tanned and she wore cream-coloured sandals, high-heeled as always, and carried a soft, cream-coloured leather bag.

"My God," she said to herself. "Italians certainly know how to make shoes and bags." She was beginning to feel better already. She loved the sensual feel of the silk against her skin. She picked up a gossamer-light, beige stole. Her make-up was applied with a rather heavy hand but *what the hell,* she thought, *it'll be dark.* She screwed in her golden hoop earrings and pouted at herself in the mirror. "Not bad for forty-five!" she said admir-ingly to her reflection in the mirror.

She went into their bedroom and struck a pose in the doorway in order for Nigel to admire her. He approved heartily, "My God, you've really got yourself tarted up. Be a good girl…don't do anything I wouldn't do!"

She could hear the slight edge in his voice and reacted to it immediately. She came closer to the bed and glared at him.

"Very funny," she said acidly. "That certainly gives me lots of leeway."

"For God's sake, Robin. Don't start on about that again. It was a long time ago. Anyway, I'm sure you've already paid me back in kind. What did you get up to while I was in England selling the house? I can't see you being chaste for two months. Well, never mind. I won't ask. We all know chastity was never your forte, my dear."

"Oh God, if you're going to go raking up the distant past again, I can't stand it."

"Sorry sweetie, but once a whore."

"Don't you dare. I hate you, Nigel, when you do this to me. I'm falling apart…can't you see that? You know that since we've been together I have never even looked at anyone else. We were talking about your little escapade, which, if I remember rightly, wasn't so long ago. You always twist things. You're guilty, but I'm made to suffer."

"Okay. Forgive me. Come and give me a kiss," he looked contrite. "No, don't, you'll catch my cold." He coughed and blew his nose again "The trouble is, you're too damned good looking and I'm an old man. And I can't bear the thought of you with another man. I think I'd kill you if you did that to me."

"Well, I haven't and I won't."

Nigel looked so sorry for himself that she added, "Darling you're not an old man. You're lovely and I adore you."

"Do you?"

She smiled at him and he continued, "All right, enough of all that. It must be this fever addling my brain. Now go! And send my love to John and Sebastian."

She blew him a kiss and picked up her bag and stole. She took the car keys from the hook and called to him, "Bye darling. I'll phone."

THE MERCEDES PURRED its way down the winding road to the coastal plain. She began to relax. Her nerves were shot to pieces or she would never have snapped at Nigel like that. She should have known how he'd retaliate. Please God, this nightmare would soon be over and things would get back to normal. She had been seeing things out of proportion because of being shut up in the house. She and Nigel must carry on as normal. Why not have a party? That would be a good way of re-establishing the status quo. It would be proof of innocence. She began to plan it in her mind.

TWENTY

HILARY CHECKED HERSELF in the full-length mirror. She was wearing a long black skirt, a red silk shirt, sandals with a medium heel, and lipstick, but no other make-up, as her tanned skin needed none. She heard the "beep-beep" that always announced Bruno's arrival. It always irritated her, and this evening even more than usual. Why couldn't he park the damn car and ring the doorbell? She grabbed her bag and hurriedly left the house. Bruno was outside in the car *champing at the bit,* as she always said.

"Ciao, you look good," he greeted her.

"Thanks, you look all right yourself," she replied tartly.

He laughed and said "Feminist! I don't see why I'm not allowed to compliment you."

"Nor I, you."

"Okay, truce. I won't do it again, it's just that I keep forgetting."

The car drove swiftly down the winding road. It was a sultry evening and Hilary mentally thanked God they would be eating on the terrace of the restaurant, and then going on to an open-air concert. It would have been unbearable to have to be inside. She felt a moment's qualm and asked, "Did you book seats for the concert?"

"Yes, I did, and the table at the restaurant. Outside on the terrace, of course."

"Lovely." They drove on in silence for a bit. "Well, how was the holiday?"

Bruno had been away for a month in the north of Italy. He

had been on a walking holiday to visit relatives, as his family came from there. He had come to live in Borgo San Cristoforo by chance.

"It was fantastic. You should have come with me. The mountains were wonderful. The silence was incredible after a year listening to kids yelling."

Bruno was the headmaster at the local secondary school. He had been transferred five years before and had liked it so much that he had decided to stay a few years. Meeting Hilary two years earlier had made him determined not to move away.

"I almost wish I had."

"Next year you must. Tell me about the murder enquiries. What do the police say? Do they have any idea who did it?"

"I've no idea. I was called in to make a statement, and was practically accused of doing it myself. Or I think I was. That Dr. Di Girolamo has a strange sense of humour. Every time I decide he must be joking he gets deadly serious and threatening. Anyway it wasn't very pleasant. They took my fingerprints, you know."

"Sounds unpleasant."

"However, I must say, he was very nice with Pia today."

"Pia. What's she got to do with it?"

"Oh, damn. I've got the feeling I shouldn't have said anything about that. No, sorry I can't tell you. It's nothing earth shattering but until I am told I can, I won't speak about it. Forget what I said please."

"I already have, don't worry."

"Sorry. Well, to continue the story…at the beginning we all thought that German had done it. But they don't seem to have arrested him, so I suppose it's not him. The burglar theory seems the most popular and as far as I can gather it's the official version. The newspapers have dropped the whole thing and everybody seems to think it will be one of those unsolved crimes. Of course they have to keep trying for a bit, but I expect they'll never know who did it."

"It can't be very nice for Nigel and Robin. Didn't Nigel get on very well with him at one time?"

"Yes, they fell out over money. Well, you know what a cheat Ettore was. It took Nigel quite a while to realise that, and then when he did, he cut Ettore out of his life."

"Well, better late than never. Ettore wasn't at all a nice person. Money was the ruling factor in his life, I think. Money and what he could do with it. He wasn't a good influence on that boy Marco, either."

"Poor kid. He seems in a bad way since his hero died. He'd had nothing more to do with the kids of his own age while Ettore was alive, so he's pretty much alone now. He looks dreadful."

"Yes, I saw him yesterday evening. I had to go out to get cigarettes. It was rather strange, actually. It was in the old town and as I turned the corner just before Palazzo Guelfi, I saw him praying, or at any rate crossing himself, in front of that little Madonna."

"Sounds unlikely. But religion is so ingrained that some people do that sort of thing automatically even if they're not religious. Don't go to church I mean. It's almost a conditioned reflex, or maybe a good luck thing."

"Maybe." They drove on in silence. As they neared the restaurant

Bruno said, "Did you miss me?"

"Yes, I did. Did you miss me?"

"Yes."

He stopped the car in the restaurant parking space. "Come on, let's go and eat. I'm starving."

As they walked into the restaurant Bruno took her hand. For some inexplicable reason, she didn't really want him to.

TWENTY-ONE

DI GIROLAMO SAT in his office, a folder open on his desk. He riffled through it. There were photographs, lab reports, statements and fingerprints. All the usual stuff. What did it amount to? Fagiolo had been killed. There was a thumbprint on the spade, which had been used to hit Ettore, a spade which had otherwise been wiped clean. The print didn't belong to anyone he had interviewed, which was why the official version was still that a burglar had been disturbed by Ettore, and had subsequently killed him.

No doubt this would be one of the many unsolved murders that were committed by delinquents every year, although a large number of these involved firearms. What was surprising about this murder was that this felon, having hit Ettore a hefty blow, should then drag the semi-conscious victim to the pool edge and throw him in. The blow to the head had been enough to stun the man, but not kill him. It would cause concussion, immobilise the man and allow a getaway. Therefore, why stop and throw him in? And by so doing, saddle yourself with an unnecessary murder charge?

Now this old lady, what was her name? Ah yes…he looked at her statement again…Pia Pieri, had come forward, albeit rather late in the day, to tell him that the Proctors had come back that night right at the possible time of the murder.

Could this just be a coincidence? Why had they not told him themselves that they had returned? He knew that reticence was not always a sign of guilt. People would omit to tell you things either because they thought they had no relevance, or because they were afraid it would make things look bad for them. He had no idea which it was in this case.

They had seemed very straightforward at the interview, so it could well be that they were so certain the murder happened after their departure that they had seen no reason to mention it. On the other hand, they may have calculated that, as it was of no importance but would look bad, it would be better to stay silent. Of course they could have come back, found him there and done it themselves. Again, why? You don't kill a man for overcharging you. You might be very angry if you found that he was using your house in your absence. And, as the ensuing argument degenerated and became a fight, you might even kill him accidentally. But would you throw an injured man into a pool? A man that you had injured in the heat of the moment? He felt not. It was far more likely you would be shocked at having hurt him so badly and try to remedy it. In his experience, the aggressor on such occasions was usually horrified. No, Ettore's death could not have been an accident.

There were no fingerprints on the spade other than the one thumbprint, which did not belong to either of the Proctors. Of course it was quite possible that this print belonged to someone unconnected with the murder. Also, if Nigel had hit Ettore with the spade, would he then clean it? What would be the point? It would be normal for all the garden implements to have his prints on them. Or had he decided to clean it for that reason, thinking that if it had been cleaned we'd think it wasn't him? Well, he'd have them in again the next day and see what they had to say about it.

He examined other possible solutions. What about the Englishwoman? Hilary Wright was a cool customer and would undoubtedly have the nerve to throw the man in, but why should she? He had asked the local police about her and they had given her an impeccable character reference. He let himself think about her for a moment. She attracted him, and he wasn't easily attracted. She intrigued him. Maybe that was it. Strange the spark that sometimes one felt, that he hadn't felt for so long. Perhaps he would find a pretext to see her again. He pulled his thoughts back to the case.

He considered the German, Herman Ganz. He hadn't totally given up on that angle, but he felt it improbable. Apart from the fact that he had been the first suspect after an anonymous phone call had alerted them to his threats towards Ettore that evening, there was no proof that he had been at the villa at all. The fingerprint was not his. Also, according to eyewitnesses, the man had been so drunk that he was falling about. He would never have had the strength or the coordination to do it. At that stage of drunkenness he would have been feeble and uncoordinated. It was impossible to imagine him coolly wiping his fingerprints off the spade and replacing it, let alone dragging that dead weight to the pool. He had a motive of sorts, though often those who yelled their intention to do so would be totally incapable of killing. No, the German might look good on paper, but Ruggero thought him innocent. His behaviour over the last few days had been exactly as requested. He had faithfully reported to police stations on the various stages of his journey and had always given the name of the hotels he stayed in, correctly.

Ruggero had asked that all reports arriving at the police station from the day of the murder be passed on to him, no matter how seemingly irrelevant. In a place this size he knew there would be few, but something interesting might turn up.

He looked at one that had arrived on his desk a few days earlier. Some rubbish disposal men had been manually emptying out one of the smaller containers in the Vicolo Buio when one of the large rubbish bags had burst, scattering pornographic videos all over the pavement. They had investigated and found another bag-load. All this material had been brought to the police station. There was quite a selection. Something for everyone: straight, gay, paedophile or S & M.

He had had two men sent up from Lucca to view them and

decide if they were the sort legally available or if there was anything that would involve a criminal offence, especially with regard to the possibly paedophile ones. They might not actually involve minors, but he wanted to know for sure. Anyway, they were checking on the suppliers, where they were named. It was possible that the videocassettes had something to do with the murdered man. They had been found in a rubbish container on the corner of the street where he had his office. That might mean nothing. But, pursuing that line of thought, perhaps someone had decided it would be better to throw them out, because they didn't want them found on the premises.

Who? They would have to interrogate the employees. Fagiolo had little family, only his parents. The father had Alzheimer's and the mother, a God-fearing old lady, looked after him. She attended every mass held in every church in town according to the local police. Would a woman like that want anyone to find porno-graphic material in her son's office? Well, the answer had to be 'no, not at any cost,' even if that meant getting rid of it herself.

He tried to imagine this tired, old woman struggling along, probably after dark, with a huge sack of porn videos, and then back again for another. If it weren't so tragic it would be amusing. He sighed. How could he ask her? What would be the point, anyway? She was bound to deny it. Also, he was very angry with himself, as he had fallen down on that one. He should have been quicker off the mark and had a look in Ettore's office immedi-ately. Of course, he had been called in the day after the murder. But the trouble was that his time here had been limited. What with tying up another case near Prato and court appearances, plus extra work covering for those more fortunate than himself who were sunning themselves in Sardinia, he hadn't been able to give this case his full attention. Obviously the old girl hadn't got round to cleaning out her son's office until after the funeral.

The burglar theory really was looking like the only solution, once the German had been cleared. It hadn't seemed possible that

Ettore had been killed because he was who he was. It had seemed to him, then, more probable that Ettore's death had been a random killing. So he hadn't looked at the office until it was too late. He hadn't thought to give it priority. The thing that worried him was that if Ettore's mother had found videos in the office, there might well have been other important material: letters, photos, phone numbers and addresses. All gone. There may have been some clue as to how this man had lived his life, and met his death. Of course this was all purely hypothetical, as he couldn't know for sure that the videos had come from the office. There were no detectable fingerprints on any of them. The old lady must have worn gloves and cleaned off everything.

He supposed there could be other explanations for their presence in the rubbish bins. It could have been an outraged wife who had discovered her husband's secret vice hidden in a wine cellar perhaps, and thrown the lot of them out. Or a deserted wife, or even, improbably, a redeemed porn addict! But intuition told him that the videos had belonged to Fagiolo, and that he had messed it up. He banged his fist on the table. He knew this was a more complex murder than it seemed, and he needed a break.

He closed the folder, placed it in a locked drawer, and left his office. He would eat alone in one of the restaurants, then he would walk through the old town, maybe have a coffee in the bar in the old town centre and maybe bump into someone he knew. Maybe someone foreign. There were an awful lot of foreigners involved in this case. If he had to choose someone to meet, it would have been someone English.

Although he walked around for quite a while, he did not see her.

TWENTY-TWO

MARCO, WITH HIS friends Andrea and Riccardo drove down the same road that Robin, and earlier, Hilary and Bruno, had taken. Their car was an old Renault with ten euros' worth of petrol in it. They were not going to the concert. All three were smoking. They talked a little about money and then fell silent. They arrived at eleven-thirty p.m. and had concluded their business by midnight. Then they walked out onto the beach and sat there for a while listening to the sea and swigging the beer they had just bought in a bar on the beach. Their cigarettes glowed in the darkness. Finally, they lethargically pulled themselves to their feet and scrunched back across the sand to their car.

HILARY PUT HER HAND on Bruno's arm "Isn't that Robin over there with those two men? But I don't see Nigel. Oh, they've disappeared."

"I didn't see anyone. Let's go and have a drink. I don't want to go home yet, do you?"

"All right. Let's go to the bar on the beach."

They sat outside the bar, looking at the sea. There was a light breeze and the sound of the sea was soothing. They stayed for more than an hour. It had been a fantastic evening and they were almost loath to get back into the car. But they had an hour and a half's drive ahead of them, and they were both tired.

ROBIN HAD MET UP with John and Sebastian, and after the concert they decided to have a light seafood meal. She had phoned Nigel who had said, *"Buon appetito!"* and not to worry as he felt better already. John knew a marvellous place that would serve them even though it was nearly midnight. Robin had promised to invite them to Villa Rosa soon, possibly to a party. Feeling much more relaxed she got into the car. She didn't like driving alone at night, so she drove very carefully and fairly slowly, letting the car ahead disappear.

She had seen Hilary and Bruno at the concert but had pretended not to, had in fact quickly drawn John and Sebastian out of sight under a pretext. Somehow she couldn't face talking to them, as she knew they would talk about the murder. They couldn't not. She frowned into the night. Everything was ruined really, as she couldn't even behave normally. She had not set foot in the garden since they got back, let alone looked at the pool. The idea of a party to exorcise the house and pool seemed a good one to her. She would discuss it with Nigel the next morning.

MARCO SLAMMED the car door and watched as it left. He'd been right to get out just before going into town. Automatically his hand tightened on the little plastic bag he was carrying. He would cut through the fields along the mule track and be home in a few minutes.

The road was dark, but there was sufficient moonlight to enable him to see where he was going, and his eyes had quickly adjusted to the light. He was about to cross the road and take the mule track when he saw a car's headlights sweep round the curve behind him. As the car came into view, he quickly stepped to the side of the road and half turned away. There was no cover and he was hoping not to be recognised.

There was a roar behind him as the car accelerated, and surprised, he began to turn his body to look at it. The lights blinded him and immediately afterwards he felt a blow as the car hit his thighs hard, knocking him upwards and backwards. Then with a thud, he hit the ground, his head bursting into a thousand fragments. He tried to turn his head, to lift it, to call, but plunged painfully into darkness. Blood trickled from his wounded head down to the collar of his white shirt, the stain slowly spreading. The little plastic bag flew from his fingers and pirouetted into the thick undergrowth.

PIETRO ARTUSI DROVE carefully round the bends. He yawned and glanced at the dashboard clock. It was nearly three o'clock and he had to get up at seven-thirty, so he wasn't going to get much sleep. Still, it was worth it. He'd had a great evening with Elisabetta. He was thinking about her as he rounded the last big curve in the road before town. As he straightened the car, his headlights lit up a white form on the ground. It was a body! He screeched to a halt and almost immediately catapulted from the car, leaving the door open. A young boy lay on the ground, his white shirt stained with blood, which came from a very ugly looking wound at the side of his head. He could actually see shattered bone among the matted bloody dark hair. He felt sick. The body was immobile and he couldn't even see if the boy was breathing. He grabbed the boy's wrist to feel for a pulse, but inexpertly could only feel the pulse of his own racing blood. He seemed to remember that the blood vessels in the neck were more reliable and, searching tentatively with his fingertips, he located one, and felt a weak throbbing. Ah, he was alive!

He rushed back to his car, picked up his cell phone and excitedly gabbled into it. Then, as he could do nothing for the boy, and had been told not to touch him, he decided to move his car as anyone coming round the bend might run into it. He took out his car's triangle from the puncture kit in the boot and walked back round the bend where he set it up as a warning. He could already hear the siren in the distance. Lighting a cigarette, he glanced down at the boy. He had long, black, curly hair; a too pale face and long, black eyelashes. Pietro peered at him, bending down closer to see if he recognized him.

Yes, it was Gino's boy, what was his name? He couldn't remember. But he did remember seeing the boy on a motor scooter. He looked around for it, but there was no sign of one. How on earth did he come to be walking here at this time of night, obviously alone, and where was the bastard who had mown him down? The sound of the ambulance became imperative, and as it braked beside him, he became aware that there was a police car behind it. He groaned. He had forgotten that one of the rewards for calling an ambulance to an accident scene was that you were grilled by the police for ages and then had to sign a formal statement. That was when he knew that he wouldn't be going to work the next day. He sighed, resigned. Well, he'd spend part of the day catching up on his sleep. He ran up to the young doctor who had jumped out of the ambulance.

"It's Gino's boy, he's got a bad head wound, but I haven't touched him," he babbled.

The doctor said, "Okay, go and sit in your car. I'll see to him now." He knelt beside the boy and lifted his eyelids, shining a light into his eyes. He felt the pulse, listened to the heart and gave a cursory examination of the rest of the boy's body. Then at a signal, two attendants helped him lift the boy onto a stretcher with infinite care as he said, "I'll set up a drip on the way down. Paolo, you phone the hospital at Lucca. We'll take him straight down there. And don't take no for an answer. I don't want to hear any crap about there being no room." Seconds later the ambulance, siren wailing, set off fast. It would take maybe twenty minutes at that time of night to do what was a thirty-five minute daytime journey.

PIETRO SAT SIDEWAYS on the driver's seat, the car door open and his legs outside, feet on the ground. He had lit another cigarette and pulled himself to his feet as the two policemen approached, but then realised that standing wasn't a good idea, so he sat down again. His hands were shaky and he felt queasy. It must be delayed shock, as he'd felt all right before. He put his head down and took a deep breath. The policemen stopped in front of him. A voice asked, "Are you the person that phoned for the ambulance?"

He heard himself answer, "Yes."

One of the policemen pulled out a notebook and took down his name and address. Then he asked for his driving licence and verified them.

He asked, "Would you like to tell us what happened?" while the other one bent over the front of Pietro's car examining it with his torch. Pietro was beginning to find the situation unreal. It slowly dawned on him that they wouldn't believe him. They would think he had run the boy over himself! He pulled himself together and said in a firm voice, "I was driving home and as I came round the bend, I straightened up and there he was. Someone had run him over and left him there." He hoped it sounded truthful.

"Yes sir. Was the boy lying as you found him, or did you move him at all?"

"No, I didn't move him. I only tried to feel his pulse at the wrist. But I couldn't find it, so I tried in the throat region and there was a pulse, so I rushed back to my car and phoned for an ambulance. They told me not to touch him at all, and I didn't." He felt he had been speaking too fast. He looked at them and hoped he was being convincing but he was beginning to feel really worried.

"Well, I think it would be better if you were to accompany us to the police station and I would prefer you to leave your car here."

They all moved towards the police car where the senior of the two phoned through for someone to come to the scene of the accident and thoroughly check his car. With a sense of impending doom he got into the police car and was driven up to the town. It was three forty-five a.m. and he didn't think he would be going to bed at all that night.

TWENTY-THREE

MORNING. THE SUN WAS shining in a relentlessly blue sky. A flock of birds screamed past before settling on a telephone wire. Shops were opening, the wooden shutters being removed by hand, carted inside and stacked against a wall until evening when, seemingly heavier, they would be replaced and the shops shut once again. Now the doors would remain open, with bead curtains in the doorway that clattered, announcing the arrival of customers, and offered effective protection against flies, creating an inner gloom, which was also cool.

A housewife was cleaning the area immediately outside her front door, swilling buckets of disinfectant to counteract the pervasive odour of cat urine, which the local tomcats would renew the next night, and the next.

The old town clung to the mountainside tenaciously. The houses were piled on top of each other and the narrow roads wound through the town, branching off into tiny Vicoli, or steep steps, all leading upwards to the Duomo, the cathedral that crowned the town. Dr. Ruggero Di Girolamo stood in the ample piazza outside the Duomo. It had a commanding view of the Apuan Alps and the valley below. The roofs of the houses were compact and often effectively hid from view the tiny, cobbled roads that ran between them, or even under them, so that some houses would have a room suspended over the road. The air was crystal clear and it was cool, the best time of day.

He ran swiftly down the steep cobbled road that would lead him to the Porta Medicea, or main gate to the old town, and then down to the sprawling, modern part of the town, which contained most of its inhabitants, and spread downwards to join the main road in the valley. He walked briskly along the main street, passing the shoe shop, which was tastefully decorated, belts snaking amongst the shoes or over the branches that made up the window display; past the ice cream parlour, which was now serving coffee and brioches to early morning customers; past the travel agency, with flights to Glasgow and London, which were the prime attraction; past the estate agent where Tuscan country houses were for sale in two languages; and turned the corner past the bank and the cinema, increasing his pace as he walked down the tree lined road that led to the police station.

He had slept in Borgo San Cristoforo, as this morning he would be interviewing the Proctors. Sitting at his desk with the case file in front of him, he leafed through the contents and fingered the photographs thoughtfully. He had asked Nigel and Robin to be at the police station for further questioning at nine o'clock. He took out the photographs of Ettore Fagiolo's body in the pool and close-up photos of the head wound that had contributed to, but not caused, his death. He arranged them to maximum effect on his desk before pressing a buzzer on his table. The door was opened by a young policeman, who was doing his military service on the force as an alternative to the army.

"Yes Sir?"

"Have they arrived?"

"The English couple?"

"Yes."

"Ten minutes ago."

"You can always trust the English to be punctual. Send in Robin Proctor."

"Yes sir." The door closed and his footsteps receded at a smart pace.

Nigel and Robin were sitting next to each other in the waiting room, looking tense.

"Robin Proctor," the policeman said, putting his head round the door.

She looked up and murmured faintly, "Yes."

"Come with me, please."

"Nigel," she said in a shaky voice, "do I have to go on my own?"

"Yes, you'll be all right. He won't eat you." Nigel smiled at her reassuringly.

She teetered after the young man, her heels slithering slightly on the polished floor.

She was ushered into the room and took a seat facing Di Girolamo. She tried a tentative smile. "*Buon giorno,* Dottor."

"*Buon giorno,*" he said crisply. His fingers tapped the photographs in front of him so that her eyes were drawn to them. These interviews would be in English as the English couple hadn't even grasped the most elementary rules of Italian grammar. They could understand well enough, but he considered they would be at a disadvantage when speaking.

"I have asked you to come today because I want to ask you one easy question." He looked into her eyes. "Why did you not tell me that you came back to the Villa Rosa on the night of the murder?"

"Was it important?" she gasped.

"Answer the question."

"Well, Nigel had forgotten some documents and we turned back. We had a lot of time in hand."

"Continue," he barked.

"Well, he went into the house, got them, and we drove off. That's all."

"I see. That is not the answer to my question. Why did you not tell me?"

"It didn't seem important."

"That was for me to judge. Did you know that omitting to give me this information could be construed as withholding evidence?"

"No, no, it wasn't that. It just wasn't important. What did it matter?" She sounded more confident now.

Di Girolamo shuffled the photos around revealing the autopsy photos, which were shocking even to him. Robin's eyes followed the movements of his hands. She looked away.

"Perhaps you didn't tell me because you knew that Nigel had killed Ettore and you were frightened I would find out."

"Oh my God. That blackmailing little shit has told you a load of lies. You can't believe him!" She sounded incredulous.

"Yes," said Ruggero firmly, having no idea what she was talking about. "I'm afraid I do. Things look very bad for Nigel."

"But surely you don't really believe him? He's a pathological liar. Nigel only paid him off because he didn't want to be hassled by this. It's not true, none of it. You mustn't listen to him."

"I have to listen to anyone who has information concerning the case and I have to investigate. You have admitted you were there, but you tell me nothing happened. My informant says otherwise," he lied.

"But he's lying. You can't possibly believe what he says. Anyway, why should you believe him rather than us? It's our word against his really, isn't it? Perhaps he did it himself!"

"Perhaps he did. Perhaps you did. How can I tell?" He spread his hands. "It seems probable that Nigel could be guilty. You see, Ettore Fagiolo was in Nigel's house, and Nigel was already angry with him. I think that he argued with him, fought with him and finally killed him."

Robin felt tears spring to her eyes. "Please believe me. There was nothing to hide, no evidence was withheld, no crime was committed. Nigel wouldn't hurt a fly and I don't see how you can prove otherwise."

"You defend him well, this husband. Tell me, why should my informant tell me lies?"

"How should I know? Everyone knows he was crazy about Ettore, so he's telling lies about Nigel because he knew they'd quarrelled."

"It is possible. Or, as you say, he could have done it himself. But again, why should he?"

"Perhaps they had a quarrel, a lovers' tiff that got really nasty."

Ruggero digested this information and replied calmly, "I think that very unlikely."

"Well, to me it's no more unlikely than Nigel doing it."

They remained in silence for a while. Ruggero judged that he would get no further information of any use from her, so he pressed the buzzer summoning the young policeman again. "Thank you for your help. I have no doubt that we will meet again," he said, dismissing her, and then, to the conscript, "See her out, you know which way. Then bring him in."

Robin was accompanied to a different room and asked kindly to wait for Nigel there. The door was closed firmly.

TWENTY-FOUR

NIGEL HAD ALMOST expected Robin to be in the room with Di Girolamo, but found him there alone. He made no comment. The photos were in evidence and the Italian kept moving them around, so he averted his eyes. He thought it was a typical police trick. It seemed obvious that this Dr. Ruggero Di Girolamo was trying to make him feel upset, soften him up, before he began questioning him. Well, it wasn't going to work. He straightened his shoulders, blew his nose and looked the policeman squarely in the eyes.

Ruggero felt like laughing at this ridiculous Englishman, who would be ready to defend the British Empire if there still was one. He was trying so hard to look as pure as snow, when, as Ruggero well knew, his life would not bear scrutiny. He remained silent for a moment while he decided on his tactics.

Then suddenly he barked out, "Robin Proctor has just confessed that she knows that you killed Ettore Fagiolo on the night of July eighth, having come back unexpectedly and surprising him in your house." He stared at Nigel, whose ruddy face took on a darker hue, which then spread down to his neck.

"Liar!" shouted Nigel, as though outraged at the enormity of this statement. His eyes bulged from their orbits, his neck was strained with all the cords in evidence as he thrust his chin even higher.

One up to him, thought Di Girolamo. It was hard to fight these people. To start with they had an inborn sense of superiority, and that gave them the confidence and the authority to bluster their way out of situations in which others would become bogged

down and swallowed up. The only way to get anything resem-
bling the truth would be to use the cunning for which Italians
were renowned ever since Machiavelli had set down instructions
to his prince. He'd held his own pretty well with Robin, but this
man was going to be very wearing. He felt almost bored at the
thought of going through the whole thing all over again. He
knew it would be more or less the same, and he was sure that he
would learn nothing new. Stifling a yawn he stared at the window,
wishing he were out in the sunshine. Perhaps tonight he would
attend the open-air concert. He had heard instrumentalists practising in the school this morning as he went past. He was fond
of Baroque music.

He glanced at the reports on his desk. There was nothing of any
interest to him. There had been an accident, a hit and run. There
had been several break-ins and quite a few people on their summer
holidays had lost valuables and electrical equipment, televisions,
VCRs and even computers. It always surprised him that these delinquents knew exactly when a family would be on holiday. Even
those who had paid for the local security service to check on their
houses had had break-ins, and their wall safes ripped out. For such
a small area it did seem rather a high rate. This intimate knowledge of people's movements would seem to indicate local offenders, but the expertise seemed very professional. He sighed, it
wasn't his problem, thank God! Just imagine dealing with irate
householders in this heat! Actually, given the summer increase in
the crime rate, he supposed that the burglar theory could explain
the Fagiolo murder. He just didn't believe it.

With a sigh he turned his attention back to Nigel, who was
looking around the room in an attempt to show how at ease he
felt. He coughed, to gain Nigel's attention.

"Why did you pay the blackmailer?"

Nigel looked disconcerted. *One point to me,* thought Di
Girolamo. He continued staring at Nigel, who was obviously
thinking furiously. Nigel finally came up with an answer.

"To avoid misunderstandings."

"Ah, misunderstandings. I see. You mean that had I known of your return to the Villa Rosa, I might have misunderstood and thought that you had been involved in this vicious murder." His hand indicated the photos.

"Yes, and I was right. That is exactly what you are thinking." He sounded more in control.

Damn, thought Di Girolamo, *I'll have to flummox him again.*

"Why do you think the blackmailer took your money, but then decided to inform me anyway?"

"I have no idea."

"Come on, I am sure you can hazard a guess."

"Well, perhaps he was feeling vindictive. And once he'd got a little money out of me, enough to immediately satisfy his habit, he decided to throw me to the wolves. I mean, I don't know what he told you, but most of it was bound to be lies."

"Why did you go down to the pool?" Ruggero decided to risk asking.

"I didn't. Did he tell you that? I think if you are going to follow this line, I should have a legal representative."

"As you wish. I am not charging you."

"No, you're not. Because you don't have any proof to back up your allegations, which are based on the lies told you by a little drug-addict."

Ruggero sighed again. How predictable this man was. He felt there was no point in continuing the interview, as there was no more to be gained.

"The police are bound to investigate all allegations. That is all I have been doing," he lied. "It would have been better if you had told me yourself, that you had returned to your house that night. Perhaps I would have been less suspicious. But you do see the position in which you have put yourself. If you are innocent then you have nothing to fear by telling the truth."

"I doubt that. But I am innocent. The truth is that I came back, got my papers and left immediately. I didn't tell you because I knew that you would think I was involved in this murder, but I wasn't. I had nothing whatever to do with it, and you can't prove that I did." He tilted his chin in a belligerent manner.

Ruggero stood up rather abruptly. "Thank you for your cooperation. Please do not leave the town for the moment." He put his finger on the buzzer. When the conscript arrived, he made a hand movement that meant "get him out of here." He then walked over to the cupboard and made a pretence of looking through the files there, leaving Nigel to go without further salutation. "Bring me a coffee," he barked over his shoulder.

Well, he had gained some valuable information. Nigel was being blackmailed and had paid up. The blackmailer was a drug addict and a friend/lover of Ettore. He had not heard that Ettore was gay. When the young conscript came back with his coffee, he asked him if Maresciallo Biagioni was free for a chat. He would be bound to know who this blackmailer was. One step at a time he was getting closer to the murderer.

AT THE OTHER END of town, Augusta Fagiolo had just taken her glass bottles to the bell-shaped glass refuse container. On her way, she surreptitiously slipped an envelope from her pocket into the post box on the corner. She had seen no one yet that morning. She did not like gossiping and divided her time equally between church and home so she knew nothing of the news spreading like wildfire through the town that Marco was at death's door. Had she known she might have thought that God had struck him down for his wickedness.

She was wearing an old pair of slippers that flapped softly on the pavement. As she walked along, she was muttering prayers and one hand was in her pocket holding her rosary. She felt evil all around her and had been sleeping badly since she had found the photographs. Images had burned themselves onto her retina, into her brain.

SOMEONE ELSE IN TOWN was very pleased to know that Marco was at death's door. That person hoped that very soon Marco would be joining his lover. In fact, had all gone as it should have, he would have already been with him.

TWENTY-FIVE

GINO AND ALDA Rossi sat side by side on the uncomfortable beige plastic and chrome hospital chairs. They had the hopeless look of those who have been waiting for an interminable time. Alda had reddened eyes and still clutched a handkerchief. They sat in silence as they had nothing left to say to each other.

At last a masked green-robed figure with sterile overshoes and head covering emerged from the swing doors, tearing at his mask. They rose together from their chairs and took a couple of steps towards him, but he stopped them saying, "No, no. Please be seated."

Alda felt her legs weaken at his words and sank back into her chair. Gino remained standing until the doctor himself took a chair and sat down facing them. "The operation was successful, under the circumstances. We have done the best we can, but the injury was very serious. As I told you before I started operating, the wound was lacerated. Fragments of bone had penetrated the brain, and there was earth and other debris in the wound. There was also a haemorrhage within the brain. We have cleaned up, removed the bone fragments and repaired everything that we could, but, as you know, the brain is the most delicate of all our organs. I'm very sorry, but I can't tell you that he will live, or, that if he does, he will be normal. These things we will be able to judge later."

"Can we see our boy?" asked Alda in a shaky voice.

"I'm sorry, but you can't see him except through the glass. I'll get a nurse to accompany you. He will remain in intensive care. At the moment he is on a respirator. He is in the hands of God."

"Thank you, doctor," they murmured in unison.

"Go home, you can do nothing here. By all means go and see him, then go home. You need to rest, and in any case I cannot allow you to stay on this ward. Hospital rules. We will call you if there is any change in his condition."

"Thank you, doctor," said Alda. Her eyes filled with yet more tears.

"Nurse! Take these people through to look at their son, Marco Rossi, in the ICU, then show them the way out." He shook hands with them and rushed off.

Alda and Gino held onto each other as they followed the nurse to the viewing window. Their son was almost invisible, hidden by the machinery that was breathing for him and monitoring his vital functions. They both had tears in their eyes.

"I know what I'm going to do," said Alda firmly. "I'm going to San Giovanni Rotondo to pray to Padre Pio. The doctor said he's in the hands of God, so there's nothing else left to do. We'll go home now, and you must stay there in case the hospital phones. I'll get Rosaria to take me there."

Rosaria was Alda's pious unmarried cousin, who had already been to San Giovanni Rotondo on a pilgrimage. The Vatican was now examining Padre Pio's case, as his intervention was responsible for at least the two, well-documented medical miracles required for beatification. For years frowned on by the Church, his stigmata considered to be of hysterical origin, Padre Pio had become a cult figure and thousands of people flocked to San Giovanni Rotondo every year. Many of these pilgrims attributed their recovery from cancer or other life-threatening medical problems, to him. Now he was receiving official recognition.

The two old people, arm in arm, continued to look through the glass at their son. They had had him so late. Were they to lose him so soon? Alda felt absolutely ferocious in her desire to make him live.

She knew that he would. It was quite simple. All she had to do was make the journey south and pray.

They left the hospital and walked slowly to the little station, the one nearest to the hospital, where they took the two-carriage train that would take them home to Borgo San Cristoforo.

HILARY HAD GOTTEN UP fairly late again. She had enjoyed the concert the evening before, but hadn't got to bed until pretty late. Unfortunately, the evening had ended badly, as Bruno had expected to stay the night with her. And quite unaccountably, she hadn't wanted him to. She didn't bother to examine the reasons for that but dwelt instead on the ugly response with which he had greeted her decision. Although, in the end, they had parted in a reasonably normal manner, and this evening Bruno was dining with her at home, it still rankled. She didn't like being taken for granted, and couldn't forget what he had said.

But it was a beautiful morning and she felt full of energy, so she decided to go shopping straight away, before it got too hot. She threw open all the windows to air the rooms. Pia would close the shutters later, before the mid-day heat entered the house.

As she walked down the road, she could hear the sound of musicians practising. A soprano sang a few bars and then repeated them. Flutes and trumpets predominated this morning. There was another six o'clock concert this evening, this time in the cloisters of the convent, so she must remember to call Bruno and maybe meet him there. She hadn't been very nice to him last night. After the concert this evening they could walk home together and dine on her terrace.

Over the next two days, there would be an opera, Baroque of course, in the theatre, and another afternoon concert given by the music students. In a few days' time it was the feast of Saint Christopher. There would be a procession the evening before, which would wind its way through the medieval town centre to end up at the Duomo, where there would be a mass, with a choir and organist. At the same time, the town was transforming itself for its annual summer festa. There would be music, jazz or pop, tables set out in all the little squares and goods for sale. There might be a fire-eater, or clowns on stilts for the children, and a lot of hard drinking and serious eating for the adults.

As she passed Gino's bar, she was surprised to see that it was closed. Something must have happened. She turned into the greengrocers to buy peppers, and was immediately told that Marco was at death's door after being run over by a hit and run car, and had been taken first to Lucca by the ambulance. Then, as his head injuries were life threatening, on to Pisa, where there was an excellent brain surgery unit.

"When did this happen?" she asked. On being told that it had been at three that morning when the boy had been found, but that he had probably already lain there for ages, she exclaimed, "But I was there myself not much before that!"

In every shop the main topic was Marco…what had happened and, most intriguing of all, why had he been there alone, and on foot at that time of night?

Coming out of the greengrocers, she bumped into Terry.

"Have you heard about Marco?" asked Terry.

"Yes, I have, poor boy. His parents must be in a terrible state."

"You know, Hilary, the kids used to be great friends with him once and he was always at the house. He was such a lovely child."

"Yes, I remember. He was a sweet child, spoilt rotten of course, but he had such charm."

"Sweet little children grow into nasty boys sometimes."

"True, but not all of them. What are you getting at anyway?"

"Hilary, I wasn't going to tell you this, but now, what does it matter? I asked the kids why they don't see him anymore and they told me that he was, and I quote, 'doing stuff,' and that he was, again I quote, "Ettore's boy." Well, that translates as 'he was on drugs and having a homosexual relationship with Ettore.'" She looked sadly at Hilary.

"But Ettore wasn't homosexual!" she exclaimed.

"They said he was bi-sexual. Look, that's not the point, that was not a matter for concern. I mean Marco was a consenting adult, and that was his choice. I may add that my kids are far more intolerant than they realise. No, what worried me was the drugs aspect. Do you think that can be true?"

"I suppose it could be," she replied slowly, remembering Marco's physical aspect. "Besides, they would be likely to know. Kids do know about each other. They don't tell us, not usually, but probably they are right."

"Hilary, do you think he could have anything at all to do with Ettore's murder? I've been thinking. If he was Ettore's lover then maybe he was with him that night. Perhaps he saw something."

"We don't know that he was with him."

"Well he usually was, so the kids told me, almost every evening, so why not that evening?"

"I don't know. Surely someone would have seen him."

"Yeah, I suppose so. You'll think I'm crazy if I tell you what I was thinking. I thought, well, as a hypothesis, suppose he was with Ettore and saw the murder, and then was run over so that he would keep quiet."

"Hey Terry, you are going overboard on this one! Listen, for the murderer to try and kill him means that he would have to know that Marco had seen him. Also, it's a bit late in the day, isn't it? I mean if Marco knew who had killed his friend surely he would have said so immediately. Why wait so long?"

"Oh yeah. I don't know, though, I just feel that somehow there is a connection."

"Look, I'm sure that if he had been with Ettore that evening, it would have come out by now. And as for the hit and run accident, well, people panic. Whoever did it probably thought the boy was dead and couldn't face the music. It happens all the time."

"What was he doing there in the first place? Maybe he had arranged a meeting with the murderer, to blackmail him, and then been killed."

"It doesn't sound very likely to me, Terry. You have an over-active imagination."

"Well, its more plausible than Ben's theories."

"Terry, for God's sake, don't go airing these 'theories,' as you call them around. And I hope you won't tell too many people about the drugs side of it, either. Or the homosexual side, come to that. The boy is probably dying. Think of his parents."

"Hey, I may be crazy, but not that crazy. No. This was for your ears only. I mean that."

"Good. Look I have to go. Bruno's eating with me this evening and I want to get everything ready this morning, as I will probably have a rest this afternoon. I want to go to the six o'clock concert."

"Oh, where is it?"

"In the cloisters of the convent."

"Great. I'll see you there, then."

Assunta rattled the bead curtain as she came out of the green-grocers and smiled at Hilary, who asked her, "How's Miriam?"

"As always. She is a very naughty old lady and I have great difficulty in stopping her drinking."

She spoke Italian with such a strong Sicilian accent that some-times Hilary found her hard to understand.

"Tell her I'll pop in soon. Send my love."

Assunta moved on. She smiled to herself: *these stupid Englishwomen talking loudly in the street, thinking no one could understand them.* She had been listening to them, hidden in the shadows at the back of the shop. It was surprising how much information she got just by moving quietly and appearing not to understand English. Not even Miriam knew that she could under-stand so much.

Hilary thought how sly Assunta looked. She had heard her praised to the sky by Miriam, but had never liked her much herself. It was true that she and Salvatore did a good job in the house and garden, but there was something about them that made her uneasy. Salvatore, driving Miriam's Mercedes with a satisfied smile on his plump face, always reminded her of the cat that had just eaten the canary.

TWENTY-SIX

GINO SAT BY the phone, staring at it, willing it to ring. Alda had left as soon as possible for San Giovanni Rotondo driven by Rosaria, who had agreed that they should go immediately. He had slept badly, a couple of hours on the sofa, and was unshaven. For the first time this year he had not opened the bar. His thoughts were going round in circles. Why was the boy there in the first place? What could he have been doing alone? Who could have done this to him and then driven off and left him? Would he survive, would he be normal if he did? He sighed. Maybe Alda was right. She was so convinced that all she had to do was go to San Giovanni Rotondo and pray there. She had great faith, blind faith. Perhaps that was the sort of faith that was needed, the kind that moved mountains. He wished he had it.

NIGEL AND ROBIN were drinking coffee in the kitchen.

"You want to do what?" He nearly choked, and clattered his cup down on the saucer.

"Have a party, to show that we aren't bothered by all this, that it isn't affecting us and that we aren't guilty."

"Really, Robin, I don't think that is a very good idea at all."

"Well, I think it's a brilliant idea. What's the alternative? We sit in here avoiding everybody? They'll all think you did it and we can't face them. Come on Nigel. Please."

"I thought we could just gently slip back into normality. Anyway, suppose nobody comes?"

"Of course they will come. For lots of reasons. The ghouls

will want to see the place and the others will think, 'Poor things, we simply must go or they'll think they're being black-balled' or whatever the phrase is."

"I just don't like it. I personally do not wish to have either ghouls or kindly well-intentioned people all over the house. Apart from that, quite frankly after this morning's do with Di Girolamo, I feel I might be arrested at any moment."

"That's exactly why you have a party, to show that you don't feel that way."

"Very clever. How do you want to word the invitations? 'In case of sudden arrest the party will be postponed for twenty years'?"

"Look Nigel, we both know you didn't kill Ettore. Make an effort. You must look serene and untroubled. What could be better than a party to show how unconcerned you are?"

Nigel spluttered into his coffee. "You really are a ridiculous girl."

"Hardly a girl, darling." She pouted and fluttered her eye-lashes in parody.

"Oh, very well. If you absolutely must, then do it. I just hope you won't be sorry."

"Okay. I'll get started on all the arrangements."

HILARY WAS MAKING aubergine lasagne. First she grilled the aubergines she had picked from the vegetable garden. Then she made a fresh tomato sauce using her own onions, tomatoes and basil, and finally she prepared a béchamel sauce. She used oven-cook lasagne. She had bought peppers to make *'la peperonata,'* which Bruno adored. They would be having grilled pork chops that were sinfully high in cholesterol, but that was not a problem for Bruno who burned up fat and had to be careful or he lost weight. The last thing she prepared was a tiramisù, which went into the fridge. The whole menu was composed of his favourite food.

In the afternoon she was going to have a rest, partly because it was so hot and, as she hadn't really slept much of late, partly to try and recuperate. Pia had been and gone, and the house was clean and tidy. The cat was rubbing himself against her legs and giving her little bites to express his love for her. She scooped him up. He was a very large, heavy Siamese, an un-doctored tomcat, whom she had named Cassius for his pugilistic inclinations. She took him upstairs to bed with her. His purring would accompany her into sleep.

DI GIROLAMO WAS LISTENING to the local Maresciallo, Giovanni Biagioni, who was saying, "The blackmailer must have been Marco Rossi. He's the son of Gino, who owns that bar in the main piazza in the old town. He was a great friend of Ettore, followed him about like a little dog. I don't know that he was his lover though. That could just be malicious gossip. As to the drugs side of it, well, that could be true. I caught him smoking a joint. But he looks awful, so maybe he's moved on to something stronger. You won't be able to talk to him, though. He's the boy who was knocked down by a hit and run car in the early hours of the morning."

"This morning?"

"Yes, I put the report on your desk."

"Yes. I remember. Is he conscious?"

"No, he's in coma on a respirator. Wired up, you know." He sounded a little embarrassed.

"Yes, I know." His own wife had had been in coma for a week before dying, three years ago. She had been driving home from work when a lorry failed to stop at a junction.

"Is he going to die?"

"Looks like it. I don't think they hold out much hope. His mother's gone off to see Padre Pio."

Ruggero Di Girolamo almost snorted in derision thinking: *really, these superstitious peasants, as if that would do any good.* They always spoke as if Pio was still alive, probably because he was supposed to have appeared to so many people after his death. "Well, that's one key witness off the scene. Or is he a suspect? I wonder. Have you any idea who did it?"

"No. We interviewed the man who found him and reported it, but it wasn't him. He'd been with his girlfriend until literally five minutes before and the doctor on the ambulance reckoned the boy had been there about thirty minutes, maybe more. Also his car was clean as a whistle, no fibres, blood, nothing, and it hadn't been cleaned, either.

"He'd been parked down by the river with his girl, and the wet sand marks were still there and had only just started drying, so we'd have seen if he'd cleaned it. We've put out a call to the good citizens of Borgo San Cristoforo to come forward and tell us if they went along that road after two-thirty, or if they know of anyone who did."

"You don't seriously expect a hit and run driver to confess do you? After all he's in the clear," Di Girolamo said.

"No, but a nosy neighbour might take the opportunity of telling us. Or, as I said, in trying to pinpoint the time of the accident, someone might say, 'Yes, I came along at two-thirty and he wasn't there.' Something of that sort, I thought."

"Let me know if you get any response. Now, you knew this boy. Could he be the killer, despite or perhaps because of his relationship with Ettore Fagiolo?

"No."

"Just no?"

"Look, I told you, Ettore Fagiolo was his idol. Now you're saying he could have been his lover, which is something I find hard to believe. Anyway, he was his friend and I can't think why he should have wanted to kill him. Also, apart from anything else, Marco Rossi is a thin little thing and Fagiolo was a biggish man, definitely much stronger than Marco. By the way, this is my area, and if you don't mind I'd rather you didn't mention anything about…any of that in your report. There's no need, especially if the boy dies. Think of his parents. It's not certain, anyway, that he was…that way inclined, I mean. This is a dreadful place for gossip."

"I agree. Was there ever any gossip about Fagiolo?"

"If you mean did people say he was left-handed, the answer is no. The only gossip about him was that he was sex mad. And now we've got all the videos so it seems that was true, if they were his. Mind you, I've been thinking about that and wondering if he might have been selling them as a sideline. There were rather a lot of them and most of them were new. I know a lot of them were homosexual, but a lot were normal. I mean…with men and women." He was obviously embarrassed at having to talk about pornography, but was making an effort to sound casual.

"It's possible he was dealing in porn, but most of those videos have turned out to be quite legitimate. So why bother to deal in something that anyone can buy?"

"Perhaps some people would be embarrassed to buy them openly and Ettore got them for his friends, for a little extra."

"Yes. Of course. To go back to Marco Rossi's relationship with Ettore…I wonder if Ettore could have been bi-sexual," he mused.

"We've not had any of those in town before," said Maresciallo Biagioni, sounding distinctly distressed as though it were a slur on the town's good name. He hadn't even liked using the word homosexual.

Bi-sexual was a word from another planet.

Di Girolamo burst out laughing. "Don't take it so hard," he said.

"Anyway, where does all of this leave us? We might think that pompous Englishman did it. But until we have proof, our hands are tied. The only possible witness is dying and I don't have any other suspects worth mentioning."

"It could have been that German."

"I don't think so," Di Girolamo said.

"Well there's always the burglar."

"Ah! The burglar. Did you bring me that list of habitual or occasional offenders?"

"Yes." He extracted it from a folder. "There's nothing very hopeful here. I asked for those with the same MO, breaking into empty villas, and only in this province. We can move further afield if you think it necessary. So here's the list: three of them are ancient, and wouldn't be up to killing a healthy young man. Several are on probation and five are on a drugs program and their parents don't let them out at night. There are a couple of others, who don't live in the province any longer and we're checking on them, but we don't hold out much hope. I should know more about them tomorrow.

"None of their fingerprints tallied with the print on the spade. There are others, but they're either in prison awaiting trial, or serving their sentences. We don't have that many break-ins in the province, or should I say, didn't have that many. But unfortunately, the Albanians have moved in on us. They work in highly organized gangs, though they haven't reached this area yet. It seems they prefer the richer pickings on the coast or in the big villas near Lucca. The other thing that should make us think that we ought to be looking in our own immediate area for a burglar, or burglars, is that the break-ins in our town and the outlying villas seem to show an intimate knowledge of people's movements. All the recent break-ins here occurred in empty houses while the owners were on holiday. And quite frankly the haul isn't that huge on any of them. I mean, there are no priceless paintings and so on. It's all television sets, computers, silver, jewels, but we're not talking about fabulous jewels, and the odd Persian carpet or small piece of antique furniture."

"In other words, these are not big time crooks. Nothing they steal is worth murder."

"That's it."

"So we don't really think it was a burglar."

"I'm not saying that. It's just that if this is a local man, then perhaps Ettore recognised him. Maybe he panicked and killed him because he knew Ettore could shop him."

"Someone that Ettore knew, and probably someone without a record," Ruggero said.

"I thought it was more likely to be someone young."

"Well, Maresciallo, that has given us further food for thought but hasn't got us any nearer to our man. Let's leave it there for today. I'm off. I want to shower and then go the concert at six. I'll see you tomorrow. Perhaps we should all start praying that the boy lives. I have the feeling that he could tell us quite a lot. If he was with Ettore that night then he might well have seen and recognised his killer, who may or may not have been a burglar. Perhaps that's why he was run over. Perhaps it wasn't an accident at all. Goodnight, Maresciallo."

"Goodnight, sir."

TWENTY-SEVEN

THE CONVENT WAS SET at the top of the old town, immediately below the Duomo. The cloisters were large and had ample room for the concert audience. There was a fountain in the middle of a paved area, and looking up one could see the delicate arches of the windows that echoed the arches of the cloisters. The building was now mainly used as a private school and there were only a handful of nuns left. Ruggero Di Girolamo took a seat at the back and watched the rest of the audience arrive. He had arrived early on purpose. He saw Hilary come in with a grey-haired, pleasant looking man, and looking at them, he felt a sudden jolt of displeasure. She looked across at him and he nodded to her. After giving him a brief smile, she turned to her companion and they chose their seats, well away from him, he noticed. Other foreigners, some of them relatives of the French, German and English music students, spread themselves around to make the audience look larger, he presumed. He was handed a computer print out programme. This afternoon it was mainly pieces by Bach and Corelli.

An energetic looking American woman strode in. She looked so healthy he felt almost ill. "Hi, Hilary," she called, her voice loud enough to make everyone look up.

"Oh. Hello, Terry. So you made it."

The American woman went to sit by Hilary and they lowered their voices.

Di Girolamo squirmed in his seat. Why did these people always state the obvious? He felt he'd had a glut of English people. Another one of them came in and was greeted as Sue. She was younger and rather good-looking, with red hair and blue eyes. Hilary called her over and whispered, "I need to see you afterwards."

She nodded and sat down in the row behind Hilary. She turned round and gave a furtive glance in his direction, before concentrating on her programme. It may have been by chance but most of the seats near Di Girolamo were still empty.

The locals were arriving now. Like most Italians, they were late, as they always added fifteen minutes onto the stated time of commencement, with the result that most programmes gave a time that was at least fifteen minutes before the actual time intended. It was a chicken and egg situation, thought Di Girolamo. A large perspiring lady with an even larger daughter, both of whom were dressed in tent-like garments, came to sit near him, fussing as they deposited their bags and shawls around them and waving at friends. Pretty soon most of the seats were taken. In the shadows of the doorway, he could see the Mother Superior who would not sit with the general public, but would listen to the concert alone, hidden from view.

At last the concert got under way, and he thought it wasn't bad. Some things were quite good. Often teachers would accompany students and the result was almost professional. Altogether it was a well-spent hour. The atmosphere was peaceful, the music charming, and the cloisters were in the shade at that time of day, so it was cooler here than elsewhere. He was not a religious man, but was sensitive enough to feel the peace in the convent.

After the concert, he decided to walk up to the magnificent Duomo, the cathedral, which dominated the town giving it an instantly recognisable contour. Several cypress trees emphasised the length of the building. He had never been inside it before.

Standing on the steps of the church, he looked again at the fantastic view of the mountains and the famous 'dead man' mountain. He went inside and was really surprised. The interior was stark and quite superb. A gigantic, almost barbaric, wooden statue of St. Christopher stood above the altar. It was painted and was the only note of colour, as here there was very little to see; no Madonnas with neon halos, nothing kitsch, just simplicity and an elaborately beautiful pulpit in marble, carved with allegorical figures and supported by splendid lions, symbols of the strength of Christian faith. Di Girolamo was very impressed. He moved into a side chapel to examine a painting which featured the town itself, and a Della Robbia. He heard other people coming into the church and their voices, though low, seemed to come nearer. It was Hilary, saying to another woman, "Look, I'm sorry. I had to tell him."

"I asked you not to. I have a pathological fear of the Italian police. I'm sure they lock people up for ages on the flimsiest of pretexts and you have no rights. And they are violent."

"Hey, calm down. Don't talk such rubbish. What is the matter with you? It's a simple statement just to say you saw him come out of Bill's house and that he had someone with him. That's all there is to it."

"Yes, but they'll probably keep me there for hours. They might think I was one of his women or something."

"I very much doubt it. Come on, Sue, don't be so irrational. That Di Girolamo is a charming, intelligent, civilised man. Not a truncheon wielding barbarian from some God-forsaken, third world backwater." She heard a man laugh and looked round the corner anxiously.

Di Girolamo stepped forward with an almost satanic grin. He bowed and said, "Good evening ladies. I am here…without my truncheon today. I find it gets in my way at concerts." Sue stood still, absolutely horrified.

"Ah, Signora Wright. Would you be so kind as to introduce me to your friend, if you think that she is up to it?" He laughed, and suddenly Sue relaxed and smiled.

"Sorry, I'm neurotic. A friend of mine had a bad experience in Naples and I've worried about the police ever since."

"As I overheard your conversation I can safely presume you are the reluctant witness I was hoping to meet."

"I suppose I must be. I mean, yes, I am. It's just that I do hate the idea of being involved in this sort of thing."

"Well, just to show you how human I am, I will ask you to write out and sign a statement at home and bring it to the station in an envelope addressed to me."

"Oh, thank you so much. Of course I will. I'll do it as soon as I get home."

"What is your name? I'll need to tell my sergeant I am expecting a letter, otherwise he might think you were attempting to send me a letter bomb and feel he had to detain you." He smiled at her.

"Oh, I'm Susan Browne."

"You are English, or rather Scottish, judging by your accent?"

"My mother comes from here, but she married a Scot so I was brought up in Scotland. I've only been back here since 1998. I've got a job translating for a pharmaceutical company about ten miles away."

"There seems to be quite a link with Scotland in this town."

"Oh yes. I think nearly every family has at least one relative in Scotland."

"Well, it was nice to have met you both here…quite a bonus after the concert. I will expect your statement tomorrow then, Miss Browne. Good evening to you both." He stared at Hilary in a discomforting manner, then he turned and left the cathedral.

The two women laughed, Hilary to cover a strange and indefinable emotion. Sue said, "God, what a *figura* I cut. I feel so stupid."

"It was so funny. When he arrived, your face was incredible. Frozen. You looked like your worst nightmare had come true."

"Well it had. Actually, he's rather good-looking isn't he?"

"I suppose he is."

"I thought he was rather taken with you."

"Nonsense," said Hilary brusquely, taking control of herself.

She left the church, said goodbye to Sue and called to Bruno who had waited outside, leaning on the low wall, gazing at the view. They set off down an extremely steep road that would bring them very quickly to the other city gate, which led to Via del Sole.

"What was all that about? Girlish confidences?"

"Don't be ridiculous, Bruno. No, it was more murder stuff. And I think I can tell you this, as I gathered in the grocers that it is common knowledge."

"Oh? Perhaps I already know then."

"Perhaps. Well, it was just that Ettore had the keys to several houses belonging to foreigners, and when they were away he used the empty houses. Sue had actually seen him doing so, so it wasn't invented gossip, but quite true."

"I see. But is this important? I mean, who cares, other than the owners?"

"It might be important. Ettore could have been using Nigel's house."

"Ah, you mean he wouldn't have been alone."

"No, and the person who was with him might have seen the murderer and be frightened to say anything."

"You mean, might be the murderer."

"Oh, yes, that as well, I suppose."

"What have you cooked for me?" asked Bruno, abruptly changing the subject.

"Wait and see. I did it for me, too, you know," she snapped.

"Of course. Heaven forbid that you should cook for me. It might smack of domesticity and female subjugation."

"I suppose that's meant to be funny."

"Not at all. I just wish you wouldn't pounce on the simplest phrase and make sure over and over again that I know beyond doubt that you are you, and you do what you please, and never to please a man or more especially, me."

"I'm sorry you feel that way, but I'm still not going to tell you what I have cooked for us."

They had reached the front door by now. She told him to go out onto the terrace, as there would be a half an hour to wait for the food to be ready.

"You can pull out the table and set it." He gave a mock salute "And don't do that either. Here take this table cloth and I'll bring out some plates."

When the table was set, she sat on the terrace and looked at the view. Bruno pulled out a newspaper and began to read it. They sat there for quite a while together, in silence.

TWENTY-EIGHT

"POSTA!" yelled the postman, opening her front door that she never bothered to lock, and hurling her letters into the house. By the time she reached the hall to pick them up, she could hear his Vespa in the distance. His nickname was "Hurricane," for obvious reasons. There was a postcard from Alex from Greece where he was on holiday (which had taken three weeks to reach her), an electricity bill and another letter with a local postmark. She opened it, took out a card and said out loud, "I don't believe it."

In several other houses there were similar scenes. Almost immediately the phone rang. It was Terry.

"Hilary have you had your post yet?"

"Yes, I have. I suppose you've got an invitation, too."

"Yes, isn't it incredible?"

"Very. Are you going?"

"Wouldn't miss it. And you?"

"I suppose so. I don't really want to, but if I don't, it will look like I'm ostracising them."

"You what? What in the world does that mean?"

"It means it would look like I wanted nothing to do with them."

"Yeah, I suppose it would."

"I wonder who else they have invited."

"I'll phone Francesca and Giulietta. You phone Anne."

"Okay." She put the phone down and it rang again immediately. It was Miriam.

"Hilary, I have had the most extraordinary invitation to a party at Nigel's house. Do you think it's a joke?" she asked.

"No, I've had one and so has Terry. It looks authentic to me."

"Darling, tell me you are going."

"Yes, I am. I suppose you are, too."

"But of course. It's too exciting. I can't wait. Normally I would have turned it down. You know how I hate little English parties. But who could resist an invitation to a murder scene, especially when the host is a suspect."

"I'll see you there."

"Bye, darling."

She looked at the invitation again, as she had hardly had time to take it in. Nigel and Robin were giving a party, a "Return to the 'status quo' party," the next evening at dusk. Thinking it over, she decided it wasn't such a bad idea.

BEN WALKED THROUGH the old town. He was wearing what he called his "English-gentleman-abroad" outfit: light coloured trousers, short-sleeved white shirt, a straw hat, sandals and a cane. This last was rather splendid, having an elaborately carved eagle's head as a handle, and was also totally unnecessary, as he walked quite well without it. He waved and called to John, who was crossing the main piazza, "Care for an *aperitivo?*"

"Good idea, let's go to Candela's bar."

"Tell me, did you get an invitation?"

"Oh boy, did I not. Terry's eyes nearly popped out of her head."

"Are you going?"

"You bet. I wouldn't miss a chance to go to the murder scene. Great idea, that. It's a good way to get back to normal, or rather the 'status quo,' like it says on the invite."

"What splendid enthusiasm you Americans always have. Actually, I agree with you. The poor things have only been back a few days and seem to have spent an inordinate amount of time at the police station. No one has seen them out. And this way they probably hope to avoid any little awkwardness that must inevitably colour any first meeting with them."

"Ben, sit down and tell me what's your poison."

"Absolutely not. I invited you, so you tell me."

A waiter hovered, "Okay, I'll take a dry martini. Thanks, Ben."

"Make that two…and bring us something to nibble, please."

"So, are you going to the party?"

"Of course, I never miss a party. At my age, life should be lived to the full. And after years of hard work and being careful about my food and drink, I have become a hedonist. I deny myself nothing."

"Have you any new theories about the murder? Or do you still favour the German?"

"Ah, thank you," he said to the waiter. He took a sip of his martini and reached out for some salty little cheesy biscuits.

"Well, it would have been nice to be right. But I think that regretfully I must cross him off my list. I certainly don't believe in the burglar theory. No, for me there is something personal in this murder. No burglar would risk being caught for murder, well not one who was just trying to steal a television set or a computer. I have the distinct feeling that sex comes into it. Let us remember that this man had quite a reputation as a night-clubber and, judging by the way he dressed, he was certainly trying to attract. In some way emotions are involved. A discarded lover? Or possibly the jealous partner theory. What about you? Have you reflected more?"

"Well, I have. And as you may remember, I always did favour a midnight tryst and possible complications arising from that. I mean just because we think he looked like a jerk, doesn't mean that women didn't find him attractive. You know he looked real flashy, but some women love that kinda thing. So, I suppose, I still kinda feel that he was meeting a woman there and that either she did it, though God knows why, or her husband did. I ask myself, why meet someone there? And the answer is, because it was clandestine. Therefore, there's more likelihood of there being a husband. And quite frankly, if my wife was meeting someone like that and I found them at it…why, I would probably do the same myself."

"John, have you got an alibi? You sound quite heated. It wasn't you, was it?" said Ben seriously.

"Really, Ben, of course not, how could you even think that…" he broke off as Ben chuckled, "Oh, I never do know when you are joking. Anyway I'm off or Terry will beat up on me."

"What picturesque phrases you use, John. I am always more amazed by the similarities in our two languages than by the differences. *Buon appetito,* and I'll see you tomorrow at the party."

John left him and Ben sat back in his chair. Soon he would order a soup made with farro and healthy vegetables. But he would follow that with a steak and very unhealthy chips. He was enjoying his retirement.

ALDA AND ROSARIA reached San Giovanni very late that evening. Rosaria had prudently booked a hotel room in a nearby village and they thankfully went up to their room. Alda was exhausted. She had been woken at four in the morning by the *carabinieri,* and had spent the day in the hospital, had then rushed home and got straight into the car with an overnight bag packed in haste. Added to that had been the journey here, which had seemed never ending. She knelt beside her bed to say the simple prayers taught her in her youth that had accompanied her throughout her life. She added one of her own. "Dear God, you gave me this child when I had given up hope of ever having one, let me keep him a little longer. Heal him, don't take him yet."

She set the alarm clock, as she and Rosaria intended going to matins. She knew this was the right thing to do, the only thing to do. She had phoned Gino and been told that there was no change in her son's condition. She took that as an encouraging sign. Tomorrow there would be a change, a change for the better. She turned out the light and slept deeply through the rest of the night.

TWENTY-NINE

"AMANDA ODESCALCHI pulled her wheeled suitcase into the hall. "Oh, it's lovely to be back. I always forget how beautiful it is here."

"You always say that. Still, I'm glad you feel that way. At least you'll always want to come back," said her mother, Hilary.

"Wouldn't anyone want to?"

"Oh, not everyone feels the same way about it. You remember Brenda Saponara? Well, her kids both went to university in England, both married there and now Brenda and Mario are going back to England for good."

"I am surprised. No, I'm not, now I come to think of it. Brenda never felt very happy here, did she? I seem to remember she never really made any friends. She was always rushing off to Tunbridge Wells to see her family. And her husband's parents are both dead now, so I suppose the only relatives they have are there. Still, it does seem a bit like burning your bridges, I mean for the girls. It seems sad that their children shouldn't know the place."

"Well, they can always come to a hotel if they feel nostalgic. You won't ever have to do that, as I would never go back to England to live now. I'd be a fish out of water. My life is here."

"How's Bruno?" asked Amanda rather abruptly.

"Fine, as always."

"Are you going to marry him?"

"Amanda, you are still standing in the hall with your suitcase in your hand and you start asking questions like that!"

"Ma, not questions like that, but that question, which you so adroitly avoid answering. And look, I've let go of the suitcase and I'm moving into the kitchen to have a coffee, I hope, so you can answer me."

"The answer is—none of your business really. But no, not in the near future."

"Ah, well, I suppose I'll have to wait for the far future and see what happens then."

Hilary prepared coffee for her daughter, a ritual when greeting her return. They sat at the kitchen table to drink it.

"So, it's my turn now," said Hilary. "What's going on in your life?"

"Well, quite a lot, actually. You remember I told you about James? Well we're thinking of moving in together. Actually he's looking for somewhere for us while I'm here. As you know we both have tiny flats, neither of which would really do for a couple." She looked up at her mother.

"Good. That sounds a good idea."

"I knew you would say that."

"Then I must be pretty predictable."

"Not always. Do you know I would have predicted that you would marry Bruno? I thought you were so suited, but you don't seem very keen now. You're so noncommittal, or do I mean noncommitted!"

"Am I?"

"There, you're doing it again." She paused, "Do you love Bruno?"

"I suppose I must do, in a way. He's certainly quite important to me. He's become an important part of my life. Does that satisfy you?"

"Not really."

"Do you love James?"

"Of course I do. Why else would I want to move in with him?"

Hilary took the cups from the table and put them in the sink. She turned back to Amanda. "At my age things are not as simple as that. Let's leave it there."

"Fine. Change of subject. What's new in town? You never tell me what's going on when you phone, or is it still the same as always?"

"Oh no. Not this time. I'm afraid there's been a murder."

"You're kidding. Who?"

"Who was the victim?" she paused. "It was Ettore Fagiolo. They don't know who did it."

"You're kidding," she said quietly.

"No."

"Oh my God. I don't believe it. Or well, I suppose I do. How did it happen?"

Hilary told her.

"And you found the body? Well, well, I don't know what to say. Was it awful for you?"

"Not too bad. There's a plainclothes policeman, well, he's the magistrate, in charge of the inquiry and he was quite kind." She wondered if kind was the right adjective.

"Do they have any suspects?"

"They seem to think he disturbed an intruder and got himself killed. Anyway that's the official version."

"I see." She thought for a moment. "I bet the town has been a hotbed of gossip. What a golden opportunity for wagging tongues and inventive minds. I can't say I'm sad about it, but it must have been a terrible blow for his parents. Well, well. I can hardly take it in," she said looking at her mother, who said nothing. "Right, I'll take my case up and then have a shower."

"Oh, Amanda, changing the subject…there's something promising on at the theatre tonight. I have got you a ticket if you feel like coming,"

"Thanks, I've brought a decent dress with me. And is Bruno coming, too?

"Of course."

"I must phone James later, as he'll want to know I've arrived safely."

"You don't have to wait until after nine o'clock anymore, I've got a new telephone line and it's the same price all day."

"Brilliant." She clumped upstairs dragging her suitcase.

RUGGERO DI GIROLAMO took the post from his desk and shuffled it. He had had some pretty disgusting anonymous letters since he'd arrived and expected there would be more. Quite a lot of people seemed to think that any opportunity to vilify their neighbours should be made the most of. Some even went so far as to cut out words from newspapers, but most were happy just to use block capitals, and two had used a computer. He was duty bound to take some note of them, but it was very rare that any contained any useful information. He opened one marked "personal and private." In block capitals it screamed at him:

"PERVERT: I KNOW YOU ARE SCREWING THAT ENGLISH COW. I SAW YOU GO TO HER HOUSE. WELL YOU AREN'T THE ONLY ONE. SHE DOES IT WITH EVERYONE AND SHE'S A MURDERESS. SHE KILLED ETTORE AND SHE WAS SCREWING HIM, TOO."

He set it on one side and opened the next. A photo fell out. It was of a naked young man who was in a state of sexual excitation and seemed to be wearing make-up. He had long black ringlets and smiled impudently at the camera. A note accompanied the photograph:

"THIS INSTRUMENT OF SATAN TRIED TO CORRUPT ETTORE FAGIOLO, A BLAMELESS MAN WHO WAS KILLED BY HIM FOR REFUSING TO SUCCOMB TO EVIL."

He smiled at the biblical overtones. The photo had to have come from Ettore's mother, who had no doubt found it amongst her son's things. He phoned the Maresciallo. "Could you come and look at a photo please? I think I can guess who it is, but it will be quicker if you come and see it."

Five minutes later the Maresciallo, with a red face, confirmed his guess.

"It's Marco Rossi. My God. I don't want this left lying around, do you understand?" he said almost belligerently.

"I always exercise the utmost discretion, Maresciallo Biagioni," he replied coldly.

"Forgive me, it's just that I can't bear the thought of his parents ever knowing of this. Where did you get it?"

"Look," said Di Girolamo handing him the note. "I think the note is the work of Ettore's mother, and I think she found the photo in his office which she cleaned out the other day. You remember the videos?"

"Yes, of course. Satan, eh? That's her all right. So you think Ettore took the photo, eh? Do you know that boy is only just 18? Ettore must have corrupted him. And it looks like you were right about him being bi-sexual." He rolled the unfamiliar word around in his mouth like something with a bad taste. He looked unhappy, as though it was Di Girolamo's presence that had revealed a maggot in the healthy looking apple that was his town.

"I never imagined anything like this here, you know. There's always been a bit of adultery, that's normal, and a couple of queers." He glanced at the other man. "I mean homosexuals. But not this sort of thing. And since you've been here there's been so many disgusting anonymous letters. We used to get them, but not so many, and now…" He trailed off and looked at Di Girolamo who seemed very composed, and thought to himself that it must be everyday stuff to him. He thanked God he would be retiring in a couple of years. They'd sent him back to his home town to finish off his undistinguished career. And although he was aware that he wasn't very popular and some of the letters had dealt at length on the subject of his lack of popularity, he had been glad to be somewhere so quiet and relatively trouble free. Di Girolamo was speaking again.

"A murder of this kind is an exceptional event in a small town. It brings out things that have been hidden, sometimes things that exist only in peoples' minds. There is a shift in the balance of everyday life, as though people think that as murder has happened and has gone unpunished, anything is licit. The letters will stop when the murderer has been caught. This town is as normal as any other, and it will return to normality. Ettore was evil. You are right, the boy was possibly an innocent. His innocence may well have been corrupted, but now he is legally a man. And if he chooses homosexuality, that is not evil; you must recognise that."

The Maresciallo sighed, "I know. Everything's allowed these days. It will be hard for his parents. If he lives, of course." He sounded hopeful, as though the boy's death would solve the problem.

"He must live. I feel sure this boy has the key, the answer. He knows who murdered Ettore, or thinks he does, and he is the witness we need. The more I think about it, the more I am convinced that this wasn't a simple robbery that escalated into murder. As you said yourself, what sort of stuff gets stolen around here? Peanuts. Certainly nothing worth killing for. I've been looking at the statistics. The only murders in this area in the last fifteen years have all been domestic, and there were very few even of those." He paused. "It could well be the Englishman, you know. We already know that things are not what they seem here, but only this boy can tell us. And if it is him, then you can feel happy that none of the townsfolk is a murderer."

The Maresciallo looked a bit more cheerful, "Oh, well, I'll light a candle for Marco Rossi myself then. We can't go losing a key witness." He stood up and his eyes glanced on the other letter there. "Shred that," he said, having taken in the contents. He looked Di Girolamo straight in the eyes, "Just somebody's idea of a joke. They love to get at the police."

"Oh yes, of course." He picked it up and put it through the shredder. "I'll put the rest of this stuff in the folder in my locked drawer, and when this whole thing is over, it will be destroyed, too. I don't think this photograph will ever be needed as evidence."

The Maresciallo nodded and left the room.

THIRTY

HILARY AND AMANDA looked at each other with approval. Amanda was wearing a very dark green dress, a sheath that made her look even slimmer. Her long red hair was freshly washed, and curled down her back. She wore earrings of jade that matched the eye shadow and gave her green-blue eyes an almost unreal look.

She said, "People will think I'm wearing coloured contacts."

She had emphasised her pallor with a creamy pale foundation and wore a fake jade choker.

"Does it look terribly false?" she asked, fingering it.

"No, but anyway, who cares? You look absolutely stunning."

"I thought you didn't go in for compliments."

"You are the exception to the rule. Who are you doing all this for?"

"For myself, of course. I should know the answer to that one by now." They both laughed. "You look good in black, Ma. You should tart yourself up more often. It's good for the ego."

"My ego is quite all right as it is."

"I wish you would wear jewellery."

"Sorry, but no way. Come on, let's go."

They walked down the steep road arm in arm, Hilary giving some support to her daughter, who had insisted on wearing high heels and was in danger of slipping.

"I always forget how steep this hill is."

"Now you know why I couldn't bear it when you used to bicycle down it so fast."

"I couldn't do that now. I'd be terrified. It's only kids, who believe they are immortal, that can do that sort of thing. Hey, I see Villa Rosa is all dark. Do you think they'll be at the theatre?"

"Possibly. Did I tell you that tomorrow evening they are throwing a 'Return to the status quo' party?"

"Really! Are you going?"

"Yes, and so, I hope, are you."

"Oh, am I invited too?"

"Yes, everyone is. All people you know, plus some friends of theirs from the coast. They told Terry when she phoned to accept and ask if they needed help. You know how Terry is."

"Well it sounds like a good idea, a sort of exorcism I suppose."

"Mmm, I suppose it is. No one's really seen them since they got back. They've been to the police station a few times, and now I think they just want to forget the whole thing, and, as they say, get back to normal. I think they want to meet everyone all together and get it over and done with."

"Why, were they suspected or something?"

"I don't think so. But as it was in their house and they knew the victim, I expect they had to clear up a few points."

"But they weren't even there when it happened."

"No."

"That sounded like a maybe, not a no."

"Well, it is barely possible that they hadn't quite left when it happened. But anyway that's obviously all been cleared up now."

"You sound like you know more than you're willing to say."

"Maybe. One can't always say everything one knows. But as I said, it has all been cleared up now."

"All right. I'll ask nothing else. You know Ma, they are a strange couple. He is unreal, and she is the pits. All that make-up and all those rings and earrings and bracelets and necklaces. Ugh! I don't really know why you're friends with them."

"I'm not."

"Then why go to their party?"

"It would look awkward if I didn't, you know. It would look as though I had something against them."

"Since when have you decided to be so diplomatic? I hardly know you."

"I hardly know myself. It's very difficult. I don't even like them and I only have contact with them because we're all British. No, don't laugh. It's awful. I was sort of hoping to keep them at arm's length, which is difficult when their garden adjoins mine. But I thought I could keep the whole thing on a very cool level and sort of gently freeze them off. But I can't do that in this situation. Do you see what I mean?"

"Yes, I do. You'll just have to freeze them off later. I thought you were all getting very pally."

"That's the trouble. You see, they are so kind and generous and thoughtful. And it's very difficult to be boorish, although quite frankly all our contacts are totally superficial. Somehow you just slide off the surface with them. It's hard to explain."

They had reached the theatre by now and joined the mass surging towards the open doors. They nodded to some friends and stopped to chat with others. Amanda said, "I'm going to leave you for a bit, Ma. Give me my ticket and I'll join you later. It won't start on time, anyway." She teetered off towards a group of younger people, waving and shouting greetings.

Bruno watched Hilary approach the door. She looked very good. Her black dress swirled around her as she moved. She was wearing heeled evening sandals and had slim tanned legs. Her blue eyes were devoid of makeup. Her face was tanned and serene. She smiled at him as he stepped forward. He knew better than to comment on her looks. She really hated it. It wasn't pretence or a form of coquettishness, but a sincere dislike of appraisal by others.

"Amanda will join us later. She's saying hello to all her old friends."

"Good. I think we have time for a quick drink if you want one."

"Oh! A very small glass of wine then, thank you." She didn't like drinking wine except at meal times and Bruno looked awkward asking her, as he knew her preferences perfectly well. She thought it would be polite to accept and then wondered why on earth she should want to be polite.

He disappeared into the throng that was tanking up before the start and re-emerged a few minutes later grinning triumphantly, holding two glasses aloft.

"I know the boy behind the counter. He lives next door to me so I got preferential treatment."

She thought, *He's trying too hard. I wonder why.*

"Cin cin." They touched glasses and drank their wine.

"Come on, let's go up to our box. I hope we haven't got anyone awful in with us."

"God, do you remember last year that awful little man with a cold, who snuffled all through the opera?"

"Well it can't happen two years running."

They handed in their tickets and went up the red-carpeted stairs to the second floor. They were in box number nine, the one next to the central box. Bruno opened the door and ushered her in. The only occupant rose to his feet and bowed almost imperceptibly. It was Ruggero Di Girolamo.

Miriam Greene watched as Hilary and Bruno entered their box. She had been very annoyed at first to find herself in a more lateral box, as she had forgotten to book until late, but she had found it was rather fun as she was able to have a clear view of others entering their boxes. She trained her opera glasses on them and saw Hilary look discomforted.

"Stupid cow," Miriam muttered. That policeman was terribly attractive, and he seemed to think Hilary was, too, judging by the way he was looking at her. What was she doing with that boring Bruno? He seemed so worthy. Deadly dull. Miriam toyed with romantic ideas. Perhaps in her next novel a policeman falling in love with a suspect would work? Of course it had been done before. It wasn't new, but then what was? She churned out the same old rubbish year after year, and no one seemed to notice how all her books were, more or less, the same.

Miriam sighed and yawned. She shouldn't have come. She had slept badly the night before and tomorrow night there was the party at the Villa Rosa, which was bound to finish late. Well, she would see what the first act was like and then maybe go home. Damn, she had told Salvatore to bugger off until the end and she had let Assunta have the evening off, so she had probably gone to the cinema or to play tombola at the church hall, a fund raising ruse copied from the Americans.

The lights dimmed and Miriam turned towards the stage. The curtain rose on a charming, if obscure, 18th century opera. The theatre was packed. It was very hot. Miriam, on her own in her box, nodded off within fifteen minutes and began to snore quite loudly. This was extremely audible during the recitatives. Hilary in a box diagonally opposite realised what was happening and nudged Bruno. "Miriam is snoring!"

"Oh my God, so that's what it is."

Di Girolamo smirked in his corner and Hilary felt that he must think Miriam and, by association her friends, a lot of hobbledehoys. Snoring in a theatre box was appalling. How could Miriam do this? It would have to be stopped. She rose and cautiously opened the door to the box and slid out. She reached Miriam's box and slipped in beside her. The noise was even worse close to her. She shook Miriam's shoulder and whispered savagely in her ear, "Wake up!" Miriam opened her eyes and looked bewildered.

"For God's sake, Miriam, you were snoring," she whispered urgently. Miriam's plump face remained blank and she looked so old and feeble that Hilary asked, "Are you all right? Do you feel ill?"

"No. I'm fine." She heaved her bulk further up in the chair. Her features came alive again and she said, "I want to go home.

I'm too bloody tired to watch this. Besides, if it's been hiding in a drawer for a couple of centuries there must be a reason. Maybe it should have stayed there." She chuckled and wheezed and threatened to cough, so Hilary took her by the arm and encouraged her to move.

"Come on out of here before you get thrown out." All of this was said in a terse whisper. Suddenly the box door opened and Di Girolamo appeared. He took Miriam's other arm and helped drag her from the box. Miriam looked delighted.

"Ah," she whispered heavily, "my hero and heroine have met. Wonderful!" She then added, "Get rid of old boring boots. You'll die of boredom with him."

It was at this point that Hilary realised Miriam had been drinking. She looked at Di Girolamo who was struggling manfully to keep Miriam upright while moving in the direction of the lift. He appeared not to have realised what the old lady was saying. Hilary said hurriedly, "I'm afraid she's had a drink or two and she's tired. We'll have to get her home. Her driver won't be back for ages. Have you got a car nearby? Mine's miles away, at home."

In box number nine, Bruno and Amanda watched first Hilary, and then Di Girolamo, grappling with Miriam.

"Should I go, too?" whispered Bruno.

"I shouldn't bother," said Amanda, thinking that if he'd wanted to help he could have done so earlier. Bruno settled down to watch the opera, looking unconcerned.

In the theatre foyer, Di Girolamo was conferring with a young policeman. Miriam had sat herself on a chair in the bar and was hopefully waving at a waiter while Hilary made signals at him not to serve her.

Ruggero came back to Hilary and said, "I'm taking her home in a police car. Will she be all right when she gets there?"

"I should think so. She has a housekeeper who sleeps in. Do you want me to come?"

"I'd love you to, but I think you should stay to watch the

opera. I'll manage alone. *Buona sera.*" He extended his hand in salutation.

Hilary shook his hand and then said, "What about you? You'll miss the opera."

He continued holding her hand and said, "That's all right. You get back to your box."

Hilary nodded and went back to the others. Di Girolamo manoeuvred Miriam into the police car with the help of the young policeman. As they drove her home, she hummed bits of opera music and sang, "plonk, plonk" to mark the end of each bar.

When they got to her house it took the two of them to extract her from the car, which she found most amusing. "Salvatore does it on his own," she informed them. They pushed and pulled her up the steps and got her to the door.

"Will you be all right?" asked Ruggero.

"I'm fine, just tired. Thank you very much. You're a good man, and bloody attractive, too," she chuckled and wheezed alarmingly. "Oh don't worry about the noise. That's normal for me. Ask Hilary…she'll tell you. She's a lovely girl don't you think?" she prodded him.

"Very lovely," he said to placate her.

"She's wasted on Bruno you know. He's deadly dull."

Di Girolamo stared straight ahead but did not answer her. The other policeman looked bored and wandered back to the car.

"Where's your housekeeper? Shall I call her?"

"No, she'll be in bed. I'm fine. I'll just toddle off to bed like a good girl. Go!" He turned to leave, but she grabbed his arm and said, "Strike while the iron is hot," and cackled wheezily at him.

He watched her open the front door and then left her. He didn't feel happy about it, but he seemed to have no choice. He wished now that he had accepted Hilary's offer, but he hadn't wanted to deprive her of her entertainment. Though he thought it would have been interesting to deprive her escort of her company.

After he had left, Miriam remembered that Assunta was out

and Salvatore was probably playing cards in a bar, whiling away the time until he had to collect her from the theatre.

"Bugger that," she muttered and began to climb the stairs. Cherry padded down to meet her. She sat down beside the dog and petted her. Hearing a noise on the landing she bellowed, "Assunta, is that you?"

After a moment and some more noises, Salvatore appeared on the landing and looked down at her.

"What the hell are you doing here?" she asked in a belligerent tone. He looked menacing standing above her, but she stood up and climbed steadfastly towards him.

"I had to come back for a call of nature," he said modestly. "Why are you here so early? Has something happened?" He moved towards her to help her, taking her arm.

"Are you all right? You're not ill are you?"

"I'm fine. The police brought me home."

"The police! I don't understand." He stood stock still, gripping her arm rather tightly.

"They arrested me for snoring in the theatre," she started laughing and wheezing. In a slightly fuddled way, she was aware that her arm was gripped in a vice-like hold.

"You fell asleep in the theatre?" He sounded relieved and loosened his hold.

"I did, and I snored, so they woke me up and brought me home."

They stopped outside her bedroom door. "Goodnight Salvatore. Lucky you were here or I might have fallen asleep on the stairs."

"Goodnight, Signora. Assunta will be back soon. Shall I send her to you?"

"No, no, I'm going to bed."

She shuffled into the bedroom and as quickly as possible got into bed and lay down. *Salvatore was lying,* she thought. *I don't know what he was doing but it wasn't what he said.* She was too tired to think anymore. Then she slept.

THIRTY-ONE

AUGUSTA FAGIOLO CAME OUT of the church, the only one where early morning mass was celebrated, and muttered to herself as she began the long walk home. Her husband would still be sleeping as she had given him a good dose of tranquilliser last night. She had been increasing his dosage recently and had got another prescription from the doctor by telling him that she had broken the bottle. He had glanced at her gnarled hands and believed her. God would forgive her. It was only a small lie, and she needed time to do God's work, to fight the evil that was in this town. She trusted no one. She spoke to no one. They all thought she was deranged by her son's death. She cackled to herself. No, she was not mad, but had been chosen by God to point a finger at Satan. Only the pure are chosen. She was keeping herself pure and had decided to fast. She knew her husband would want to do the same, but as he was unable to decide for himself, she had made the decision for him. That was partly why she had increased his medicine. He wasn't as strong as her now and needed help. Perhaps God would soon take him to his bosom. He was very weak, and in a sinless state, insofar as any man can be free from sin.

She arrived home and let herself in. A strong smell of bleach pervaded the house. Everything was spotless. She went into her husband's bedroom. He lay still, almost as white as the bed linen. She had opened the window before leaving, and the cool morning air had given the room a freshness that she approved of. She smoothed his hair. It was snow white and his pale scalp was visible between the thin strands.

"The wicked shall be punished," she said to him. But he slept on.

She took off her black jacket and headscarf and put them away in the small wooden wardrobe, which had been made by the local carpenter for her marriage. In the mirror she saw a gaunt old woman dressed in black, but for a moment she remembered how she had looked in this mirror as a young bride, never really beautiful but with a certain prettiness and a determined look about her.

"All is vanity," she muttered.

She moved out of the room, closing the door behind her, and went into the kitchen. She opened the door of the credenza, and stooped down to lift the bills to one side. There was a newspaper wrapped around an envelope, which she picked up.

"God forgive me. I will never look on this instrument of the devil again, but I must warn others of the evil." Sitting on a chair, she rocked to and fro, murmuring "Evil. Evil. Evil." She placed the package on the table and then prepared a sheet of paper and a pencil.

"Thy will be done." She bowed her head.

Slowly and carefully she began to write, printing the block capitals in a legible manner. Her hands were in pain, but her task was a glorious one. That other instrument of the devil had been struck down, and she knew what God wanted her to do now. She had set aside this photo and had not burned it with the others. She did this without knowing why at the time, but all was made clear to her now. She had been chosen to fulfil this task.

When she had finished, she placed the letter in the white envelope containing the photograph and sealed it. She addressed it and put on a higher value stamp than was usual for a letter. At the top she wrote, "URGENT. PRIVATE AND PERSONAL."

Then she picked up the small bag of rubbish she had prepared earlier and tucked the letter in her black cardigan. She shuffled out of the kitchen door, leaving it slightly ajar, and made her way down the Vicolo to the rubbish bins.

There was the usual mess littered around the big green containers, and someone had stuck a used syringe into a bursting bag on the ground. She placed her own small bag beside it and moved on to the post box on the corner. She looked around her; there was no one in sight. The letter was quickly pulled from her front and posted. She then turned back to the house.

ALDA AND ROSARIA PREPARED to leave San Giovanni. Alda was clutching a *santino,* a photo of Padre Pio, and felt elated. Marco's condition was stable and that was enough for her to feel sure that Padre Pio was intervening. She had smelt a wonderful perfume as they approached the sanctuary area and knew that this was the sign given to the faithful that He would intercede.

MIRIAM PICKED UP the phone, *"Pronto."*

"Miriam, it's Hilary."

"Darling, I am so sorry about last night. It was unforgivable."

"Are you all right?"

"Of course I am."

"Miriam, I have to tell you that I know you had some booze last night. Now I know you're going to say it's none of my business, but you really mustn't do it, it's so bad for you."

"Yes, I'm afraid I was a bit naughty, but it wasn't much. Assunta sometimes lets me a have a drop of gin in my tonic, and last night I must have been extra convincing. I wasn't drunk you know, just very tired. I'd had a foul night the night before. Anyway, last night I slept like a dream, so I shall be in good form for the party."

"As long as you're feeling okay. Dr. Di Girolamo wasn't very happy about leaving you there alone. He said that you told him Assunta was in, so he felt reassured. But I heard from Pia this morning that she was at the church tombola so you were alone, and I just wanted to check that you were all right."

"Ah, Dr. Di Girolamo, now there's a man for you. He said you were a very lovely girl."

"That doesn't sound like him at all. You shouldn't put words into people's mouths."

"Well, all right, I said it. But he agreed with me."

"I'm sure he didn't have much choice."

"My dear, he's a gentleman."

"No doubt."

"Well, anyway, you're obviously not going to give me any satisfaction so let's leave it. To go back to last night. To tell you the truth, I wasn't alone. It's rather strange, but Salvatore was here when I got back. I don't know what he was up to, but I feel sure it wasn't just a 'call of nature' as he so modestly put it. Anyway, he helped me up the stairs and I got into bed and fell asleep immediately."

"Well what else would he have been doing?"

"I don't know."

"After all, he does live with you, and perhaps he was embarrassed about having to explain his presence to you."

"Perhaps. Anyway, I'll see you this evening at the party. Thanks for phoning and don't fuss so."

Amanda came into the kitchen as Hilary was saying goodbye to Miriam.

"How is she?"

"Fine. I do worry about her. Also I know you'll think I'm silly, but I don't like that couple she's got living with her. Assunta has a very sly look and Salvatore a very smug one."

"She's happy with them. That's what counts." They both started eating their breakfast. "Ma, you know I thought that Dr. Di Girolamo was quite fascinating."

"Did you, dear." Hilary deliberately kept her voice bland.

"Well, he's very attractive, and he was very kind with Miriam."

"Yes, he was." Hilary turned a page of her newspaper.

"I'm surprised Bruno didn't help."

"He doesn't really get on with Miriam, and actually it's a good thing he didn't help, as she was a bit offensive last night."

"What did she say?"

"Oh, nothing much. Just that he was boring. Anyway, it wouldn't have been very nice for him to hear."

"I suppose he is a bit. Boring, I mean. He never says much, and he's fairly predictable," Amanda said before sipping her coffee.

"He's restful to be with."

"Restful is just a kind way of saying boring."

"Really, Amanda. He isn't boring, he's…comfortable."

"Comfortable! Maybe you should try something more exciting. I mean, you don't want to marry him, and I think you don't really love him. It's hardly a passionate affair now, if it ever was. You shouldn't stay with someone just because they're comfortable."

"Thank you, Amanda, when I need your advice I'll ask, but it won't be at breakfast." She folded her newspaper, and stood up. "I'm going shopping later. Are you lunching in? And if so any special wants, longings, cravings, diets or whatever? I'm willing to spoil you today, as it's your first day home."

"How lovely. Yes I am lunching in. In fact, I'm staying around the house all day today. I'm going to sunbathe in the garden and read and laze, and I am longing for grilled pork ribs and Italian sausages. So I suggest a barbecue, just for the two of us."

"I see you're not into healthy food at the moment."

"No, I'm not. By the way, get some of those lovely soft rolls from the bread van. And we could have a mixed salad with the grilled meat. That's healthy."

"Well, as I said, it's your first day home so I'll pander to you, but after that you know the rules. You eat what I'm having or do it yourself, and I'll want to know in advance when you're going to be in for meals."

RUGGERO HAD PHONED the hospital early and had been told there was no change in Marco's condition. Obviously Padre Pio hadn't pulled it off as yet. He felt very frustrated, as he was certain that this boy was going to give him the information he needed. *I need this miracle as much as the boy, in a different way,* he thought.

IT WAS A DAY OF waiting, an interim day. The air was heavy and humid and increasingly so as the hours passed. Hilary felt slowed down, and was glad to have a lazy day with Amanda. They lolled in the shade replete with a too large lunch, too tired even to talk or read. No one phoned. The whole town seemed silent and during the afternoon thunder could be heard in the distance. It rumbled around for the whole afternoon, but came to nothing.

"I shall have to water the plants before we go to the party," Hilary yawned.

"That'll make it rain," said Amada.

"I hope so," her mother said.

"What time is the party anyway?"

"It says nine o'clock on the invitation, but I certainly don't want to be the first there," Hilary said.

"No one will want to be, so I predict a mass entry at roughly nine-twenty."

"It should be a bit cooler by then."

"It's funny how I think of this place as hot, but never have a correct perceptive memory of the entity of the heat," Amanda said.

"It's the humidity that makes it seem hotter than it is."

"I know. But I still find it surprising, the heat, I mean."

"Do you? It will probably rain during the night. A good thunderstorm will clear the air. I'm going in to shower," Hilary said, getting up.

"Again?"

"Again."

MIRIAM LAY ON HER BED supported by several pillows in a darkened room, a ventilator stirring the pudding-like air. She was unable to read, as she was too tired, but she was not asleep. She was thinking about Salvatore's face, or rather the expression on his face, the evening before. There was no doubt about it; he had had an air of guilt. She remembered his fingers painfully digging into the flesh of her upper arm. She remembered the noises she had heard and puzzled over their provenance. What had he been doing?

Salvatore and Assunta sat in the kitchen, a fan lazily purred from the ceiling.

"I don't think she believed me. I can't tell you why, but there was something in her attitude."

"You're crazy. She was just embarrassed for you having to mention your natural functions in front of her."

"I suppose so. What about tonight, do you think it's safe?"

"Of course. What could be safer? Besides, you have to do it now, we've got others lined up for next week and if we don't do them now it will be too late."

"I'm getting really pissed off. There's not much in this area. We've been here three years, and if you add it up..."

"We'll move on soon. I'll invent an elderly relative who needs help and we'll get her to write us an excellent reference. Then off to new pastures. This place is dead." She paused following her own train of thought. "You know that kid that got run over? I heard two women talking about him. It seems he was on drugs, and queer to boot!"

"Well, there's nothing to do here, so it's sex and drugs and so on…"

"Poor kid, his mother's gone down to Padre Pio."

"They're saying in the bar it will take a miracle."

The fan churned on. Assunta shuffled the cards and they began to play.

Miriam finally fell asleep, and Hilary walked naked from the shower to her bed. She too flicked on the fan as she passed. The shutters were closed and a dull golden light filtered through them and striped her bed. The thunder rumbled and the sky grew gradually darker. The air was stiller than ever, waiting.

Everything was waiting.

THIRTY-TWO

AT NINE-FIFTEEN Hilary and Amanda joined Bruno, who had called for them. The thunder still rumbled and now there was a breeze. Occasionally the skyline was lit up by distant lightning. Vast areas were suddenly as bright as daylight. Both women had taken a shawl and Bruno was prudently carrying an umbrella.

"Really, Bruno, you'll bring us bad luck carrying that damn thing," said Amanda. "It will never rain with you all prepared like a Boy Scout. We really need it to rain."

"I don't care if it doesn't. But if it does, I've no intention of walking home in the rain without an umbrella."

Terry shouted, "Hi everybody!" and joined them. "I see we've all timed it perfectly. Tom and Anne are just behind us and I think that's Miriam's car arriving. Goodness Bruno, an umbrella! It will never rain now."

The car drew to a halt beside them and Salvatore jumped out to open the door for Miriam. She emerged from the car swathed in a shimmering golden caftan. Little golden slippers peeped from beneath the hem.

"Oh my dears, isn't this fun? As you can see I'm wearing my party frock, and I'm going to enjoy myself." Salvatore heaved her to her feet. "Thank you, Salvatore, come back for me at half past midnight. I think I can safely say I'll last that long. I had a good snooze this afternoon and I feel fit as a fiddle. Bruno, you can take my arm and escort me in. Hilary won't mind, even if you do." She attached herself to Bruno and began to slowly waddle up the drive with him, the others following. She spoke to them over her shoulder. "Darlings, I saw Sue Browne and that divine Ruggero Di Girolamo talking together in the street. He really is devastatingly attractive. Do you think he's been invited as well?"

"Hardly," said Bruno.

"You sound a bit acid this evening, Bruno. Am I impeding your progress?"

"Not at all," said Bruno stiffly, helping her negotiate the two steps that led into the house. Robin was greeting guests at the door and was more heavily made-up than ever.

"Come in, everybody, go on through. Nigel's serving drinks on the terrace. I'm so glad you've all come. Thank you, thank you."

Amanda nudged her mother, "I think she's been tanking up on the party spirit already!" she whispered, "And she's actually wearing false eyelashes!"

"Be quiet!"

Two obviously homosexual men came in after them, and were greeted with cries of joy from Robin. "Nigel, Nigel, come and see who's come to see us."

Nigel came out to greet them. "John, Sebastian! Jolly good, so you found us. Wasn't too difficult was it? Great to see you, come on through, drinks are over there."

The room and the terrace soon filled up. The 'status quo' party was in full swing, and any doubts that Nigel had had about it soon vanished. He grabbed Robin in the kitchen and hugged her.

"You clever girl! You're wonderful. This was a brilliant idea. It's really working."

"I'll admit I wasn't sure they'd all come, but they have and I'm so happy. It will all be all right."

DI GIROLAMO WALKED THROUGH the old town. He had bumped into Sue Browne and taken the opportunity of thanking her for her statement and she had told him about the party. If he had been surprised he hadn't shown it. If the Englishman was innocent, then the party would clear the air and bring their life back to its former level. If he was guilty, then it would look as though he were innocent, and could be considered a good tactical move.

Ruggero was more or less certain, in his mind, that Nigel had done it, and wondered if his companion was an accomplice. It would have been easier for two people to drag the body to the pool, and the evidence showed that it had been dragged there. However, it seemed unlikely, especially as Marco Rossi had specifically blackmailed Nigel, or so he had understood from his interview with the Proctors. Of course, he had no proof. Not a shred of evidence. Strangely, Nigel did not have that elusive air of guilt that he usually detected in cases like this, and he had to admit lack of motive. But often the heat of the moment was motive enough. Not that Nigel looked like a man prone to violent rages, but perhaps his foreignness was what he could not come to terms with.

Ruggero knew his Italian murderers because he knew his countrymen. He couldn't know Nigel, because he was an unknown element. Until now he had thought certain character-istics international. For him there had been no frontiers for guilt, and murder. He had actually believed in the invisible mark of the murderer. He had found he could apply it even to the Moroccan and Senegalese criminals he had encountered, and he had been right. Perhaps it was a question of latitude. He laughed to himself. Thank God he'd never made his ideas public.

He stopped at the bar in the centre of town for a coffee, but he didn't linger. Nobody loves a policeman, and his presence would dampen other people's enjoyment. He sometimes felt he could hear a sigh of relief when he left a bar. It was depressing when everyone was unnaturally polite and well behaved. Perhaps he'd have done better to go back to Lucca. He still had work to do there, and the Prato thing was dragging on. But he kept making excuses to stay here without really knowing why. He told himself he was waiting for Marco Rossi to regain consciousness, but that wasn't sufficient motive to remain here. Depending on what the boy said, he would either leave or conclude the case with an arrest.

He was feeling lonely tonight. Silvia's death had left him so totally alone. He worked and did little else, apart from the occasional concert or cinema, alone of course. Even his work, which he loved, left him feeling isolated.

He was well liked, though he didn't realise it, and he had managed to keep his sense of humour, which helped his social contacts at work. It was living his own life he found difficult. He didn't really have his own life, only Silvia's death.

There had been no children, as Silvia had been working and struggling with her career as a hospital doctor. "I'll have children when I'm forty," she had said. "I won't have time until then." But there hadn't been time. What would he have done with a child alone, anyway? He felt neither glad nor sad about the lack of a child. He was apathetic about most things. Only his work, the solving of riddles, gave him any pleasure. He walked slowly on towards the other end of town.

"WHERE'S JOE? He was supposed to be here at ten," asked Assunta.

"Don't panic. He'll be here, I've left the gate open." They were both wearing gloves and standing by the kitchen door. On the floor beside them was a heap of stuff: a computer, CD player, two televisions and some boxes. A light shone from the garden. It beamed towards them twice.

"Here he is. Hurry up. Let's get loaded up." They began to move towards the light carrying boxes. Just outside the garden gate was a small black van.

"Joe, the stuff's ready. Move it."

They made a few hasty journeys to the van within a few minutes.

"Quick Assunta, back you go."

He sat her down on the kitchen floor and tied and gagged her. He took her gloves and put them in his pocket. He lay two chairs on the floor and moved the table a bit.

"Good girl. See you later."

He went out of the back entrance, leaving the kitchen door

with its damaged lock wide open. He sprinted towards the main bar in the new part of town. He had been away exactly eleven minutes. Assunta had done everything except carry down the television. She had trashed the house and broken the lock from the outside, wearing gloves. Any fingerprints of theirs would have been normal anyway, but Salvatore was taking no chances.

He had been in the bar from 9:25 until three minutes to ten. At the back of the bar was an area of tables and chairs where on Saturday nights there was usually a dance. Other nights, people sat there as it was cool, but it remained in semi-darkness. He had moved there at about 9:45 with his beer, taking good care to sit in a very dark spot. He was sure that he had left unnoticed. If someone had seen him go they would have thought he'd gone for a pee, as his direction had been that of the lavatory.

By the time he unobtrusively regained his seat, he had been absent for a total of sixteen minutes. He would remain there until it was time to fetch Miriam and they would enter the house together. Poor Assunta would have to sit there for two and a half hours, but that was all to the good, as she would have quite deep rope marks on her by then and everything would look authentic.

They'd had to do it early, as he didn't trust Miriam. It had given him a shock the night before when she had turned up early, just as he was about to start. He'd had to annul it, leaving the "no go" sign for Joe. So this time they'd decided to leave Assunta tied up, certain proof of his non-involvement. Normally he would have just left the door open for Joe and had the stuff ready, but the whole MO had been changed tonight.

DI GIROLAMO HAD REACHED the other end of town. Going through the Medici Gate, he was ambling along the road towards Lucca. He was about to turn back, having decided that bed and a book was the best way to pass what was left of the evening, when he was almost knocked over by a dark van that shot out from the lane at the back of Miriam Greene's house. He cursed and looked after the van, which he now realised had been without lights.

Di Girolamo began to walk quietly on towards Miriam's house when he saw a man emerge cautiously from the lane. He froze and merged into the hedge at the side of the road. The man then ran at top speed down the hill towards town. Despite the dark, Di Girolamo instantly recognised the plump short figure as that of Salvatore, Miriam's chauffeur/gardener. *What's he been up to?* he wondered.

Ruggero reached the house and looked up through the main gates at the windows. The house was in darkness. He turned to the left and took the small lane that led to the back of the property. There he found the garden gate and saw that there was a light at the back of the house. Taking care, he walked quietly up the garden path to the kitchen door, which was wide open. He cautiously stepped to one side of it and peered in. Chairs were lying on the floor and the table was skew-whiff. He could see a pair of legs bound with rope. Silently, he stepped into the room and saw that Assunta was lying on the floor, gagged, her arms bound behind her back and her legs bound together. As soon as she saw him, strange noises began to issue from her throat, and she wriggled her body, her eyes blazing. He ignored her and tiptoed past her to the stairs. It took him a very short time to realise that the house was empty apart from a small, white dog that gave a half-hearted bark from under the bed in Miriam's room.

For a moment he had wondered if the old lady had been in there, but he realised pretty quickly what this was. A scene had been set, and very efficiently, too. And had it not been for his aimless wandering it would have been successful. He returned to the kitchen where Assunta still lay, making more noises, hoping he would untie her.

He grinned at her and said, "All in good time my dear. I rather like you as you are at the moment."

Her eyes glowered, enraged at him, and he burst out laughing.

There was a phone in the hall, which he used before going out through the main door to wait. Five minutes later the lights of the police car blinked at him and he opened the main gates with the internal command.

Maresciallo Biagioni joined him and said, "We'll have to wait for the fingerprint man to arrive. I put through a call immediately so he'll be here in about twenty-five minutes. Where's Signora Greene?"

"Oh, she's not here. There's nobody here, only the thief's accomplice and he very kindly tied her up for me."

"Where is she?"

"Where he left her, and as he left her, tied up on the kitchen floor."

Maresciallo Biagioni laughed. "I'd better go and untie her or they'll have me up for police brutality."

"Be careful. She looks dangerous. That's why I left her. I couldn't possibly handle her on my own. I'm sure you understand."

"Oh, I see. Well, I'll need a witness or she'll accuse me of trying to rape her or something. Michele," he bellowed. "Come down to the kitchen."

"Let's keep her sweet till we get her down to the police station. I don't want her to have an inkling until then that we know she's in on it. I'll tell the lads. We can get him after you've dealt with her. He was sprinting down to town, so I expect he's in the main bar. Again, I do not want to arrest him until we've got him in the police station."

They went down to the kitchen followed by Michele, a young policeman.

"Assunta! Oh dear, what's all this about?" said the Maresciallo, not unkindly, as he began to loosen her bonds. He pulled off the gag and she immediately began to shout. "There was a burglar. Look what he did to me! Why didn't you set me free immediately?" She stood up rubbing her chafed wrists. "Look at me, and that other man just ignored me. I was so frightened," she almost sobbed.

"Police rules my dear. You can't touch people when you're alone. You have to wait for reinforcements."

"Rubbish, I was suffocating. I could have died and I'm an important witness!"

"Well, I think we'd better get you down to the station to make a statement as soon as possible. Where's the Signora? She'll have to be informed."

"She went to a party at the house of that English couple, you know, where the murder took place. She'll be so upset, *povera* Signora, all her things gone. There were two of them…look what they did to me. They could have killed me, like that poor Ettore. I just thank God the Signora was out. She would have died of fright, like me. I feel ill. That man left me there and laughed at me. He must be crazy."

"I'm sorry," said Di Girolamo from the doorway. "I'll go to the party and explain what's happened to the Signora.

Assunta gave him a withering look. "You should have freed me immediately. It's unbelievable. What are you a racist or something? If it had been anyone else you would have rushed to free them. It's because I am a Sicilian. You just stood there and laughed at me while I was suffocating to death."

"Police regulations," he said tersely.

"No, it was discrimination. You northerners always treat us Sicilians like shit, as if we were gypsies or something. I'm not trash like some Albanian. You haven't heard the last of this. It's a disgrace."

"I'll go and meet the others, they should be arriving soon." Di Girolamo turned and left the room. Afterwards he would walk to Nigel's house and tell Miriam what had happened. It would probably be quite a blow. To be defrauded by people you trust is a form of betrayal. Assunta was still raging. He could hear her voice rising and falling as he walked down the drive. *Quite a performance,* he thought. She hadn't realised that they were on to her. As he reached the main gates another police car with two men in it turned towards the drive. He stopped it and gave them their instructions.

"The Maresciallo is in the kitchen with a witness, who is actually an accomplice. I want her to be taken to the police station immediately. She doesn't know we're on to her. Keep it that way. I want her arrested but not until you get there. Until that moment you will treat her as a witness. Is that clear? Oh, and make sure there are always two of you with her, or you'll find yourself facing rape charges. Got it? Don't breathe a word of the arrest until you've got her safely tucked away. Then I want a strict compliance to the letter of the law. Arrest her properly, and let her call a lawyer if she wants one."

The door of Nigel's house was open. Music and laughter poured into the street. All the lights were on and through the windows he could see people dancing. He went in and was met by Robin who was coming out of the kitchen with a tray of pizza.

"Oh my God, what the hell are you doing here? Have you come to arrest us?" She began to laugh hysterically. "Nigel, Nigel," she called. "Guess who's here!" He followed her into the room and for a moment the whole scene seemed frozen, before movement and noise began again, but on another, lower, level.

"I need to speak to Miriam Greene," he said to no one in particular.

Robin began calling, "Miriam, Miriam."

He realised she was drunk and began looking for Miriam himself. He moved through the throng and out onto the terrace.

"Miriam Greene," he called quite loudly, and several faces turned towards him. Hilary said, "She's over there at the table in the corner." She had appeared from nowhere to stand beside him. She smiled and pointed out the direction he should take.

"Thank you, Signora Wright."

"A pleasure, Dottor Di Girolamo."

They let him pass and he stood before Miriam, who was re-splendent in gold, a fork in one hand suspended halfway to her mouth. She put it down and exclaimed, "I said they should have invited you, sit down and grab a drink!"

He sat down opposite her and said gently, "I haven't come to the party. I've come to see you. There's been a break-in at your house."

"Oh." Her face sagged.

"It's all right, nothing too terrible and we've caught them."

"You have?"

"Yes, luckily I was going for a walk and caught them at it."

"Good work!" she rallied and added, "You deserve a drink, then. Bruno, get a drink for Doctor Di Girolamo." He stayed Bruno's movement with a wave of his hand.

"Please don't. I haven't the time." He turned back to Miriam.

"Perhaps your friends will accompany you home, in a while. I will eventually need a list of the missing items, but there's no hurry. At the moment my men are examining the house for fingerprints and so on. Please stay here, and later, is there someone who could perhaps stay with you for the night?"

Hilary, standing behind him, said, "I will, don't worry."

"But I don't need anyone. I've got Assunta at the house."

He hesitated and then said, "All the same I should prefer you to have someone with you. And if you agree, I think that Signora Wright would do very well." He looked seriously into her face and said, "It is often quite a shock for people when their house is broken into." He gave her a compassionate look.

"Could I speak to you alone, maybe in the driveway, please?"

This last phrase was said very softly to Hilary, as he was rising from his seat and turned away from the others. Hilary took her cue and said, "I'll see you out."

"Buona sera a tutti, Signori, Signore," he said formally and left, following Hilary out. In the driveway he told her that Assunta and Salvatore were responsible for the break-in. "It will be hard for her to accept that they have done this to her. She is old, so she will take it even harder. Also she is not a fit woman. I am tempted to call a doctor. What do you think?"

"No. I don't think that's necessary. I think this is the sort of thing she can manage to cope with. She is tougher than you think. I'll stay with her and if she seems unwell, I'll deal with it then. I do think she'll be all right, really."

"I'll leave it in your hands then, and I'll see you later, as I will have to go back to the house. Goodnight for now and thank you." He pressed her hand with his and looked intently at her, then he disappeared down the driveway, his dark suit blending into the shadows.

THIRTY-THREE

RUGGERO WENT BACK to the villa. The fingerprint men had arrived and were at work, so he left them to it, certain that there would be nothing for them to find. He phoned down to the station and was told that Assunta had been arrested.

"I'll go and get Salvatore myself. See you soon."

He felt very pleased and was going to enjoy himself with Salvatore. The wind was quite strong now and the lightening nearer, the rumbling of thunder was louder and before long there would be a torrential rainfall. Ruggero was still on foot, and he reached the main bar in a few minutes. Outside the bar Miriam's car was conspicuously parked. As he entered the bar he was aware of being looked at and looked around without seeing Salvatore. Then he remembered the area at the back and walked out to look for him at the tables almost hidden in the dark. Leaves swirled as the wind strengthened. He saw his man in a dark corner and approached him. Salvatore got to his feet and asked, "Are you looking for me? Is something wrong? Has something happened?" His plump face was creased with anxiety.

"Yes," replied Di Girolamo. "I'm afraid something has."

"What, for God's sake?" The man looked genuinely worried.

"I'm afraid that your wife has had an unfortunate encounter with a burglar," he said ambiguously.

"I don't understand. Is my wife hurt?"

"I'm sorry I wasn't very clear. Your wife is fine and is making a statement at the police station at this very moment."

"I still don't understand, a statement about what?" He was looking and sounding very uneasy.

"About the burglary."

"What burglary? What are you talking about?"

"Oh, I'm sorry. It's been such a hectic evening, and I'm obviously not making myself clear. There has been a robbery at Miriam Greene's house. Your wife was tied up by the burglars, but luckily was set free shortly afterwards. She is understandably a little shaken, but quite well and is making a statement about what happened."

"Oh. I see," he said in a faint voice.

"I thought I'd come and tell you as I'm sure you would like to see her as soon as possible. And perhaps you would be kind enough to give me a lift to the police station, as I am without my car this evening."

"Of course. Let's go." The wind almost swept his words away and the first drops of rain splattered onto the tables.

"Let's make a run for it!" Ruggero sprinted towards Miriam's car while Salvatore broke into a waddling run behind him. He unlocked the car with trembling fingers and they both jumped in.

"Just in time!" said Ruggero, as the rain began to batter on the roof of the car. In a few minutes they arrived at the police station. A young policeman rushed out with an umbrella and escorted them in. Di Girolamo grinned at him and said to Salvatore, "Wait here."

He knocked on the Maresciallo's door and went in. "I've got him. He drove me here, and he doesn't have a clue."

"Right, I'll go and do the rest then, shall I?" said the Maresciallo with relish.

"If you would." He held the door open and the Maresciallo, pulling down his jacket, walked through and approached Salvatore. Di Girolamo closed the door and remained in the room, the rest was a boring formality, and he felt tired. The fun was over.

HILARY WATCHED MIRIAM, who seemed fairly calm. The weather was getting rapidly worse and she thought that before long it would be better to leave. She murmured to Bruno, who promptly disappeared. She went up to Miriam and said, "We should think about leaving very soon. Bruno's getting my car to save time. It's going to pour with rain. In fact there's going to be a storm. So let's go and say our good-byes and thank-yous now."

"I agree. I haven't really taken it in you know, but I suppose there will still be the police at the house, and the sooner I get it over and done with the better. I'm feeling a bit done in, my dear." She looked tired and older than usual, and Hilary was concerned at the news she would have to break to her before they reached the house. It would be better, she felt, for her to do so on their way there, rather than to wait until they reached the house and have the police do it. She took Miriam's arm.

"Come on. Let's find our hosts."

They took their leave of Nigel and Robin. Robin by now was looking the worse for wear, with strands of hair falling from her elaborate hair-do, which had been piled on top of her head making her seem even taller. Her eye make-up was looking tacky, and she suddenly reminded Hilary of those sad creatures one often sees at night, on the roadside plying their wares, their bodies. She was quite drunk and slobbered on Hilary's cheek, her "thank you for coming" was barely comprehensible. Nigel seemed stiff as ever, if a little redder in the face. He said anxiously to Hilary, "I think it went quite well, eh? Jolly good show. All Robin's idea, of course. I don't have the imagination. I'm a bit of an old stick in the mud, you know."

He sounded rather sad and, for the first time, sincere. She realized he must have had quite a lot to drink as well to sound so forlorn and found herself reassuring him.

"Nigel, don't put yourself down. It was marvellous, and I'm sorry to leave but I must get Miriam home. It's starting to rain already, and there's going to be a downpour."

Bruno arrived at that moment and she settled Miriam into the front seat.

Bruno asked, "Do you want me to drop you off and bring the car back here, or do you want to drive yourself and keep the car." Hilary managed to bite her tongue and not say that she would have preferred a third alternative. He could have offered to stay with her and Miriam, at least for a while.

"I'll keep the car."

"Right." He got out of the car leaving the door open for her." See you tomorrow then. I'll stay on here a bit I think. I've got my umbrella, so I'll be fine."

Hilary was amazed. He so obviously felt that he was her prime concern. She got into the driver's seat, slammed the door and set off, quelling the anger she felt. Miriam seemed very subdued. Halfway there she stopped the car and faced her.

"I've got to tell you something, and you won't like it a bit," Miriam said. The rain began to hammer on the car as she spoke.

SALVATORE FUMED IN his cell. It was unbelievable. *There must be some way to get out of this,* he thought. After all he was a first offender, well, technically at least. Everything had gone wrong and he still didn't really understand why. Worst of all was the fact that they wouldn't let him speak to Assunta. He knew he had nothing to worry about there, as she would deny everything and admit nothing. Even so he would have liked to speak to her. He was examining an idea in his head at the moment. He wondered what they would give him in exchange for information, vital information that would solve their murder case. Would it be worth his while in the end to admit another, albeit failed, burglary, and tell them what he had seen? What about if he got the goods back for Miriam? He could do that if he acted quickly enough. He could shop Joe. After all, Joe would do the same to him in a similar situation. There would be no repercussions either, as Joe was a loner. He had to decide quickly.

Ruggero drove up to Miriam's house in a police car and reached it just as Hilary and Miriam arrived. His men had finished and were ready to leave. He sent them off before going up to Hilary's car. He helped extricate Miriam from the small car and then assisted her up the steps to the house, covering her with his umbrella. Hilary, holding Miriam's other arm, was grateful. Miriam had perked up considerably as soon as she saw him and now she offered him a nightcap.

"You must have a drink. I insist."

"Well, if you insist, then I am obliged to accept."

"Hilary, could you do the honours. I think I'll sit down." She lowered herself into a large armchair and smiled at Ruggero. Hilary went out to get glasses and a bottle of brandy.

"Hilary's a wonderful person, you know," she confided.

"Yes, I can see that she is."

"A pearl without price. Someone should snap her up."

"I rather think that someone has."

"Oh him. It won't last. He's a pathetic little man, and not at all the sort of person she needs. Now a fine man like yourself is more the sort of thing…" She broke off as Hilary came back into the room with a tray and three glasses.

She poured a little brandy into a glass and handed it to Miriam, who protested, "That's not much. I can hardly see it." She peered into her glass and looked miserable. Hilary, who was handing a somewhat larger glass of brandy to Ruggero said, "It's a medicinal quantity, Miriam. You've already had a few drinks this evening."

Ruggero took the glass from her and said, "Thanks. I think I need a drink. Perhaps it will help me sleep."

"Oh, do you have trouble sleeping?" she asked.

"Yes. Sometimes." He meant "often," but wasn't inclined to talk about it.

"It's so wretched, isn't it? I hate it. Either I don't get off, or I wake up at three and that's it for a couple of hours. I hate it, sitting in the kitchen till dawn. It's so lonely."

"Oh, do you do that, too?" He sounded surprised.

"Frequently."

Miriam stirred and said, "I know an excellent remedy for getting to sleep, but I don't expect either of you would consider it."

"Miriam," said Hilary in a warning tone.

"All right, all right. My lips are sealed. But what is life without love?"

"Is that a quote?"

"No, a rhetorical question."

"Which I won't answer."

Di Girolamo drained the last drop of brandy from his glass and stood up. "I must leave you two ladies now. Will you be all right?"

"Yes, fine," replied Hilary standing up, too. "I'll see you out. I need to lock up."

"Good girl," said Miriam, giving her a knowing wink, which Hilary ignored, praying that Ruggero had not seen it.

In the hall, she suddenly felt shy and embarrassed. Miriam's blatant efforts at playing the go-between were easier to ignore in her presence. Now that she was alone with Ruggero, she felt the full weight of them.

"Miriam's a bit naughty," she said apologetically.

"I suppose she is, but I rather like her."

"Oh, so do I, of course. I love her. But, well, she can be a bit…" she failed to find the right word.

"Ruggero smiled at her and slowly ran a finger down the side of her cheek, just touching the corner of her mouth. "Goodnight, Hilary. Sleep well tonight." He wanted to kiss her.

She murmured. "Goodnight. Sleep well, yourself."

She shut the door behind him and touched her cheek. She wondered what his gesture had meant.

THE STORM GATHERED strength. Now the thunder made the windows rattle and the lightening was almost continuous. Miriam still sat in her enormous armchair in the drawing room. Hilary had given her a glass of warm milk, and she sipped at it suspiciously.

"This tastes very healthy, Hilary. Are you sure you laced it with brandy?"

"Quite sure."

"Hmm. You know, Hilary, I knew Salvatore was up to something. I told you so, didn't I?"

"Yes, I suppose you did. How do you feel?"

"Quite all right, my dear. He's only taken things, you know, and there was nothing that can't be replaced. All my precious stuff is in a security box at the bank. There were just a few baubles here, and the hi-tech stuff isn't important."

"Good. I knew you'd be brave."

"Well, I wouldn't have liked to have been in the house when they did it, but there was no question of that. They aren't violent people, I'm sure. Although I must tell you that it has crossed my mind, that they, well Salvatore, could have been responsible for Ettore. What do you think?"

"Oh, you mean the burglar theory? I suppose it is just possible, but really, would anyone risk a life sentence when all they were aiming to steal was a computer and a television?"

"Of course, it could have been an accident. I can't see Salvatore killing a man in cold blood. But he might have done so accidentally. I've no doubt it will occur to Di Girolamo to look into it. He seems very on the ball to me."

"Yes he is. Miriam, if you feel like it, we can go up now. Everyone left ages ago and we don't have to make a list of what's missing till tomorrow. I'll help you with that, anyway. You must be tired. I know I am. I think it's pretty late."

"Yes, I think it's already tomorrow. That's what they used to say to us when we were children, if we stayed up after midnight, on some special occasion. I suppose this counts as a special occasion, in a way."

"Yes, I think it does."

THIRTY-FOUR

THE STORM RAGED until dawn. An incredible amount of water had fallen, swelling small torrents to raging proportions. A few minor landslides occurred where the dry earth was unable to cope with such an enormity of water, but none were large enough to do any real damage. The rain washed the dusty roads and was gratefully sucked in by the thirsty earth. A few roofs had lost some of their tiles, and the streets were littered with leaves and twigs, and even branches. Then the sun rose and the land steamed as it dried. Everything green sparkled with a new vitality and stood firmer. Vegetables appeared to have grown rapidly overnight.

The air was clear and several degrees cooler than on previous mornings. Everybody in town threw open their windows and let the clean air wash through the houses.

The phone rang. Gino picked it up on the second ring, muttering an inward prayer.

"Pronto."

"Signor Rossi, this is Doctor Baroni from Pisa hospital. We thought you would be pleased to know that your son has regained consciousness."

"God be praised! Is he all right?"

"Well, it's early days yet, but he is fully conscious and asking for you."

"Asking for me," repeated Gino with wonderment. "I'll be there as soon as possible."

"Good. I'm on duty till two this afternoon, so if you would

like to come and see me before I leave, there are one or two things I would like to discuss with you."

"Of course doctor. Good-bye, and thank you."

He put the phone back and brushed at the tears that were coursing down his cheeks.

"Alda! Alda, the boy's woken up! Quick, wake up! We must leave immediately."

"Gino, what did you say?" came a distant voice from the bedroom.

"I said, Marco is awake. He's woken up and is asking for us!" he shouted as he clambered up the stairs. The door burst open and his wife rushed out and clasped him to her. They wept together.

Di Girolamo was in a good mood. He whistled as he opened his mail and called through to his colleague, "Have we got the results of that check yet, the fingerprint on the shovel with Salvatore's prints?"

"Not yet."

"Phone down and chivvy them along a bit. I feel very hopeful about it. I feel very positive this morning."

The phone rang and his colleague answered it.

"Yes, I see. Thank you very much, doctor. Do the parents know? Good. Yes I'll tell him. Good-bye."

He came in and said, "The boy, Marco Rossi, has woken up. They won't let us to talk to him yet, but felt you should be informed."

"There, what did I tell you? I knew that today would be a good day. Excellent. All we need now is the confirmation about that print and I'll feel really happy."

He picked up an envelope marked "URGENT. PERSONAL AND PRIVATE." There was a photograph and a note. He tipped them out and pulled on a pair of rubber gloves that he kept in his desk drawer. He glanced at the photograph, then picked it up and examined it carefully. He put it down and picked up the note. It was laboriously printed. In places the pencil had gone through the paper, but even so the writing was shaky and wavered across the page.

SATAN IS AMONGST US. HE HAS TAKEN ON THE FORM THAT IS NEITHER MAN NOR WOMAN: HE IS HERE!!! WE MUST BE VIGILANT. THE BEAST IS AMONG US!! FAST AND PRAY. YOU MUST SEEK OUT THE BEAST AND DESTROY HIM. HE HAS KILLED THE INNOCENT. HE HAS CORRUPTED THE INCORRUPTABLE. SUFFER LITTLE CHILDREN TO COME UNTO ME SAITH THE LORD BUT THE BEAST HAS TAKEN THE LITTLE CHILDREN HAS CORRUPTED THE INCORRUPTIBLE. MINE EYES HAVE SEEN THE GLORY OF THE LORD MINE EYES HAVE SEEN THE CORRUPTION THE FOULNESS OF THE BEAST. SEEK OUT AND DESTROY THE BEAST. WE MUST FAST AND PRAY BRETHREN. ONLY THE PURE SHALL BE SAVED. DEATH WHERE IS THY STING? WE SHALL ALL BE SAVED THROUGH GOD. IN PAIN WAS HE BROUGHT FORTH. THE LORD GIVETH. THE LORD TAKETH AWAY. HIS ONLY SON DIED FOR US. THE BEAST HAS TAKEN THE ONLY SON.

FAST AND PRAY. THE LORD WILL GIVE STRENGTH TO THY HAND. FAST AND PRAY.

DI GIROLAMO OPENED the file on his desk and took out the letter that had come with the photograph of Marco Rossi. It looked like the same hand to him, but no doubt an expert could say so with absolute certainty. The writing was shakier than in the first letter, and the contents less coherent. Even so he felt sure that this was from Augusta Fagiolo. If he was right, then she was obviously deranged. He was uncertain what he should do about it.

"Call the Maresciallo for me, ask him if he'll see me," he called. "Preferably now if possible." He took off his gloves. The photo laughed up at him. Who was it? It reminded him of someone, but the red wig and the wide-open mouth distorted the features. Was it really important or had this photo so unhinged the old lady that she had chosen to send it to him as emblematic of evil, rather than as a clue for the solution of her son's murder?

MIRIAM WANDERED THROUGH the house talking over her shoulder to Hilary who walked behind her with a notebook and pen.

"Both the televisions of course, but the only thing that really makes me angry is the computer. It's got my latest book on it, and I'm over halfway through it."

"Didn't you save it on a disk?"

"Well I did for the first few chapters so they're somewhere in the desk, but then I didn't bother."

"Well, I think that's the lot Miriam. We've done all the rooms now, so I'll take this down to the police station. Do you want to come with me, or are you going to stay here and get depressed?"

"Oh, I'll stay here, but I won't get depressed. I've got to start thinking about a new couple to help with the house. I'll phone around some agencies."

"You'd better vet them very carefully this time."

"Oh I will. You know, I think I might offer a very large reward for my computer, and no questions asked. What do you think?"

"Ask the police what they think first."

"You ask them for me. My dear, it will give you an excuse to see Di Girolamo. He's such a fascinating man, don't you think?"

"I'm going. I see you're back to normal. Don't forget you're coming to me for lunch. I'll send Amanda for you."

"SALVATORE! *Buon giorno,* I have wonderful news."

"For me? Dottor, am I getting out of here?"

"No, no, no. Wonderful news for me! Your thumbprint was on the shovel that was used to hit Ettore Fagiolo, contributing to his death."

"What?"

"You heard."

"Oh my God! I want a lawyer."

"Do you?"

"Yes I do! Now! Get me one. I'm saying nothing till I've spoken to a lawyer." He turned his back on Di Girolamo. He was going to be forced to barter now, or he would be facing a murder rap. But he needed expert help.

Di Girolamo returned to his office but stopped in the corridor when he saw Hilary. He walked towards her, offering his hand to shake hers, and smiled. "Good morning. Have you brought the list of missing items?" He looked down at her hand, it was tanned, and her fingers were fairly short with short, unvarnished nails. A working hand, which held his firmly.

"Yes, here it is." She waved it at him.

"Thank you. How is Signora Greene?"

"Oh. She's fine, in good form. Actually she's asked me to talk to you about something."

"Oh yes? Well come into my office and you can talk to me there. We could even have a coffee. Do you like coffee?"

"Who doesn't?"

"Send in two coffees please," he called. "Right, come in and sit down." She did.

"Now what do you want to talk to me about?" he smiled again. She was quite surprised he looked so good tempered.

"You're in a fine spirits this morning, are you?"

"Oh very."

"Well, it's just that one of the missing things is her computer and she desperately wants it back. It's got half a novel on it."

"Half a novel?"

"Yes, she writes. Didn't you know?"

"No, I didn't. What sort of thing does she write?"

"Romantic novels. She's quite well known and sells very well, so this half a novel is rather important."

"I see. Romantic novels!" He laughed. "So you want me to speak to Salvatore about it? Yes, come in. Thank you." He took the tray of coffee and set it on the table between them. He handed her a cup of coffee.

"Thank you. Well, she's pretty desperate. She was talking about advertising for it, you know, a large reward and no questions asked."

"I don't really think that will be necessary. I'm sure Salvatore will be reasonable. He's not in a very comfortable situation. I feel certain he will do anything that might make things a little less unpleasant for him. Tell her to do nothing for the moment. By the way, thank you for helping me out with her, you know, explaining the situation to her last night. I was worried I wouldn't do it well and she seemed rather fragile."

"Yes, I suppose she is in a way, though she hides it well. But this hasn't been too bad. It could have been a lot worse. Besides, they've taken nothing of sentimental value. She'll be fine now. She's phoning the agencies already, looking for another couple."

"Good, and thank you once again. You're a good woman to have around."

"You mean you don't suspect me anymore? Are you sure I'm not dangerous?"

"Not quite sure, but let's say, not in that way."

After she left, he said to himself, *I must be crazy. What kind of a stupid remark was that? She must think I'm mad.*

There was a knock and the Maresciallo came in.

"I faxed the letters to Rome and the handwriting expert looked at them straight away. He says the letters are by the same hand."

"It's always nice to have official confirmation. So, Ettore's mother is at it again. What did you think of the letter?"

"Crazy."

"Yes, but should we intervene? Would it be more harmful to intervene or leave her to stew?"

"I'm generally against intervention. 'Time will heal,' is my motto.

She's still grieving, so I say give her some time. She'd die of shame if we interfered."

"She's looking after a senile old man on her own, so either she's still got some contact with reality, or she's a danger to herself and to him. Is there any discrete way of knowing if she's capable of looking after him?"

"I suppose I could get a neighbour to look in with some excuse. My niece lives nearby, so I could ask her."

"Is she tactful? Does the old woman know her? Does she like her? Because if not, she won't like some busybody neighbour poking her nose in."

"Well, I think she doesn't mind her. She doesn't like anyone much. She doesn't have any real friends. My niece is a school-teacher and she's involved in the church council, so she would be acceptable, and she does know her better than most."

"Get your niece to come here at lunchtime and I'll talk to her. By the way, get a lawyer for Salvatore and fix up a taped inter-view as soon as possible."

"Do you think he did it? I mean, the thumbprint points that way."

"I don't know. If he didn't, then he knows something, or he's involved in it in some way. I don't see him as a murderer, but he must have been there that night. And he must have touched the shovel. How else can you explain the thumbprint? He could well have done it. It fits with our theory. But if so, then why did the boy, Marco, blackmail Nigel? If he blackmailed him, that means he was there, in the area of the pool. How else could he have seen him? He seems to think Nigel killed Ettore, and until we've spoken to him, we can't discard that possibility. Of course, I may well be wrong."

"Assunta is still ranting about police fascist methods. She wants to see her husband, and she's going to sue us all."

"Let her stew. Don't forget to send your niece along. Let me know the exact time she's coming and I'll grab a snack around then. Today we are going to get a lot done. I knew it the moment I woke up."

"Really?"

"Yes, I felt it in my bones. No. It was just that I had the feeling that the thumbprint would be positive and a lot hung on that.

Everything moves forward from it."

Five minutes later the phone rang, "My niece, Teresa Carradini, will be along at one-fifteen and I didn't tell her what you wanted. I just said you needed help."

"Thank you."

THIRTY-FIVE

TERESA CARRADINI FITTED his image of a schoolteacher. She was about forty; wore thin, gold-framed glasses; had frizzy hair piled on top of her head and looked benign and worthy. Her figure was a little lumpy, and her plump bosom was modestly covered with a flower-printed blouse. She wore a gold chain and cross. He asked her to be seated and began to explain what he wanted.

"I believe you know Augusta Fagiolo fairly well."

"As well as it is possible to know someone who has almost no interest in social contact. I have worked on church activities with her. She has always been a willing helper, though our contact was brief and only concerned the work at hand."

"I'll tell you frankly that I am concerned for her. I understand that to lose one's only son must have a devastating effect on anyone, and it would be normal for a religious person to seek a greater contact with God. However, there are cases when this sort of thing goes beyond the bounds of what is considered normal behaviour, even for someone who has been so recently bereaved."

She looked at him with no change of expression.

He ploughed on, "What I am trying to say is I am convinced that her behaviour is no longer normal. As she is the sole person responsible for her husband's well-being, I ask myself whether she is able to carry out this onerous task as well as she did before."

She still looked at him waiting for him to finish. He would have welcomed a word of comprehension, but none was forth-coming. She still sat like a flowery pudding, skirt modestly pulled down, hands in her lap, gazing at him like a pregnant cow. He was very worried that she might think he was delving into realms that had little to do with his job, and he realised that he feared her judgement.

"This is purely my own interest, not a police concern, you understand. I am worried that Signor Fagiolo may not be receiving the treatment that his case deserves. There is no way that I, as a police officer, could find out what the situation is in the house without causing mental anguish to this lady, but all the same, I very much need to be reassured that all is well, and that is why, after discussing the situation with your uncle, I decided to ask your help."

He waited.

There was a rather lengthy silence before she said, "You want me to go to the house and see if her husband is being looked after properly." It was a statement, flat, and said totally without inflexion.

"Yes, I do. I feel that you could go to the house without upsetting Augusta, and perhaps, with the interests that you have in common, she would speak to you and even let you see her husband."

"Is that all?"

"Well, yes."

"I will go straight away." She rose smoothly and left the room immediately.

He almost mopped his brow. She was either very intelligent, and parsimonious with her speech, or she was a stolid unimaginative half-wit.

Maresciallo Biagioni popped his head round the door, "Did you speak to Teresa then?"

"Oh yes, I spoke for hours, she hardly murmured."

"Ah well, Teresa is not what she seems. She always makes people feel like they're back at school. You're always waiting to see what mark she'll give you," he laughed.

"Well, I think I got a pass mark. Anyway, she's gone to see Signora Fagiolo. She just said, 'I'll go straight away,' and walked out."

"Teresa doesn't waste words. She'll do a good job. You can set your mind at rest. By the way, I fixed for four-thirty with Salvatore."

"Good. I'm off out to grab a sandwich. Call me on my cell phone if Teresa comes back before I do."

"Oh, by the way, Assunta says she's sure she's pregnant, so we must let her go."

"Get a gynaecologist. I don't believe her, but best to be sure."

He walked out into the blinding sunshine and quickly put on his sunglasses. He was wearing a beige linen suit with an off white shirt. His tall slim figure and brisk way of walking made him look more youthful than his age. Only his short greying hair betrayed him. Amanda drove past slowly with Miriam stowed in the front seat beside her. It was late because Miriam had insisted on finishing her phone calls and had then decided to take a shower before changing into a fresh caftan.

"He's a good-looking man," she said with relish, looking at Di Girolamo. She waved a plump arm out of the car window at him and he waved back, raising his sunglasses and smiling at her. The car moved on.

"I wish I were thirty years younger," she sighed.

"Really Miriam. Do you fancy him?"

"Of course I do. Don't look so surprised. My dear, you still fancy people even at my age. It's just cerebral, though. I mean, you can't do anything about it and you wouldn't have the energy even if you had the opportunity."

"How old are you?"

"None of your business. Let's just say, too old. But your mother isn't. She could have him at the drop of a hat, my dear, but she won't of course."

"Why? Do you think he fancies her?"

"Of course he does. She's a good-looking woman, and she's wasted on Bruno. The man looks like a bloody priest."

"She says he's restful."

"Restful! My dear girl, that means 'boring as hell.' She should go for Ruggero Di Girolamo. He looks like a man. I might be too old to have a man, but I can certainly recognise one when I see one, and I bet you he'd be better than Bruno in bed."

"Really, Miriam, it's not just sex, you know. There are other considerations."

"Of course there are, my dear. That's what I'm saying. Bruno is probably as boring in bed as he is out of it."

"I'm going to pretend I haven't heard you. Come on, I'll help you get out of the car."

They went into the house, where Miriam was annoyed to see Bruno.

"Oh, I didn't know you were here for lunch. I do hope I didn't keep you waiting," she smiled at him unpleasantly. Then turning from him, she gushed, "Darling Hilary, forgive me. I'm late." She proffered her cheek for a kiss. "Now while we're eating tell me all about your meeting with that divine Dr. Di Girolamo."

Amanda raised her eyebrows at Hilary over Miriam's head.

"Hilary very kindly took my list in this morning," she continued, looking at Bruno. "I wanted to give her an excuse to see Dr. Di Girolamo again." She gave him a satisfied smile.

"Yes, she is a kind person," he said mildly, ignoring the implications.

On the table was a huge bowl of *farro*. It was a cold dish, a salad of grain and mixed in with it were olives, finely cut peppers, cucumber, onions, capers, runner beans, and herbs. In another bowl were tomatoes with basil, and on separate plates, were Parma ham and cold roast pork. There was fresh wholemeal bread and red wine.

"Help yourselves, everybody," commanded Hilary

"This is splendid," said Miriam serving herself first with the *farro*.

"Pass the tomatoes please, Bruno," she said in English, which she knew would annoy him.

"Here you are, Miriam," he replied in Italian.

"Oh, I'm sorry. I always forget that your English isn't very good.

Ruggero Di Girolamo speaks English very well, you know. Tell me what he said, about the computer, Hilary."

"Oh, nothing much, he just said that you should wait a while before advertising. He thinks he can get Salvatore to get it back for you."

"That would be splendid. I simply must have it back. There's half a book on it."

"Yes," said Bruno, "you mustn't deny your public the chance to read yet another of your literary pearls."

"Don't try and be funny, Bruno. It doesn't suit you. It just sounds rude." Miriam's tone was scathing. "Stick to what you are good at. Just continue being your usual boring self and don't try and dazzle us with your wit."

Bruno stood up grating his chair on the floor. "I'm sorry Hilary, I can't stay. Your friend seems to be determined to be as unpleasant as possible."

"Yes, well, you weren't being very nice yourself."

He threw down his serviette and left the house.

"You would be well rid of him, Hilary. He's been around too long and he's getting proprietary."

"Miriam, you are being very naughty and not really fair to poor Bruno," Hilary scolded.

"My dear, when one uses the adjective 'poor' about one's lover, then he already has one foot out of the door."

"Let's drop the subject," said Hilary in a determined manner. "Tell me, did any of the agencies have anything promising?"

"Well there is a couple, housekeeper/chauffeur, with some gardening skills, who will be free in September, as the family they are with are moving abroad and they don't want to leave Italy. I'm interviewing them next week. Otherwise there's nobody free until the end of the year. There's the possibility of filling in until then with temps. They are more expensive and only stay for short periods. Anyway, for the present I shall carry on using my local domestic help, eat out and use a taxi if and when."

"Good. Please, don't just take this first couple just because they are available. Find out why they are available. I mean check their story and all their history."

"It's no guarantee, you know. Assunta and Salvatore had excellent, verifiable references."

Amanda said, "By the way, I heard this morning that Marco Rossi has recovered consciousness, and they think he'll be okay."

"Thank God for that. Who told you?" Miriam asked.

"His father, he was rushing off to get the car out, and go to see him," Amanda said.

"My dear, we'll never hear the end of it. Alda went off to see Padre Pio you know, so no doubt they'll attribute the boy's recovery to him," Miriam sighed.

"Yes, they probably will. Where's the harm in that?" said Hilary.

"None, I suppose. It might even make the boy feel special, make him mend his ways," replied Miriam.

"What ways?" asked Amanda.

"Oh you know, dissipation my dear."

"Miriam that's such an old-fashioned word. What do you mean?" Amanda asked.

Miriam shifted in her seat. "Well, Assunta told me he was on drugs, and queer to boot. He had a thing going with Ettore."

"Ettore wasn't gay!" cried Amanda.

"Oh, I know that! No one knows better than you about his sexual proclivities. But take it from me, my dear, he was into men as well. Utterly depraved."

Amanda looked at Hilary accusingly.

"No. It wasn't your mother told me. It was Ettore who blabbed to Salvatore," Miriam said.

"I wonder who else he told," she said bitterly

"Rise above it. The past is over and no one wants to hear about it. It's as appetising as cold, congealed spaghetti. Besides, he's dead, so you're safe." She paused, "My dear Hilary, this is a charming meal. I'm sorry I upset Bruno. Amanda, my dear, would you take a gossiping old lady back home straight after coffee? I need to sort out my temporary help and I mustn't leave Cherry for too long."

"Of course. Do you want me to stay with you a bit?"

"No, I expect I'll take a little nap. I usually do when it's so hot in the afternoon."

They had their coffee at the table and then Amanda helped her out of her seat and took her back to "the Mausoleum." She left her there alone, a plump, rather forlorn figure. She was never really vicious and often quite kindly. Her voracious love of gossip filled the vacuum left by lack of family.

THIRTY-SIX

When Amanda got back, she reheated some coffee while her mother finished clearing up the lunch things.

"Ma, do you think Marco was on drugs?"

"It's probable. He always looked pretty bloody."

"And homosexual?"

"What's wrong with that?"

"Oh nothing. But if he had an ongoing thing with Ettore, then do you think he was with him that evening?"

"I have asked myself the same question. Again, I think probably."

"So, you think he is involved?"

"I wouldn't go that far. You didn't see him after Ettore died. He was distraught. I suppose he might know something, but he would never have killed him."

"Do the police know about their relationship?"

"I don't know, and anyway, it's only hearsay."

"I would never have thought Ettore was gay, or well, bi-sexual."

"Why shouldn't he be? It's a private thing you know, one's sexual 'proclivities' as Miriam calls them." She finished stacking the dishwasher and set it going.

"Yes. I suppose it is. What are you doing this afternoon? I'm going into the garden to sunbathe, coming?"

"No. I'm going up for a rest. I didn't get much sleep last night, what with one thing and another."

Amanda wandered into the garden. It had a rather parched look despite the storm the night before. The grass was still yellow and dry. She looked down towards the pool, and saw that Robin was sunbathing there. She was wearing a bikini, the lower half of which was minute, a mere cache-sex.

Amanda walked further down the garden to look at the bougainvillaea she had bought for her mother the summer before. It had survived the winter encased in straw and plastic and was now flowering. She knelt down to examine the weeds at its base, and with strong fingers felt along the stalk of one, down to its roots. It took a while to uproot it, but finally she stood up, triumphant, with the whole weed in her hand.

A movement caught her eye and, as she watched, she saw that Robin was standing up and turning towards her. She hadn't seen Amanda, and as she didn't want to seem a nosy neighbour, she pressed herself against the wall remaining hidden by the plants. Then she saw Robin do something so shocking that she almost couldn't believe what she was seeing. She wondered if it was a hallucination brought on by the lunchtime conversation. Robin then returned to the sun-bed and lay immobile again. Amanda went silently back into the house.

TERESA CAME BACK to the station and was far less calm than before. She seemed to have been running, despite the heat, and her hair was falling down. Crinkled tendrils stuck to her cheeks.

She mopped at her pink face with a spotless handkerchief and said breathlessly to Di Girolamo, "I'm afraid you were right. I got there and she didn't want to let me in at first, but I managed. The whole place reeked of bleach, and she told me that she had high standards of cleanliness. So I thought it was okay. Then I asked if I could see her husband and pray with her for him, and she took me in, and I realised he was dead. She didn't seem to realise, so I said a prayer with her and then she accompanied me out and said that I should be very careful as Satan was among us, and that I should fast and pray."

"You're quite sure he was dead?"

"Oh, quite sure. I touched his hand and it was quite cold." Her eyes filled with tears. "It was a terrible shock. Will you go there?" She sat down rather abruptly in a chair and took a few deep breaths.

"We'll deal with this. I'm sorry you had to do this, but you do see it would have been difficult for me, and I could have been wrong. I should have realised that it could have been upsetting for you. Please forgive me."

"What will happen now?" she asked.

"It's a medical matter. She'll be looked after, don't worry."

"She's so thin, I think she has been fasting. She's always been keen on fasting. I remember when the missionary sisters came round…they had quite a discussion about it. Of course fasting is a part of one's religious life. It's a discipline, but it should never be carried to extremes. Do you think she made him fast, too?"

"It's possible. There will have to be an autopsy of course, but even if she did, what does it matter? She is a deranged old woman suffering from religious mania, with nothing to live for. I can safely predict that she will probably join her husband before too long. I've seen it happen before."

"You sound so cynical. Do you believe in God?"

"No," he replied curtly.

"But you are a good man. I will pray for you." She stood up as she spoke, touched him briefly on the shoulder as though blessing him, and left the room.

He banged his fist on the table softly. These bloody Catholics. They made him seethe. He never interfered with their beliefs. He respected them and avoided arguing with them, and in return they pushed their religion onto him, whether he liked or wanted it or not. He did not want anyone to ever pray for him. He wanted nothing to intercede between whatever power may exist and the huge rage that he had felt ever since Silvia had died. It swelled within him, threatening to burst inside him and smash him apart.

THIRTY-SEVEN

MARCO HAD WOKEN slowly. Like a diver surfacing, his head had broken through the waves and the light had penetrated painfully. He closed his eyes again and perceived strange surroundings: noises, a quiet conversation in technical jargon and the sound of wheels, no, a trolley. The stiff white sheets reflected the light as he opened his eyes again. His mouth was dry and he felt incredibly tired. There was a rhythmic pumping noise and a continuous "beep-beep." A hand touched his forehead and then his wrist was held in a professional manner. A young woman's face loomed into view and observed him dispassionately. She moved out of his visual field. He couldn't turn his head so he closed his eyes again. Then he heard rapid footsteps approaching and a man's voice said, "I see you are awake. Good. Excellent."

Marco looked at him and saw that a man of about forty, clean-shaven and with dark curly hair was smiling at him. Marco realized he was a doctor.

"You are in hospital. You've had an accident. Keep still and don't try to move. You have several fractures, so you are more or less immobilised anyway. There is a drip going into your right arm, so keep that in mind. The other arm is in plaster. Don't worry. You'll be fine. You are young, and the young heal fast."

Marco looked at him blankly. He felt the stethoscope move on his chest and then the sheets were readjusted.

"You are on a respirator, but I think we can take you off it now. If you understand please blink twice." Marco did so. "Good. We'll have you off it in no time."

Half an hour later, freed from the respirator, and after a sip or two of water through a straw, Marco managed to speak.

"Who did it?" he whispered.

"Oh you mean, who ran you over? It was a hit and run, I'm afraid."

"My parents?"

"They're not here. We sent them home. Hospital rules. I'll phone them now. They'll be delighted to know you have regained consciousness." Marco closed his eyes and went to sleep again.

"Marco, Marco. Are you awake?" It was his mother's voice. As soon as he heard it, a tear rolled down his cheek.

"Marco, *mio,* don't cry. You'll be all right. I went to Padre Pio for you and he has saved you. It's a miracle. You must rest and get well. Don't talk if it tires you."

He looked at her kind, plump face and tired eyes. She smiled encouragingly at him. Love shone from her face. It beamed down on him, this tremendous, weighty love that suffocated him and bound him to her. Somehow it felt surprisingly safe and reassuring. More tears rolled from his eyes. She mopped them with a handkerchief.

"Mamma…" He didn't know what to say to her.

"There, there, you will be all right. I'll leave you now, as your father is coming in to see you."

His father! Lately they had hardly spoken. His father's looks had been hard to bear and his own guilt was so awful to him that he had avoided his father as much as possible. He felt sure his father knew about the drugs, knew that he was somehow involved in Ettore's death, and perhaps even thought he had killed him. He closed his eyes again. He could feel more tears bursting through his closed eyelids.

He heard his father's voice. "Marco, why are you crying? You have nothing to cry about. You are going to get well. Everything will be all right. We are here. We will help you in every way."

He looked at his father and said, "Babbo, help me."

His father looked down at his son's bare arm. A plastic tube emerged from a vein on the wrist and was connected to a drip. But further up, the arm bore the marks of other, earlier, needle tracks. He patted the boy's hand.

"Marco, you have been through a bad patch. But now, as your body heals, so will your spirit."

"I must speak to the police." His voice was merely a croak.

"The police! What about?"

"I must tell them."

"Tell them what?"

"I know who killed Ettore."

"Then, of course you must. I'll speak to the doctor about it. Rest now. You mustn't tire yourself."

DI GIROLAMO EMERGED from the interview room. He felt very pleased with himself and with the events of the day. It was funny how a case would drag on and almost peter out, with no new avenues for exploration, and then a chance event would send you a multitude of information, and give you the solution, laying it in your lap. Salvatore had been a godsend. He had been at the Villa Rosa the night that Ettore was killed and his testimony was, to say the least, extremely important. To avoid a charge of homicide, he had offered up Nigel on a plate. Of course he could be lying. He could have done it himself, and be offering Nigel up as a sacrificial lamb. Di Girolamo knew that his forthcoming interview with Nigel would be of paramount importance, and he would have to play a very careful hand.

"Telephone sir. It's the hospital at Pisa."

"Yes, Di Girolamo here. Yes, I see. Excellent! Did he say anything else? Is he up to it? Right, I'll either come myself or send someone as soon as possible. Yes, I understand, a very brief interview." Decidedly an abundance today!

He thought briefly, then picked up the phone again. "Di Girolamo here, from the Province of Lucca. I am the P.M. in

charge of a murder case in the Commune of Borgo San Cristoforo. Yes, that's the one. I'm phoning because I have an important witness in hospital in Pisa. He's been in a coma and only
just come round, so he's pretty weak. I want someone tactful and
quiet to take a statement from the boy in the hospital. Yes, the
main hospital. He's on the brain surgery ward. The name is
Marco Rossi. Now, your man is to speak to the doctor in charge
and find out how long he can stay. This boy's testimony is vital.
He will give me a name. Yes, he can give a complete statement
when he's stronger. Phone as soon as you have it. Of course I
want it taped! Thank you."

Among other things, Salvatore had shopped his partner in
crime, so Di Girolamo had passed all that information on to the
Maresciallo. Perhaps Miriam would get her computer back
sooner than she thought.

AMANDA HAD CHANGED into a two-piece costume and
carrying a large towel she went back out into the garden. She
pulled a sun-bed into a good position and began to lay her
towel on it.

"Amanda! Amanda!" It was Robin. "Come on down for a
swim. The pool is fine. It's been exorcised, I promise."

Amanda hesitated and then walked down to the end of the
garden, climbed over the strand of wire and joined Robin at the
poolside. She stood over Robin and looked at her opulent bust,
her flat muscular stomach and long slim legs. "Not bad, eh?" said
Robin. "I don't tell everyone, but I'm forty-five."

"You look great. Do you exercise a lot?"

"Well, a fair amount. I don't want to get flabby."

"You look very strong. Do you do bodybuilding?"

"You guessed. Yes, I do. I'm not fanatical, but I feel that at
my age I should really make the effort. I'm a member of the Saint
Andrea Health and Beauty Centre. You should try it. I pay a
monthly sum and can go as often as I like. It's got a well-

equipped gym. They've got the full works there. There's also a sauna. Let me tell you, it does wonders for you."

"Well, there's not many women of your age could wear a costume like that."

"Oh, that's just for sunbathing, I don't go out in public like this."

"What about Nigel. Is he a member, too?"

"Nigel! Good God, no. He stays in the shade and the only exercise he gets is the swimming, unless you count raising a glass to his lips," she laughed.

"Oh, I thought he looked pretty fit."

"He's not in bad nick actually. He swims a lot, and it really is the perfect exercise. All the muscles of the body are used in harmony in swimming, but he doesn't go in for bodybuilding and he doesn't sunbathe. He's got very fair skin and he burns easily. I'm lucky, I soak up the sun."

"Robin, can I ask you something?"

"Mmm."

"Did you like Ettore?"

"Not much. Do we have to talk about him? I'm trying to forget."

"Sorry."

They had a quick swim and Amanda tried hard not to think that only a short while ago Ettore's body had been floating here.

Afterwards they lay side by side on the sun-beds in the brilliant sunshine, the empty pool winking at them as the sunlight hit the water. Amanda's mind was in turmoil as she thought about what she had seen earlier. Robin looked so marvellous. It was unbelievable that Robin should…it wasn't possible. She dozed.

The late afternoon sun slowly moved through the sky, and the temperature became slightly cooler. The house threw its shadow across the pool and Nigel came out wearing a pair of swimming shorts. He walked down the steps into the pool and began to swim methodically round and round without stopping. Robin stirred on her sun-bed and Amanda woke up.

"I told him the pool was the wrong shape for long-distance

swimming, but he would have it this way. And the colour! He adores pink. Well, I had to let him have his way. He let me choose everything else."

"I'm not very fond of pink myself."

"Darling it's pure kitsch. I've tried to tone it down with the urns and the plants, and then look what he did. He bought those awful umbrellas. That was in his Ettore period."

"His what?"

"Oh, you know, when they were such good pals. Unfortunate, aren't they? As soon as the pool was ready, Nigel whipped them out of the cellar where he'd been hiding them. He was so pleased with them I hadn't the heart to say anything. Of course Ettore had terrible taste. All those black shirts unbuttoned to his navel, and gold medallions."

"Yes, and yet he looked almost effeminate sometimes," Amanda dared to say.

"Hardly surprising."

"Why, was he gay?"

"Straight, gay, anything and everything. Oh, am I shocking you? I thought all you young people were un-shockable."

"No, you're not shocking me in the least, but how do you know?"

"Oh, one just does, you know. One sort of senses these things." She got up as she spoke and moved towards the pool. "I'm joining Nigel. Coming?"

"No thanks. I think I'll go home now. See you."

She watched Robin dive smoothly into the pool and set off in pursuit of Nigel. The two figures swam round and round until it was difficult to see who was following whom.

THIRTY-EIGHT

"Di Girolamo here. Yes. Good. He's quite sure? Yes. Oh I'll probably come down tomorrow if they think he's up to it. Send me the tape, ASAP."

It was six-thirty. Tonight there was the famous procession. It was the eve of the feast of St. Christopher, the patron saint of the town. The town was filling up already and before long there would be hundreds of visitors thronging the streets. It was already pretty full most evenings with the annual festa in the old town, but tonight would be especially crowded. The procession would wind through the streets of the old town and finish up at the Duomo, where a Mass would be held.

Ruggero Di Girolamo reflected. By the time the tape arrived and he had listened to it, it would be late and the town packed to beyond its capacity, so he decided that the best thing to do was to be patient and make an arrest at dawn. Well, not at dawn maybe, but early enough to get the man out of bed. That always gave one such an advantage. He smiled at the thought. He was going to enjoy himself tomorrow. Tonight he would eat a leisurely meal, watch the procession and go to bed early. But first the tape.

AMANDA AND HILARY had decided to eat out and then watch the procession pass by. They would not be going to Mass.

"Let's go to a restaurant where it's quiet. There's too many people in the old town."

"I think we should go to Arcobaleno in the new part of town. There's more chance of a table there. I don't really fancy sitting on a bench in the old town and eating scorched spare ribs off a plastic plate."

"Really, Ma, you sound a bit sour. Okay, we'll go to the Arcobaleno, though I'm rather fond of spare ribs myself."

"Yes, I know, but it'll be hell tonight…far too many people. You'd have to wait ages to be served and the food wouldn't be up to standard."

They walked downtown and stepped into Arcobaleno.

"Is there room to sit outside?" Hilary asked the waiter.

"Yes, plenty of room. Go on through."

They went out to the garden at the back, where there were several empty tables. The waiter followed them.

"Take whichever table you want. We haven't had so many customers since the festa in the town centre's been on. Still, only one more night to go, then things get back to normal." He handed them two menus and disappeared.

"It's very nice here, Ma. This was a good idea. Actually, I wanted to speak to you about something."

"You could have done that at home," Hilary responded.

"Yes, but I've only just decided."

"I see. Tell."

"It isn't easy. I know you'll think I'm crazy," she sighed. As the waiter reappeared she asked him for some water and ordered some *tagliatelle* with a wild mushroom sauce. Hilary asked for the same. She looked at her daughter and waited.

"Let me say it all and don't say anything until I've finished," Amanda began.

Hilary nodded.

"Well, you remember I went into the garden this afternoon? I could see Robin sunbathing. And then she stood up, and I didn't want her to think I was spying on her so I hid behind a plant, and then…" she stopped while she tried to find the words.

"And then…" said her mother.

Well, she did something that should be impossible. Except

afterwards I thought about it, and I suppose it is possible." She took a deep breath and told her mother.

Footsteps approached their table. They looked up and saw Di Girolamo. He smiled at them.

"May I join you? I'm at a loose end. Everyone seems to be rushing through the streets in the opposite direction to me, so when I saw you both going in here I thought I'd risk butting in."

"Please do," said Hilary feeling absurdly pleased. Her face was slightly flushed.

"You can tell me to go, I won't be offended."

"No. I see no reason to. Please stay with us," Hilary said.

"Yes, do," said Amanda, feeling that her mother wanted her support, but uncertain as to the reason. Actually, she thought her mother was looking very, very pleased at this unexpected intrusion.

"Have you met my daughter Amanda?" Hilary asked.

"Ruggero Di Girolamo," he said formally, offering his hand. "We shared a box at the theatre for a short while, I believe."

"Oh, yes, till Miriam started snoring," Amanda said.

They both laughed at the memory.

Hilary said, "I was sure you were very disapproving and including us all in your disapproval."

"Not at all. I thought it was hilarious."

A waiter hovered at his elbow. He ordered and then sat back and looked at the two women.

"I've had an interesting day. Many things have been revealed to me, and I think this case will be closed very soon. Then I will leave Borgo San Cristoforo, until the next murder of course." He smiled at them.

While Amanda wondered if this was some kind of occult message that should alarm them, her mother said quite calmly, "Well, we don't have many of those, so I should think you won't be back for a few years."

"I may come back now and then to visit. Yes. I may well do that," he looked directly at Hilary as he said this.

Hilary surprised herself by saying, "I hope you do."

Their food arrived and they started eating. Amanda felt at a loss for words. She had wanted to discuss things with her mother and now of course that was impossible. She wasn't even sure what one usually talked about to policemen. In the end they talked about food and wines, and cinema. All quite normal things, yet somehow, the situation didn't feel normal to her. She wondered for a moment if he was playing some subtle police-man's game with them, but then she realised that Ruggero Di Girolamo's reason for joining them was quite obvious and had nothing to do with murder. Otherwise her mother would hardly be so relaxed and happy. It seemed advisable to leave them alone, so as soon as she had finished her meal, she stood up and said, "I'm off, so I'll say good-bye. I won't have coffee with you as I fixed to have it with friends."

She shook hands with Ruggero and patted her mother's shoulder in a gesture of affection and left, feeling relieved. A glance over he shoulder at them as she reached the door showed that her absence had barely been noticed. They were talking and gazing at each other in what she thought a rather embarrassingly intimate manner. She had had no idea that things had moved in that direction and so fast! She shrugged and thought, "Well, I can see where this is leading all right, but what about poor Bruno?"

Ten minutes later, when Bruno put his head through the door looking for Hilary, he saw her talking earnestly to Ruggero, their heads almost touching across the table. He turned on his heels and walked straight out of the restaurant feeling as one of his pupils might if his girl were to dance in the disco with another boy. He had thought himself too old to feel this kind of emotion. He mingled with the crowd, saying hello to people he knew, but his mind was turning over the events of the last few days and the distancing he had felt. He had no idea how to mend matters, or how to make them return to their normal comfortable status. He felt distinctly threatened.

HILARY WALKED HOME with Di Girolamo. It felt natural. It felt natural that he should come into the house for a nightcap. She herself had drunk several glasses of wine, as he had insisted she help him finish his bottle, and then they had broached another. He took her arm as they walked up the hill, and she felt herself lean against him. She had obviously had too much wine.

As she opened the door, she saw a note on the doormat. It was from Amanda, saying she was staying the night with friends as the next morning they were leaving at daybreak for a trip to the mountains. She smiled at it and passed it over to him. He read it and put it on the table. They looked at each other. Hilary knew it had to be her choice so she said, "Come, let's go upstairs."

THIRTY-NINE

IT WAS JUST before first light when he left. She called him back and said, "Amanda told me something last night. It has to be true. She's no fool. I don't know if it's important, but it could be a motive for blackmail I suppose." She told him and he gave a satisfied nod. Another piece of the puzzle was put in its place.

THERE WAS AN insistent ringing and banging that finally penetrated Nigel's dream and was incorporated into it as a telephone which he couldn't reach and a man knocking on his door which he was unable to open no matter how he tried. He opened his eyes to the half-light. The noise continued and there were more voices. He pulled on a pair of pants and, after glancing at the clock, went down to open the door. The early morning light hit him in the face so that he had to shield his eyes. Outside were three policemen and a police car. They pushed him into the house and closed the door.

"Get dressed. You are to come to the police station now," said one of them. "I will accompany you to your bedroom."

"But it's only six-thirty in the morning!" he exclaimed, overcome by the enormity of it.

"Yes, we decided to let you sleep in a bit. Aren't we kind? Come on, hurry it up."

"You can't do this, you have no right."

"I'm afraid we can and we do. If you prefer we will take you there in your underpants. Will you get a move on and get dressed?"

He was hustled out of the house before he really had time to wake up. His last memory was of Robin clutching the sheet to her naked body, a scared look on her face. He had tried to reassure her, but was thrust out of the room after saying only a couple of words. He felt a little frightened, but he was angry as well. This was hardly the sort of police behaviour one expected in Europe. It seemed to him far more like that of some third world country, where your rights were automatically trampled on, or non-existent in the first place. He felt a shiver of fear. What did he know about this country anyway? For all he knew, he was going to disappear into some legal black hole from which he might never return.

DI GIROLAMO WAS WAITING in his office impatiently. Dressed in a dark blue linen suit and medium blue shirt, freshly shaved and showered, he was impeccable. He knew his opponent would immediately feel at a disadvantage. Unshaven, unwashed and dressed in haste, he would be hustled into the room where Di Girolamo had deliberately left his empty coffee cup and the plate with the crumbs from his breakfast. These would be removed before the prisoner's eyes, reminding him that he had not breakfasted.

The tape recorder was at the ready. He threw the window open so that the room would be fresh. When they arrived, he remained seated. He let his officers manhandle Nigel to his chair, and watched them remove the handcuffs. He indicated the breakfast debris with his eyes and they removed it. One remained seated in the room behind Nigel, at a table in the corner with the tape recorder on it. The other two closed the door and stationed themselves audibly outside.

Nigel felt too defeated to bluster in his normal way. He eyed Di Girolamo with loathing and pressed his lips together, as though to indicate that he had no intention of speaking. Di Girolamo nodded to the young officer, who switched on the tape recorder. He intoned the date, time and named those present in the room. Di Girolamo leaned forward and said "You are Nigel Proctor, born November the thirteenth, nineteen thirty-eight in

Hastings, in the county of Sussex, Great Britain? You are a computer consultant and are actually resident in Jersey, with a temporary resident's permit in Italy?"

"You know perfectly well that…"

"Answer the question," interrupted Di Girolamo in a cold voice.

"Yes."

"On the night between the eighth and ninth of July, at about one o'clock in the morning, did you return to your house, having previously left it at about midnight, to collect some forgotten documents?"

"Yes."

"Now, answer this question very carefully. Did you meet Ettore Fagiolo at your house on that occasion?"

"No."

"I have a witness who will swear that you did meet him then and that a heated discussion took place, and finally, that after a physical confrontation with him, you attempted to hit Ettore Fagiolo with a shovel. You failed, and returned to the house as you had a nosebleed. Later you returned to the pool to find that someone else had hit him, which was most convenient for you. Then you deliberately pulled his semi-conscious body to the poolside and threw him into the water, causing his death."

"Lies. I did nothing of the sort."

"Would you prefer to have a legal representative with you?"

"No, I have no need. I am innocent, so I have nothing to fear." He pulled his chin up and looked Di Girolamo squarely in the eyes. "Did that blackmailing little bastard tell you this rubbish?"

Di Girolamo nodded to the other officer who turned on a small tape player.

A weak voice hesitantly gave its testimony.

"…I was at the house with Ettore. He had the keys. We were in the bedroom, when we heard a noise. He went down. I heard shouting and banging. Downstairs. Then outside. I looked out. They were at the poolside. He was fighting with Nigel…"

The breathing was laboured, the words came out slowly.

"...then Nigel fell into the hut. Came out with a shovel. He tried to hit Ettore, but fell over. Ettore kicked his face. He laughed. Nigel got up and went into the house. I went under the bed. More noise outside. I look out and see another man dressed in black. He is cleaning the shovel, Ettore is on the floor. Then the man in black runs away and Nigel—" There was a burst of coughing, and the tape was switched off. He took up the story with a stronger voice as the machine was switched on again. "Nigel came back and pulled him into the pool. He ran back to the car, and drove off."

"That is all that interests us. Could you understand all that?

"Enough." ·

"Would you like to comment on what we have just heard?"

"It sounds like the ravings of someone in delirium."

"I can assure you that the boy is quite sane and was anxious to offer this testimony."

"I bet he was. He probably did it himself. Did you know that the man, Ettore Fagiolo, was his lover?"

"I must tell you that his story has been corroborated by another witness. If you can't understand it all, I will translate for you."

Again he nodded to the man at the tape recorder. This time the voice was quite strong and had a pronounced Sicilian accent.

"I knew that the Proctors were going away at midnight so I planned to do the job at about one a.m., just in case they were late leaving. Joe was nearby with the van, and when I was ready with the stuff I was to call him with my cell phone and in a few minutes we would load up and he would be on his way. That's how we worked it.

"That night, as I approached the house via the garden of course, I realised, a bit late to tell the truth, that there was someone in the house. I had to hide pretty sharp, as at the same moment a car drew up with two people in it and a tall man got out and went into the house. A few seconds later he came out brandishing a big pot and chasing another man, who I recognised as Ettore Fagiolo. He threw down the pot, maybe to run faster, and caught up with Ettore near the pool, which was pretty near me, too. They started fighting. The other man got pushed against the shed, the door burst open and he fell in. He came out brandishing a shovel.

"He was shouting *'Bastardo'* and *'Testa Di cazzo'* and English words. I couldn't understand it all, but I heard the words, 'Screw you,' which I recognised. Anyway, he took a swipe at Ettore, and missed…it was pathetic. He even fell over. So of course Ettore kicked him in the face.

"Then his nose starts bleeding and Ettore starts laughing at him. I'm not surprised. I felt like laughing myself. It was like slapstick comedy. Anyway, I now realised that this bloke was Nigel Proctor. He went back into the house dabbing his nose and shouting, in his horrible Italian, something about, 'You'll pay dearly for this. I'll sue you for this,' and Ettore laughs and shouts, 'I wouldn't do that, your wife wouldn't like it.'

"Anyway, he goes back to the house and Ettore starts to follow him and I think the moment has come to hook it. I start creeping away from the pool area, and damn me if I don't tread on a bloody great branch, and it gives an almighty crack and that's me in big trouble. Ettore comes rushing down towards me. I don't know who he thought I was, but he was in a filthy mood, so he really went for me. He chased me and when I reached the shovel, I picked it up, only to threaten him, you understand. I am a small man and not that fit. He was big, younger than me, pretty fit and angry, so to defend myself, and for this reason only, I picked up the shovel and shouted 'Leave me alone or I'll hit you!' but he took no notice of my threats and rushed towards me shouting 'I'll kill you, you bastard.' So I was forced to try and stop him from injuring me with the only possible defence available to me, the shovel.

"It was not my intention to injure him, only to stop his advance on my person. Unfortunately the shovel made contact with his head and he fell to the ground. I cleaned the shovel, which I had handled with my bare hands, and put it back in the shed as he lay on the floor groaning. Then I saw someone approaching and I ran away as fast as I could. I didn't look back. I could not be sure as to the identity of the person approaching Ettore as I left, but I think it was Nigel Proctor."

The machine was stopped with a click, which sounded loudly in the room. After a moment's silence, Di Girolamo said, "You will note the careful way this man explains his intention to halt, but not kill Ettore. I may tell you that we believe this to be the case. He is a small time house burglar, and not a killer. I have now let you hear two separate witnesses, both of whom indicate you as the aggressor of Ettore Fagiolo. I am willing to hear your version of the facts. Are you able to shed any further light on what happened?"

Nigel groaned. He put his hands to his face and covered it, then removed them abruptly as though he had washed it, and took a deep breath.

"It would be pointless to deny I was there. I was there and I went into the house for the documents, and that damn dago was in there. He came downstairs, zipping up his trousers, and looking as though he owned the place. Well I saw red, I yelled at him, told him what I thought of him, and picked up the pot to threaten him with. That frightened him. He changed the look on his face then and rushed out through the French windows into the garden. I followed. I looked bloody silly with a flowerpot in my hands, and it was heavy, so I jettisoned it, and I caught him at the pool. I went for him. He is a lot younger than me, was, I mean, so he threw me off and I fell back into the shed. I grabbed a shovel from the shed and swiped at him with it, but I missed and fell over.

"That bastard kicked me in the face. I mean it's not on, to kick a man when he's down. That started a nosebleed, so I went back to the house for an ice pack, and I told him I'd go to the police. I hadn't got the time then to do anything else, except make it clear that he wouldn't get away with it. I couldn't risk missing the plane, so I said that I'd do it when I came back. I went to the fridge got an ice pack, bunged some cotton wool up my nose, grabbed my documents and left. That's all. I did, categorically, NOT, go back and throw the blighter into the pool. I didn't see the burglar who made that statement, or any of what he says went on. I was in the house at that point trying to stop my nosebleed. I had blood down my jacket so I sponged it with cold water. I was seething. I felt like throttling Ettore, I admit it, but I didn't kill him."

"I see, but if you didn't, then who did?"

"I've told you who. That little boy, his pet dog, the one who is trying to lay it on me."

"Why did you pay Marco when he tried to blackmail you?"

"I've already told you that, too. I didn't want you to know I'd been back to the villa."

"You have lied all along, there is no reason why I should believe you now. I do not believe you and I am going to arrest you for the murder of Ettore Fagiolo."

The correct formula was pronounced and Nigel was formally arrested. He was sent down to the main prison in Lucca later that morning.

FORTY

ROBIN SAT IN bed alone. Nigel had gone to the police station ages ago, and she sat immobile, clutching the sheet around her for comfort, waiting for a phone call or for his return home.

"Why had they come for him? What could have happened? Had they got new evidence?" she asked herself, feeling an increasing wave of panic.

Finally she decided to get dressed and pop in to see Hilary, for tea and sympathy. She had to talk to someone or she would go mad. She left a note on the door for Nigel and tripped up the road. When Hilary opened the door, still in her dressing gown, she found Robin wearing a smart dress and full make-up at nine o'clock on a festa morning.

"Good heavens! What's happened, Robin? What's wrong?"

Robin burst into tears, "Everything. That fascist policeman has arrested Nigel, I think."

"Oh, I am sorry. Come in. I'll make some tea, or do you prefer coffee?"

"Tea would be lovely." She blew her nose and followed Hilary into the kitchen. Hilary put the kettle on, turning her back on Robin who was still sniffing, so that she could get a hold on herself. Robin obviously had no idea that she had been sleeping with the enemy.

She busied herself with cups and teabags. She set everything on the table and sat down facing Robin.

"It won't take a minute. Now, what happened exactly?"

"At the crack of dawn those fascist bastards nearly knocked

the door down, and took Nigel away, and I haven't heard anything since. I'm so worried. They can't arrest him. He wouldn't hurt a fly. They can't possibly think he's killed Ettore. Should I get in touch with the Consul or the Ambassador or a lawyer or…oh Hilary, what shall I do?" she wailed.

Hilary let her rant on, and said, "Have a good cry Robin and then we'll talk." She stood up, made the tea and brought it to the table. She poured a cup for Robin and said firmly, "Blow your nose and drink your tea."

Robin gulped at her tea and still looked weepy, then she gave a small smile and said, "Good thing my make-up's waterproof. What must I look like, all red eyed and probably with a red nose to boot."

"You look splendid, as always. Now you've calmed down, tell me exactly what happened. He was taken to the police station early this morning, is that right?"

"Yes. That's all I know. They accompanied him to the bedroom to get some clothes, watched him dress and ignored me, even though I kept asking what was going on. He said, 'Don't worry Robin, I'll be back soon,' and off they went. Hilary, they put handcuffs on him." She burst into loud sobs again and buried her face in her handkerchief.

"Oh my dear, how awful. I'm so sorry. Well, I think you should wait awhile and then find out if he has actually been arrested, or if they are just interrogating him. Then you can decide what to do."

"Yes, I suppose you're right. I mean they can't just arrest people on suspicion, can they? They have to have proof, witnesses, something. He didn't do it so there can't be anything. Of course someone could be lying to protect himself. That's a possibility."

"They have to investigate all testimonies Robin, and then if they are proved false, they're ignored. I'm sure he'll be back soon. Go home and wait there. Phone me if you've heard nothing by lunchtime, okay?"

"Thank you, Hilary. You're so sensible. I'm sorry I burst in on you like this, but I was panic-stricken. I feel better now. I'll phone you later then."

She left and Hilary washed up the cups thoughtfully. Ruggero had seemed so sure that he was going to arrest the right person. He had obviously got new evidence. He had seemed certain. She puzzled over it. Robin had been so distraught, so sure that Nigel was innocent. Who was right? Maybe they hadn't arrested Nigel. Maybe they needed him to nail someone else. She decided that she had found the answer to the puzzle and put it on one side.

She had other things to think about. Her emotions were in a turmoil. Last night! She felt a thrill inside. Last night had seemed so inevitable, so right and so good. It had been really good. Poor old Bruno. What had Miriam said about that adjective? Ah yes, one foot outside the door. Well Bruno had been moving away for some time, or she had. Either way they had moved apart. She had been glad, initially, when he came back from his holiday. She had missed him but, when he was there all the time, she hadn't felt anything much. No passion at all, and restful wasn't enough.

DI GIROLAMO WAS SUNK in thought. His elbows rested on his desk and his chin was cupped in his hands. Why did he still feel uncertain about that Englishman? He had two concurring independent witnesses, which was more than enough. Something kept niggling at him. He was missing something. It had slipped through his fingers. He picked up the phone and called the hospital.

"Di Girolamo here, investigating magistrate for the province of Lucca. I'm enquiring about Marco Rossi. Yes, that's the one. How is he this morning? I see. Could I come, do you think? I would be careful. Yes, I see. Well, after lunch then. I'll call in on you of course. Thank you, doctor."

Maresciallo Biagioni was at home today. It was the town's patron saint's day and he wanted to be home with his family. Besides, he understood the case was more or less closed, and the burglaries had been wrapped up, too, so he felt quite content. Di Girolamo phoned him at ten o'clock.

"I've arrested him. He didn't have a leg to stand on, but he denied doing the actual murder."

"Well, they all do that don't they?"

"I suppose so."

"Aren't you sure about him?"

"Yes, I am, but I keep feeling I've missed something."

"Ah well, we're never a hundred percent happy are we? Have you told Robin Proctor that he's been arrested?"

"No. I'll do that now."

"By the way 'Fritzy' is back. I forgot to tell you. He signed in yesterday afternoon."

"I'll see to him tomorrow. Enjoy your day off."

He dialled again. "Di Girolamo here. I am calling to inform you that Nigel Proctor was arrested and will be taken to the prison in L—shortly. The charge was murder."

He heard a sharp intake of breath, then, "Can I see him?"

"Not here I'm afraid. You can in Lucca. Also you will want to sort out a legal representative. Anyway, I advise you to contact the prison authorities, as this case is now out of my hands,"

"I see. Thank you for phoning."

He put the phone down, and put all thoughts of the case on one side. He thought of Hilary and what had happened. He picked up the phone and dialled again.

"Hilary, it's me, Ruggero."

"Hello Ruggero. Come to lunch. I'm alone."

"It will compromise you."

"That's fine. I don't mind at all, in fact I think I shall quite like being compromised. I'll see you later."

ROBIN RUSHED OUT of the house, holding an overnight bag. She had prepared this for Nigel, but was uncertain what would be allowed. She had phoned a top lawyer that had previously been recommended to her should she ever need one, and was meeting him in Lucca at twelve p.m. She bumped into Alda, Marco's mother, on her way to the parking area where she had left the small car. She didn't want to use the Mercedes, as it was too cumbersome for parking.

"Hallo, where are you off to?"

"Oh, I'm going to Pisa to see Marco. I have a train at ten-forty-five, so I must rush or I'll miss the bus that goes to the station."

Robin heard herself say, "I'm going as far as Lucca. Do you want a lift? Then you can get a bus to Pisa from there."

"Oh how kind. Yes that would be lovely."

She prattled on gaily for the whole journey, and after a short while Robin was sick to death of her and Padre Pio and that little shit of a son of hers. Screw you, Padre Pio, she cursed inwardly. She hoped that blackmailing little shit, Marco, would keep his mouth shut. His mother obviously knew nothing, so maybe he was just waiting his chance to start blackmailing Nigel again.

She let Alda out at the Lucca bus station and sent her best wishes to Marco. That would surprise him! It was a damn shame he hadn't died in the accident. He must have been hit a terrific blow, but the resilience of the young was something quite incredible. And, against all the odds, he had survived. He was free to blackmail them again, free to invent whatever he liked and try and pass it off as the truth.

She parked the car and walked into the medieval town centre to meet the legal representative. She knew Nigel was innocent. It was just a question of convincing others.

THE CASE FILE was open on his desk. He flicked through the pages putting it into order, checking there were sufficient copies. He checked the German's statement. He read the letters from Augusta again. A copy of the second letter would have to go into the file for the inquiry into her husband's death, so he made a note. He pulled out the photograph that had accompanied it, tapped his finger on it a few times and then carefully put it back in its envelope and numbered it. The other photograph, he was undecided about. He remembered his promise to the Maresciallo, but was loath to destroy it yet. H replaced it in the file but did not number it. Today was a festa so he would finish all the paper work the next day. He felt deflated. All the adrenaline had gone. The end of a case should be triumphant, not flat like this. He locked his office and walked out into the sunshine. Several people said *"Buon giorno"* as he walked through town. He felt he was becoming part of this town, but now he would have to leave it and go back to his lonely flat in Lucca. Perhaps that was what was making him feel so edgy.

He arrived at Hilary's and was watched by at least two neighbours as she let him in. *These small towns certainly limited your freedom of action,* he thought. Hilary opened the door and smiled at him.

"I'm sorry, but your reputation will be damaged by this," he said.

"Don't worry. You are a policeman and it is lunchtime, so I think I'll be fairly safe."

"Well I won't stay too long."

"Stay as long as you like. If anyone asks, I'll say the police department is commissioning the translation of the testimonies, so there'll need to be frequent consultations."

"Perhaps it could be true."

"I've worked for them before, so who knows."

"I should have brought a briefcase with me."

"Never mind. Bring one next time."

"And the next, and the next."

They smiled at each other. Then they kissed. He pressed her body to him for a brief moment. She gently released herself.

"Come on, we're lunching under the pergola, it's cool there and hidden from the public view."

"I have to leave fairly early as I'm going to Pisa this afternoon to take down a signed statement from Marco Rossi, if he's up to it."

"Robin was here this morning in a terrible state about Nigel. She said she thought he was being arrested. I haven't heard from her since. Has he been arrested?"

"Yes. She has been informed. In fact, I expect she's on her way to Lucca now. It's out of my hands."

"You mean the case is closed?"

"Yes. I'll be leaving myself before long and then I expect I'll have a few days off before I'm assigned a new case."

"Oh."

"Hilary, will you come away with me? We could go to the mountains. I have a small chalet. It would be very primitive. There's no electricity, and only a freezing mountain stream for water."

"Yes."

"Just yes."

"Yes."

FORTY-ONE

MARCO WAS FEELING better. He had been taken out of intensive care and was now in a private room. His parents were going to stay in a hotel at Pisa and spend the whole day with him. They had bought him tapes and magazines and new pyjamas and they washed him and fed him like a baby. They looked older to him than before and seemed more tired than he remembered, but despite that, they were happier now and their kindness overwhelmed him. Their joy at having him alive seemed boundless. Probably because he was so aware of this, he kept finding himself weeping, and felt ashamed. He had several fractures and would have to remain immobile for some time. The only pain he had was caused by the fractured rib, which had punctured a lung. He looked up as Di Girolamo came in with a young policeman.

"Marco, I hear you feel up to making a proper statement today."

"Yes, I slept quite well. Talking doesn't seem so tiring."

"Okay. Now I'll tell you what we'll do. I am going to tape this interview, then Roberto here will pop into the doctor's office and type it up for you to sign. After that we can leave you in peace." He looked kindly on the boy. His long hair had been cut off, his head shaved for the operation. He was pale and thinner even than before. He was very small boned and delicate looking, and his green eyes looked huge in his little white face. A waif. He reminded Di Girolamo of the photos he had seen of refugees.

"My parents don't have to know what I'm saying, do they?"

"No, this is between us. It will probably have to come out in court, but your parents do know what the situation is, you know. You mustn't let that interfere with what you say."

"Fine."

"Shall we start?" He read aloud the date, time and place, and named those present.

"Where were you on the night between the eighth and ninth of July?"

"I was in the Villa Rosa with Ettore Fagiolo."

"Tell us in your own words what happened that night."

"Ettore had the keys to the Villa and had said we could go there, as the Proctors were leaving at midnight. We often used other people's houses, as they left him their keys."

"How did he come to have the keys to the Villa Rosa?"

"Nigel gave him the keys last year when Ettore rented the place for them, for the summer."

"But they no longer had that kind of relationship."

"Oh, no. Nigel was right off Ettore. He'd had an argument with him a while before, and he wasn't speaking to him. Nigel must have forgotten about the keys. Anyway, we set off, and that crazy drunken German was running behind the car bellowing in German. Ettore was laughing like a drain. In fact, we hadn't been there long when there was this almighty crash, and old Fritzy was falling about down by the pool, knocking over chairs, so Ettore went down and got rid of him. He even kicked him up the arse and Fritzy scuttled away on all fours. God, that was a sight." He smiled sadly as he spoke.

"You didn't mention this in your previous statement."

"Well it didn't have anything to do with what happened afterwards. We went upstairs and we hadn't been there long when we heard someone in the house. Ettore said it must be that crazy bastard again and went down to see. But it wasn't. It was Nigel Proctor. He had come back, so then there was this terrible row. Nigel was furious. I thought they must have gone outside, because I heard a pot smash, so I went to the window and saw Nigel chasing after Ettore. They stopped at the pool where Nigel charged at him, but Ettore shoved him backwards and he fell into that shed thing. He still hadn't had enough, and came out with a shovel and swiped at Ettore, but he missed him by a mile and fell over. It was quite funny. Ettore kicked him in the face then and his nose must have started bleeding 'cos he was mopping at it. Anyway he decided to give it up as a bad job and was coming back to the house. He held a handkerchief to his nose. He was yelling at Ettore, 'I'll see you in court' or words to that effect. Ettore was wetting himself laughing."

"Did Ettore reply?" interrupted Di Girolamo.

"Yes, he shouted, "I wouldn't do that if I were you, your wife wouldn't like it.""

"I see. Did those words mean anything special do you think? Why did he say his wife would not like it?"

"I think he had something on her, that, you know, he could use as a lever to shut Nigel up."

"Was he blackmailing her?"

"No, I don't think so, but it certainly sounded to me as though he could do if he wanted to."

"You tried to blackmail Nigel yourself, I believe."

"I was going to shop him, I just wanted to make him suffer first for what he'd done to Ettore. Anyway, I needed the money then." He refused to meet Di Girolamo's eyes and said nothing more.

"I understand. Carry on, Marco. I want you to think very carefully about everything you saw and heard from this point on. Close your eyes and try to tell me everything in sequence."

"Nigel came into the house and I scuttled under the bed. I thought he was coming to get me, and he's a big bloke. He frightens the life out of me, but he stayed downstairs. I went to the top of the stairs and I heard the faucet running in the kitchen. Then I heard more noise outside so I ran and looked out of the window again and saw Ettore lying on the ground, and there was a fat, little man cleaning the shovel with something. He ran off when he saw Nigel coming back. Then Nigel pulled Ettore into the water. That's all."

"So Nigel must have been waiting for the fat little man to finish and go so that he could get rid of Ettore for good. How long after he ran off did Nigel come out?"

"Almost immediately, I remember thinking that it was quick. He just appeared. It all happened very fast, you know." He frowned, concentrating. "Maybe the fat guy ran off because he had seen Nigel."

"So, we have Ettore at the pool being swiped with a shovel and Nigel in the house with the tap running—right? Then the little man runs off and Nigel rushes up to the pool and pulls Ettore to the edge and tips him in. Is that right?"

"Yes."

"Do you know who the fat little man was? You said the first time that he was dressed in black."

"Well, if he wasn't dressed in black, it was another very dark colour. I didn't recognise him. Do you know who he was?"

"Yes. Anyway, please go on."

"Well, then Nigel ran back to the car and drove off."

"Did he have some documents in his hand when he went to the pool the second time?"

"No."

"Now, think hard, did you see him stop to pick up any documents on his way back to the car?"

"No. Perhaps he already put them in the car."

"No matter. What I am trying to get clear is the timing here."

It was the timing that was worrying him. It wasn't right. He asked the last question, "Are you quite certain that the person you saw was Nigel Proctor?"

"Oh yes. Quite certain."

"It couldn't have been the German?"

"No way. That fat slob was so drunk he was falling about all over the place. Besides, he's different. I mean, he's enormous. You'd recognise him anywhere."

"How well could you see from the house?"

"Pretty well. The pool is just below the house and there was a full moon that night."

"Marco, did you go down to the pool, afterwards, to try to get Ettore out of the water?"

"No. I knew he must be dead and I was frightened. I ran away and left him there." His eyes filled with tears.

"It's not your fault."

"I can't even swim, you know."

"It wouldn't have helped much, even if you could."

"I suppose not," he sighed. "I want Nigel Proctor to be punished for what he did."

"Good. Well, we'll get this typed up and you can sign it. You realise you are a very important witness." He smiled at the boy, patted him on the hand and added, "Get well soon."

In the car on the way back he worried over the timing. It had all happened too fast by his reckoning, but maybe the boy's perception of time was incorrect. He had been quite certain as to the identity of the murderer, and that was the important thing.

FORTY-TWO

"I WANT FRITZY here as soon as possible," barked Di Girolamo as he walked towards his office, "and as soon as possible, which probably won't be till later this evening, I want Robin Proctor."

He opened the folder and reread several of the statements very carefully, and began cursing under his breath. He opened the door to the office in the next room and shouted through, "And Roberto, bring up Salvatore immediately!"

"Yes sir." He jumped to his feet and went to close the door. "What's got into him? He rushed in here like a whirlwind, and now he wants to see them all again?" he grumbled to a colleague.

Five minutes later, Salvatore sat in front of Di Girolamo. "What's up chief?" asked the little Sicilian.

"I want to go over your statement with you." He paused and asked, "Did you see the German known as Fritzy at any time that evening?"

"Well, I saw him when everybody else did, drinking in the bar and shouting about Ettore. Not after that."

"You never saw him at any time at the Villa Rosa that evening?"

"No."

"Are you quite sure that it was Nigel Proctor you saw coming towards the pool as you left?"

"No, I said so in my statement. I think it was him, but I won't swear to it."

"Could it have been the German?"

"No way. That guy is like a mountain. I'd recognise him anywhere."

"Please think very carefully. Close your eyes and try to visualize the scene. What made you think it might not be Nigel?"

The little man sat quietly and remembered that night. It had been dark, but there was certainly enough moonlight to see by. He was cleaning the shovel and he looked up as he put the shovel down on the ground. He saw a dark figure separate itself from the house, or was it the house? Perhaps it was the bushes? No matter, the person had walked lightly towards the steps and turned sideways to step down the first one, and he had fled. He had had enough that night.

"It was the way he walked."

"It wasn't the way he usually walked?"

"Well, it wouldn't be. I mean he was tiptoeing quietly. He thought I hadn't seen him."

"Tell me how…no…show me how he walked."

The little man tiptoed across the floor almost mincing, and then he turned, and said "Like this, and then he turned sideways to take the first step."

"He turned sideways."

"Well it was dark. It's safer that way, I suppose."

"I see. But something about the way he walked made you think it might not be him."

"Yes."

"All right, what made you think it might be him? Think carefully and visualise the scene again."

"He was tall and the right build. He was wearing a dark suit. I couldn't see his face, you know, but, well, it had to be him. I won't swear to it, as I said, but I'm pretty certain."

"Thank you. That's all for now." He opened the door and called, "I've finished here. Take him down."

"You will remember that I've given full cooperation."

"How could I forget? Oh, and by the way, your wife isn't pregnant. My condolences."

"Fritzy, I mean Herman Ganz, is here, sir."

"Send him in."

"Good afternoon, Maresciallo." The German lumbered in sweating profusely.

"I am not a Maresciallo. Sit down. You lied to me. Roberto, come and tape this."

"Yes sir." He scuttled into place and turned on the tape recorder.

"Did you go to the Villa Rosa on the night between the eighth and ninth of July? Answer truthfully this time. Remember, I have evidence that you lied in your previous statement."

"Yes," the German sighed disconsolately.

"Ah! Now tell me what you did there and what you saw. Take your time, think carefully and answer truthfully."

"I can't remember much, I haff a lot to drink, but this you know. I haff seen Ettore with that kid from the bar und so I followed the car, but it took me a long time, as it vas I that vas falling down and about. I remember I get to the Villa and I am creeping through the garden, but I haff fallen down all the steps to the swimming pool and knock over all the chairs, I think. Anyway it must haff made much noise because suddenly there vas Ettore and he kicked me up the arse, the behind, jah? It was so humiliating, because I cannot even stand up and run away. I haff to crawl away on all fours, like a dog. Now that is really my last clear memory, for then I haff fallen asleep behind the hut. I did hear the thuds, and bangs and the voices, but it is all so very far away, you know, like in a dream. I keep being awakened up by all these disturbances. I remember a voice was shouting about to tell someone's wife, but I do not really remember anything so clearly." His thick German accent made his tale strangely sad.

"I want you to try harder, to remember anything you heard. Although you may have dozed on and off, you were there when the murder took place. Did you for example hear the splash as the body hit the water? Did you hear footsteps? Did you see anyone?"

"I am behind the little hut, so I can see nothing. I hear things, but I haff not really remembered much." He sat and thought.

"I remember a voice. It says a bad vord. I don't remember so vell. I think it vas perhaps a *cazzo* vord. Maybe *testa di cazzo*. I don't know vhen this was, though. I know I haff heard the splash because I remember I am thinking it is a funny time to go for a swim and it was cold, too."

"No footsteps?"

"Vell all the people that vas running and shouting, clumping about and then the tic-tac, tic-tac, tic-tac, so fast. I don't know vhen it all is, though. The sequence, I don't know it. I vake up in the early morning. Ach it is so cold and then somehow I go home, but I do not see the body. I see nothing. There vas nobody there. They haff all gone in the car. I hear the doors slamming and the car drive off so I see no man. They haff all gone. Jah!"

"The car door, or doors."

"They are the doors, bam, bam, first one then another one, jah, more than one."

Di Girolamo unlocked the desk drawer and pulled out the German passport, "You are free to leave the country, you may be called to give evidence, though quite frankly the testimony of a drunk is not likely to stand up in court. Wait until Roberto gives you this new statement to sign and then you are free to leave."

HE LEFT THE BUILDING. It was early evening. He should eat now, as he wanted to see Robin Proctor later. He used his cell phone.

"Hilary, meet me in ten minutes time where we ate yesterday?"

"I'll be there," she said.

When she arrived, he was looking at the menu.

"I don't have a lot of time, I'm interviewing someone later, but I must eat, and so must you, so here we are."

"The case is still open?"

"Yes and no. Let's just say I must be sure. Technically the case is closed, but this is just me wanting to dot all the *Is*. I have this niggling feeling that I might have missed, or forgotten, something."

"I see. Well, let's order quickly and then you can get back. I'll have *tagliatelle all'uovo con salsa di gamberetti and panna*, you?"

"Oh I'll have the same. I'm not really hungry, but if I don't eat my brain stops working."

"Well that would be tragic, especially now." She smiled at him. "Take my advice, let's talk about anything you like, but not the case. Relax and forget it, then when you least expect it, you'll find that the elusive something will come to you. That's what I do when I'm trying to remember something, and it works."

At the end of the meal they separated, Hilary was going to play cards with Ben, Terry and John.

"I'll be back at midnight, but I think Amanda will, too, unless she phones and says she staying out again."

"I'll phone you."

He walked away, immediately lost in thought. He was hoping that Robin would clear the way for him. Her testimony to date had been very sparse. He should have called her again earlier. To do so now, when Nigel had been arrested, might not be so useful as she was bound to be resentful, angry, aggressive and possibly taciturn. He felt he had already made too many errors in this investigation. He strode through the corridor towards his office. It was half past eight. Robin should surely be back by now. "Roberto, has Robin Proctor come back yet?"

"No sir."

"I want a car there at her house, and she's to be brought in as soon as she arrives."

He opened the case file again, going methodically over each statement. He reread the letters and looked at the photos and then, quite suddenly, he knew. How stupid he had been. It was clear as daylight. He smiled to himself, and murmured, "Before I go to bed tonight, I will have remedied all my errors."

It was getting late, nearly ten. She must have stopped to eat. There was a knock on the door,

"Avanti."

"Sir, Robin Proctor is here." He ushered her in. She looked tired. Her dark blue trouser suit looked crumpled, her hair was drawn back from her face, rather severely, her make-up applied with a lighter hand today. She looked her age. She folded up her long legs as she sat down gracefully. Placing her hands on the desk in front of her she said, "I am exhausted. I was woken at the crack of dawn by your men, and I see I am going to finish this dreadful day in your company. You've arrested Nigel, what more do you want?" She slumped back in the chair her hands on her lap.

"I am taping this interview," he nodded to his subordinate, who started up the tape and repeated the usual formula."

"On the night between the eighth and ninth of July 1998, did you return to the Villa Rosa with Nigel Proctor to collect some forgotten documents?"

"Of course I did."

"What did you do when Nigel left the car to go into the house?"

"I waited for him, of course."

"But he was away quite some time?"

"Was he? I was reading a magazine and didn't notice."

"Didn't you hear any noises while you were sitting there?"

"No, I was listening to the radio."

"Do you know what Nigel did while he was away from the car?"

"He collected the documents."

"Come on, Robin, we know that he disturbed Ettore Fagiolo. He has admitted that much himself."

"All right, he told me afterwards that he found Ettore in the house, and he sent him packing. It got a bit physical. Ettore hit him and Nigel had a nosebleed, but he didn't kill him."

"Yes, we know that he had a fight with him. I have two witnesses to this fact. Would you like to hear what they have to say?"

He signalled to Roberto who played the two tapes, first Marco, then Salvatore. He translated where she did not understand.

"Nigel has also signed a statement admitting the same facts, with the exception of the homicide."

"Nigel wouldn't hurt a fly. It's all hot air with him. You don't know him."

"Convince me that he didn't do it. One witness saw him pull the body to the pool and tip it in, the other saw him approach the pool.

You see, I have no alternative but to believe he did it."

"They're lying."

"No."

"It was that Marco. Since he's admitted he was there, I don't see why you don't think it was him. He must have seen Ettore and Nigel fighting and when Nigel left, he killed Ettore."

"Why should he?"

"How should I know? Maybe Ettore had a new boy, or perhaps he was cutting off the supply of drugs. Drug addicts will do anything when they have a need."

"I agree, but they don't usually kill their supplier. I'm sorry, but the facts are clear. Nigel killed Ettore."

"It must have been someone else."

"There was no one else." He raised his eyes to her face, "Except you."

"Prove it," she snapped at him. "First it's Nigel and now it's me. Why don't you think it's Marco? Why us? You're a bloody racist that's why. You don't want it to be an Italian, do you, so you'll push it off on us, the foreigners."

"It's no good, Robin. I'll tell you what really happened after Ettore was knocked to the ground by a blow with a shovel, shall I?" She shrugged her shoulders and remained silent.

"I think you had heard some noise and got out of the car to see what was going on. I think you saw Nigel go into the house with a bleeding nose, and I know you heard what Ettore shouted at him. You were meant to hear it. Then you heard the branch break under Salvatore's feet, yes it was Salvatore who had come to do a bit of housebreaking, and you saw what happened. He defended himself from Ettore with the spade and struck him a hefty blow. Ettore fell to the ground, but he was not dead, nor would he have died from that wound.

"You were standing in the shadows at the side of the house, quite near to the pool, really. As Salvatore finished cleaning the spade, you came out from the bushes by the garage. He says he saw a man in a dark suit, coming down the steps to the pool and he thought it was Nigel, so he made off as fast as he could. He was right, wasn't he? It was a man, but it wasn't Nigel. It was you. You went down to the pool and saw Ettore, lying there groaning. He was stunned and very weak, but he saw you and when you bent over him, he said *'Testa di cazzo'* to you. You saw it was the perfect opportunity to rid yourself of a man who had something on you and could use it whenever he wished.

"So you pulled him to the edge of the pool and tipped him in. It only took a minute. It was easy for you. You are strong, much stronger than Nigel. Nigel was older than you and had just about exhausted his energies. He had been kicked hard in the face and his nose was bleeding copiously. While he was up at the house in the kitchen, cleaning his jacket and trying to stop the flow of blood with a cotton wool plug, you were at the pool killing Ettore. Ettore, the man who had shouted to Nigel, 'I don't think you'll do that.' He meant, tell the police about his presence there in your house. He said, 'Your wife wouldn't like it.'

"Nigel didn't know the meaning of those words but you did. Ettore had shouted them for you to hear. He had bellowed them, in fact. Every witness heard them. You knew what he meant. It was a warning. He wanted you to quieten Nigel down, because if you didn't, he was going to tell Nigel about this," with a flourish he tipped the photograph on the table. Robin began to weep.

"After you killed Ettore, you rushed back to the car and you were there when Nigel arrived from the house. Did he ask you what Ettore meant, I wonder?" He paused, but Robin refused to look at him. "Ettore was bi-sexual, and I'm sure that someone like you must have fascinated him. Nigel was often away, and Ettore was an attractive young man. You thought no one would ever know. But I think that if Nigel had known, he would have thrown you out. So when you killed Ettore you were trying to save yourself, and your life with Nigel. One word and the whole tissue of lies would fall apart. You would be revealed to Nigel as unfaithful, and even worse, unfaithful to him with the man he hated. You would have been revealed to the world as a trans-sexual, something you had carefully hidden for years, behind a mask of femininity." He paused again, then added, "I am seeing Nigel tomorrow, his testimony will, no doubt, be conclusive. I will ask you to make a statement now and sign it. Robin Proctor, I arrest you for the murder of Ettore Fagiolo…

HE WAS TIRED. Sometimes he found his work so sordid, this delving into other people's sex lives, their intimacies laid bare, picked over, exposed to public censure. This case would be like that. People would read their newspapers with glee, gloating over every scabrous detail that earnest journalists would lay before them like prime cuts of meat in the butcher's window, all in the pursuit of truth. The truth will out, but he felt pity for the broken creature he had arrested. She/he would be exposed like a circus freak. The first murder had precipitated dementia in an already fragile old woman, and this in turn had been the cause of another death. We are all responsible for our actions, so now Robin Proctor would pay the price.

He phoned Hilary, "It's over. I'll tell you everything, later."

"Amanda phoned, she's staying overnight with her friends. Have you been bribing her?"

"No, but I'll remember to do so in the future. I'll come then."

He opened the case file, picked out the photo of Marco and put it through the shredder. The photo of Robin in her red wig he returned to its envelope and then closed the folder and locked it in the drawer. He turned out the light, locked the door and left.

DURING THE EARLY HOURS of the next morning, the earth rumbled and like a duck shaking water from its feathers, tried to shake the parasites from its back. It was only a half-hearted attempt, and a few roof tiles were dislodged, a few cracks appeared on pristine walls, and a little loose plaster fell from old houses and smashed in the street below. Many people spent the rest of the night in their cars as a precaution, but Hilary and Ruggero didn't even feel it.

The sun entered the window at its usual time, and Hilary opened the shutters as she always did and looked out on the same world as always. She looked down at the pool, and thought it seemed different today. There was something... She went back to the bedside table for her long distance glasses, put them on, and brought it into focus.

"My God!" she cried.

"What is it?" Ruggero sat up in bed, alarmed.

"The pool, it's cracked, all the water is leaking out."

He jumped out of bed and came to stand beside her. They looked down at it. There was an ample, and widening, crack in the swimming pool. And as the water seeped out, it was causing subsidence, so that the pool itself was moving and seemed about to start an inevitable slide into the valley. A stream of muddy earth flowed down below it, and was still moving.

"It's going down. The whole thing is going to slide down the hill. The supporting wall must have given way. That's Ettore's shoddy work for you."

They stood together and watched, fascinated, as half the pool broke away from its place and began to slide down into the valley. At the same time, a wave of water burst from the pool and at great speed seemed to push the broken-off section along, so that it bounced and boomed its way rapidly down to the valley floor, smashing into pieces as it hit the rocks at the bottom, near the stream. The remaining piece was moving slightly and would inevitably follow on.

"Incredible!" cried Ruggero. "Absolutely unbelievable!"

Other windows had been opened and heads appeared, necks craning to see. There was a kind of excited babble, which rose up and increased in volume, culminating in a great "Ah" as the pool smashed.

"A fitting end, wouldn't you say?" commented Ruggero.

"I never did like it, anyway," said Hilary.